I0633099

THE
GOLDEN
DAGGER

THE GOLDEN DAGGER

by

E. R. Punshon

RAMBLE HOUSE

First published (GB) 1951
Ramble House reprint 2008

ISBN 13: 978-1-60543-178-9
ISBN 10: 1-60543-178-8

Cover Art: Gavin L. O'Keefe
Preparation: Gavin L. O'Keefe

THE
GOLDEN
DAGGER

CHAPTER I

THE 'PHONE CALL

COMMANDER BOBBY OWEN, Scotland Yard, was very busy indeed. Almost as busy indeed as bored. For all the huddle of papers on his desk, all his overflowing 'in' and 'out' trays, all the letters he had been dictating and all the reports he had been signing, all dealt with such matters of detail, routine, procedure as any fairly intelligent boy of twenty could have dealt with almost as well.

It was with alacrity therefore, in the hope that it might presage something a little more interesting, that he answered a tap on his door with an invitation to come in. Detective Constable Ford appeared.

" 'Phone message just received from a Lower High Hill call box," he announced. "Sarge said he thought you ought to see it."

He laid a paper on the desk as he spoke. Bobby picked it up and read it aloud.

"Begins: 'Speaking from call-box on road X79, near Lower High Hill. There's been a murder at Cobblers if that interests you. Goodbye.' Ends."

Bobby laid it down again and looked annoyed.

"Some silly ass trying to be funny most likely," he said.

"That's what Sarge thought, sir," answered Ford.

"Better check up all the same," Bobby said. "Ring up our Lower High Hill man and ask him if anything unusual has been happening. Let me see. Cobblers? Isn't that Lord Rone and Saine's place? The chap the *Daily Trumpeter* keeps calling 'Export Dictator'?"

"That's right, sir," agreed Ford. "*The Trumpeter* has a piece about him every day nearly. Extra big headlines this morning."

"What about?" Bobby asked.

"There's a long letter from him, nearly a column of it, to say calling him Export Dictator, or any other sort of dictator, is too silly to need a reply. So they've put a big photo of him on the front page and a whole lot inside about Cobblers and the Carton family history. Especially the scandals, and there've been lots of them—very old family. Old-world pomp and state, they say, and the finest private art collection in the world, outside America. Worth thousands of pounds."

"Trying to be nasty, I suppose," Bobby remarked. "A tall poppy and ought to be cut down."

"That's right, sir," agreed Ford, though it is to be feared the classical allusion was lost upon him.

"Well, let me know if you get anything from Lower High Hill," Bobby said.

Ford retired. Bobby yawned and signed another report—on the style, cut, and colour of the ties the police are now permitted to wear on duty, and told himself that a drive out to Cobblers by way of the famous Cobblers Oaks would be an agreeable change, even if only to uncover a mare's nest.

"Ought to have had sense enough to take the opportunity," he, reflected, and put out a languid hand to collect the next triviality which had been 'passed to you' for consideration.

But before he could apply his mind to the particular problem involved, Ford reappeared.

"Sarge said to inform you at once, sir," he announced. "Constable Yates, Lower High Hill, states: '*Re* 'phone inquiry to hand, Mrs. Jane Williams, Rose Cottage, this parish, reports finding knife, one, fancy handle, apparently bloodstained, in call-box near village, on road X79.' He asks for instructions."

Bobby sat back in his chair, a little startled. It might, of course, be part of some elaborate practical joke. The knife, with its 'fancy' handle, might have been used for skinning rabbits or killing pigs, or something of that sort. It might even be some new stunt of some specially enterprising young gentleman on the staff of the *Daily Trumpeter*, since that journal announced almost every day that Lord Rone and Saine was 'murdering' British exports. But then again it might not. What, he wondered, did 'fancy' handle mean?

"This private art collection the *Trumpeter* talks about," he said slowly, "doesn't it include what is supposed to be the finest collection of arms and armour ever got together? I seem to remember reading something of the sort."

"I didn't notice the *Trumpeter* said so much about that," Ford answered. "It talked a lot about Dutch interior pictures and about a stamp collection Lord Rone has got together himself recently and worth thousands."

"Dutch interiors, old arms and armour, and postage stamps," Bobby remarked. "Seems to show a catholic taste. Well, you know, I don't much care about bloodstained knives turning up after a 'phone call about a murder. Report back to your sergeant and tell him I think I had better drive out to Lower High Hill and have a look round, and I would like to take a man with me, just in case.

Most likely it's a leg-pull, but one can't be sure. Ask your sergeant to spare you if he can."

"Yes, sir. Thank you, sir," said Ford, looking very pleased—so pleased indeed that Bobby wondered if his message would not reach Ford's sergeant in a slightly more peremptory form, as regarded at least Ford's personal share in the proposed excursion, than Bobby himself had given it.

Not that he minded if that did happen, since Ford was an intelligent and reliable young man, who had already proved himself useful in emergency.

So he entered in his diary what he proposed to do and why, left a message or two with his secretary, and went out to find Ford had a car ready and waiting.

"Shall I drive, sir?" he asked when Bobby appeared.

But Bobby thought he would prefer to drive himself, and soon they were out in the country, both of them secretly aware, though neither of them would have admitted it for worlds, that even in a policeman's life there are moments less arduous, difficult, and trying than others.

Lower High Hill is one of those oddly placed villages produced by modern conditions. It remains remote and solitary, living its own life in sleepy, content, and it is in close touch with all modern developments. Television sets even are not unknown, and a good 'bus service puts the village within half an hour's ride of two fairly large towns, west and north-west. London itself is not more than an hour away by motor coach, though this runs at much rarer intervals. True, the main road along which these 'buses and the coach pass is nearly two miles away over wooded and hilly ground, but an active walker can cover this distance in half an hour. On a bicycle even less time is required. This wooded and hilly country serves to act as a kind of curtain—not iron—between the village and the outer world and so helps to preserve much of its original character as a self-contained entity.

The village itself—there is hardly a building in it less than a century old, and gas, electricity, and piped water are alike unknown—is dominated by the enormous bulk of Cobblers, almost entirely rebuilt soon after the Napoleonic Wars, when a disastrous fire destroyed its Carolean forerunner. It is approached by a stately avenue of ancient elms, and if the house has small claim to architectural beauty, its very size gives it an imposing air.

"You wouldn't think anyone could manage to keep a place like that going in these days," Bobby remarked as it first came into view. "It must need a regular army of servants, and they aren't so easy to get."

"Well, sir, I suppose everything's easy if you've got the money," observed Ford, and Bobby in reply spoke those two dreadful words that in these days weigh so heavily on all.

"Income tax," he said simply; and in the depressed silence that followed the utterance of those two sad words he drove on past the open entrance to the avenue of elms—the iron gates formerly guarding it had gone long ago to make munitions—past a lodge still clearly in occupation, and on to the village, where he drew up before the cottage that served both for police station and for the residence of Police Constable Yates, who represented law and order in Lower High Hill.

Yates was expecting them and the weapon found by Mrs. Williams of Rose Cottage was carefully laid out for their inspection on a clean sheet of paper.

It looked both a lovely and a deadly thing with its long, narrow blade, inlaid with gold, tapering to a point of needle sharpness, and showing on it ominous brown stains at which both Bobby and Ford looked doubtfully. The handle was in the shape of a nude woman in ivory and gold—a magnificent piece of work. Italian, Bobby thought, of the Renaissance period, and at once a work of beauty and of death—in that, typical of its time.

"You can't identify it in any way, I suppose?" Bobby asked presently.

Yates shook his head.

"No, sir," he said, "though they do say as up at Cobblers there's the like of it as was used before guns were thought of." He paused and added: "That handle now, there's times you could swear she was smiling wicked like, telling you to do the same and why not?"

"Why not what?" Ford asked, and Yates answered sombrely:

"Kill."

"Oh, well," Ford said.

Bobby had taken out his notebook and was putting down a full description of the weapon. He went on to make a sketch of it, and as he did so he, too, began to be aware of something of the same sensation that Yates had just spoken of. There were moments when it was as though the figurine was watching him as he worked, watching him with a sort of secret, hidden glee. He could almost have believed that the stains upon the blade had wakened it from long sleep to a life of its own, and that from it was proceeding waves of impulse imploring, urging, demanding that this fresh life imparted to it should be strengthened and continued in the same way.

"And the sooner, my dear," he said as if he were addressing it and it could understand, "the sooner you are back again safe in your glass case, the better."

Neither Ford nor Yates seemed to find anything strange in this remark, and indeed they were both of them regarding the thing with much the same sort of uneasy mistrust.

"No chance of finding any useful finger-prints on it, I suppose," Bobby remarked as he finished his sketch. "I expect the woman who found it didn't think about that."

"No, sir," agreed Yates. "I asked her. She had handled it quite a lot, wondering what it was and showing it to neighbours. Some of them said to take it straight back to Cobblers, but she thought I had better see it first—and quite right, too."

"It'll have to go for expert examination at Hendon," Bobby 'What about the call-box?"

"I've shut it up," Yates answered. "Stuck up a sign 'Out of Order,' but I couldn't see anything to notice. I had a look round, but it all seemed as usual. No bloodstains, no signs of a struggle. I hadn't time to make a proper search."

"Good," Bobby said approvingly. "You've done all you could. I'll go and have a look at the call-box myself, though I don't suppose you've missed anything, but I may as well see what it's like; and then we'll see if Lord Rone can identify the dagger as his property. If he can't identify it from my sketch, I'll bring him back here. Keep it safe, and above all don't let anyone touch it. There may be a dab or two somewhere that might be useful."

"There's some young gents staying up at Cobblers," Yates said. "I did think as it might be some of them up to their larks."

"If it's that," Bobby said, hoping that it might be so, "they'll be sorry for it before I've done with them. There is such a thing as causing a public mischief." He paused and added, almost against his will: "I don't believe it's that way, though," and when he turned to look again at the knife lying on the table he could almost have sworn that the features of the figurine had only just returned to immobility from a smile of evil, secret joy.

CHAPTER II

HENPECKED HUSBAND

BOBBY'S VISIT TO THE indicated call-box brought him in fact no fresh information. He was able to see for himself that the telephone directory whereon, according to the finder, Mrs. Williams, the dagger had been lying, showed no trace of blood. Presumably therefore any stains on it, whether of blood or not, were dry before the weapon was placed there. But blood dries so quickly that that piece of deduction seemed of little practical value.

They drove on to Cobblers, and Bobby noticed again, as he drove up the long and splendid tree-lined avenue, how well the place was looked after. Nearer the house, lawns and flower beds, looking all the better for the heavy rain-storms of Monday after-noon and evening, showed that the same skill and care and labour were being spent upon them now as before the war. And the enormous house itself was clearly receiving every care and atten-tion. The exterior had even been given recently a fresh coating of paint, in itself no inconsiderable expense. Again Bobby wondered how that expense was being met.

"I've heard it said that no one can have more than six thousand a year clear," he remarked to Ford, "but I should guess the keeping up of any house this size must run well over four figures, and then there are the grounds as well."

"There's ways and means," answered Ford darkly. "A big Stock Exchange kill, and then there's expenses and suchlike."

"Well, it's evidently managed somehow," Bobby said.

All the same, he thought it strange; and he was inclined to ask himself if there could be any connection between this apparent freedom from the general austerity and whatever it was had hap-pened here—or not happened. For after all, there was as yet nothing very much to suggest that anything serious had really taken place.

He was destined, however, to receive another mild shock when Ford's knock was answered by a tall young woman attired in that uniform of small lace cap, frilly apron, white cuffs, black frock, which was by no means unbecoming as an everyday working cos-tume, but which now is considered rather worse than the wearing of handcuffs and leg-irons.

Not a pretty girl, with her broad, flat face, eyes hidden behind spectacles with heavy rims and thick lenses, and a mouth that seemed to be permanently half open, as if to show off at their worst a set of large, protuberant teeth. But tall, well built, and quick in her movements, and plainly capable of any amount of hard work. More suited, Bobby thought, for work on a farm than as parlourmaid in a rich man's house. When he asked if Lord Rone and Saine was at home and could they see him, she inquired in a voice unusually deep and heavy for a woman if they had an appointment. So Bobby said "No," but that their business was important, and he produced his official card. The girl took it, glanced at it. The lower jaw of her permanently half-open mouth dropped suddenly, she gave a little gasp, and scuttled off like a frightened rabbit, leaving them standing on the doorstep.

"What's biting her?" Ford asked suspiciously.

Bobby was wondering about that, too. The girl had clearly been very much startled, even frightened, and that suggested a bad conscience, a knowledge or suspicion, even complicity in, some sort of wrongdoing she now feared had come to light.

The door had opened on a small entrance hall. From the interior into which the girl had vanished issued now a loud and angry masculine voice.

"Well, good heavens, suppose they are. What about it?" the voice was saying, and there appeared a small brisk, active-looking man, with a reddish-hued, square face, snow white hair and plenty of it, and a small white moustache and beard of the kind that used to be known as an 'imperial.' A distinctive figure, and with about it that air of sharp authority which comes naturally to those who have exercised it with little questioning all through their lives.

"I am Lord Rone," he said. "I understand you want to see me?" He looked at Bobby's card he was holding. "Police business? Scotland Yard?" he said. "You've scared that fool of a girl half out of her life. What's it all about? Come this way."

He led them through a spacious and lofty inner or lounge hall, lighted from above by a dome of coloured glass, less admired to-day than when first erected, and down a narrow corridor into a large and pleasant room, lined with books and overlooking through an open window a lawn on which three or four people were sitting. The murmur of their voices could be heard through the open window, though the distance was too great for words to be distinguished. But the quick glance Bobby gave suggested that one lady with wagging forefinger was very much dominating the conversation—if indeed it was not so much conversation as the delivery by her of a lecture for which she was demanding close attention. From the direction of the house a man was hurrying towards them as if anxious to miss no word of what was being said.

Bobby noticed, too, that the books on the shelves had very much the air of being in frequent use, as is not always the case in the libraries of large country houses. A desk near the window had on it many papers, all neatly arranged. There were two filing cabinets, a card-index cabinet, a telephone, a typewriter, all the accessories, in fact, needed by a busy man of affairs. Also there were several pictures on the walls, and even the hurried look Bobby gave them as he entered told him that they were probably of considerable interest and value—the Dutch interiors, probably, of which he had already heard. One of them, hanging above the mantelpiece, was of a horse against a pastoral background, and Bobby thought it might perhaps be Paul Potter's well-known 'Young Stallion,' the companion to his even more famous 'Young Bull.'

Lord Rone as they entered indicated two chairs for his visitors, extracted a box of cigarettes from a drawer of the desk, offered it to them, seated himself at the desk, and said:

"Well, now, what's it all about? Nothing to do with that girl, I hope. She had excellent references and it's the devil's own job to get hold of any staff."

"I noticed she seemed rather upset," Bobby agreed. "I haven't the least idea why. General principles perhaps, though of course we always wonder if there's any reason for it if people seem too disturbed when we call."

He was interrupted from without by a voice raised in loud and angry protest. The man he had seen hurrying towards the lecturing lady had reached the group, and she was now addressing him with great vigour, at the same time holding aloft some sort of wrap. From a word or two that reached them through the open window, it appeared that he had been sent to the house for a wrap and had brought the wrong one, for which he was being suitably rebuked in very loud tones. Apparently he was offering apologies which were not being received with any very good grace, and now he went off at a trot back to the house, presumably to retrieve there his unfortunate error. The gesture with which the injured lady turned to her two companions as he departed was plainly a kind of resigned demand for sympathy.

Lord Rone, looking half amused, half annoyed, tapped on the desk, rather like a schoolmaster demanding the attention of an inattentive pupil. Bobby, thus recalled to the business of the moment, went on:

"We are making inquiries about what seems to be an Italian dagger of some value. The blade is inlaid with gold and the handle is a figurine representing a nude woman. The workmanship is very fine. It has been suggested that it comes from your lordship's collection."

"Sounds," Lord Rone said in a surprised tone, "very much like my Cellini dagger—the golden dagger, we call it. But that's upstairs in the Long Gallery. Why are you inquiring about it?"

"Can you identify it from this?" Bobby asked, producing his notebook and showing the sketch he had made therein.

Lord Rone took the book, examined the sketch carefully.

"Did you do this?" he asked.

"I did it half an hour ago," Bobby answered.

"I don't understand," Lord Rone said, and he was looking now very puzzled indeed. "What from?"

"I made it as accurate a drawing as I could," explained Bobby, "of a dagger now in the possession of the police. But the sketch does not show stains on the blade that look to me very much like blood. That, of course, will have to be tested."

"Blood?" repeated Lord Rone, and now he was positively gaping as he stared bewilderedly at Bobby. "Nonsense. That's impossible."

"It is, however, a fact," Bobby said. "We have also had a message by 'phone stating that a murder has been committed here." This time Lord Rone seemed inclined to laugh.

"Oh, come now," he exclaimed. "Really. This is simply fantastic. I can assure you no one has been murdered in this house. Someone has been trying to make fools of you—and I am afraid succeeded very well."

"People do try occasionally," Bobby admitted. "That is what is meant by 'public mischief.' It may turn out to be like that this time. But we must make sure. There is this to be accounted for," he said, and showed again the sketch he had made and the description he had written.

"It certainly has," agreed Lord Rone. "There is, of course, a description of the Cellini dagger in one or two works of reference. Is this sketch made from one of them?" He picked up the telephone. "I'm dialling 999," he remarked, rather with a suggestion in his voice that Bobby and his companion had better run for it before a reply came.

"It'll take a moment or two to get through," Bobby remarked. "I could have given you the Commissioner's private number, but no doubt it is more satisfactory for you to do it yourself. A very sensible precaution to take," he added, deliberately making his voice a little patronizing. "If everybody took it, a good deal of trouble would be saved very often."

Lord Rone grunted. He did not like being approved of. He felt that it was slightly presumptuous for anyone to approve of anything he did. They ought simply to show their respect—a respect he was not sure Bobby's tone adequately expressed. Fortunately he did not notice the tiny smile that Ford permitted to creep round the corners of his mouth. Bobby turned to look out of the window. The little man he had seen before was returning at the same anxious trot towards where the three ladies were sitting on the lawn. He was short and fat, with a disproportionately big head. His hands were empty, and when he reached the waiting ladies he held them out with a kind of a deprecating, apologetic gesture. The one of the three women to whom he addressed himself rose with melancholy resignation in every line of her body and began to walk towards the house. The little man trotted in her wake, evidently still apologizing. They were nearer the house now and Bobby heard the lady say, loudly and clearly—she had a high, carrying voice:

"Oh, for goodness sake, William. I know you looked. I know you always look. Unfortunately, you never seem able to find. That's all. Of course, it's not your fault. I wouldn't have asked you, only I felt so chilly and I couldn't very well go myself while Lady Rone was so interested in what I was saying."

Lord Rone had got through now. He was saying into the mouthpiece:

"I have a visitor here. He describes himself as Commander Owen, one of your staff. He has a companion. He tells an entirely incredible story. I want confirmation."

Bobby's attention was still on the little scene outside, where the lady had evidently gone on to the house, while her companion was returning dejectedly towards the two still sitting on the lawn. But he could hear the 'phone squeaking in reply. Lord Rone said:

"They are putting me through to the Commissioner," and his tone now was a little less expressive of an expectation that Bobby and young Ford would take to instant flight.

The telephone squeaked again. Lord Rone hung up the receiver. In a voice that now sounded slightly disappointed, he said:

"I am asked to give you every assistance."

"I was, of course, always well aware that we could rely upon that," Bobby assured him.

"I still don't in the least understand," Lord Rone continued. "It is certain there has been no murder here. Absurd. But this sketch of yours . . . you say you made it half an hour ago from an original in your possession?"

"Might I suggest as a first step," Bobby said, "that we make sure that your Cellini dagger is still in its place?"

CHAPTER III

MISSING DAGGER

LORD RONE APPEARED to reflect upon this suggestion, as if it were not very welcome. Probably he was trying to persuade himself that it was all so incredible there was no need for any test. However, he got up and went to the open window.

"Maureen, Maureen," he shouted. "I want you."

The lady who had so unfortunately been forced to return to the house to fetch for herself her wrap her emissary had failed to find was now back in her chair on the lawn, apparently holding forth with as much eloquence as before—at least so one might suppose from her still-wagging forefinger. The little fat man, her disgraced emissary, was listening intently. The two other women rather less intently, Bobby thought. One of them at Lord Rone's summons sprang to her feet and came running at full speed. A swift, eager obedience, Bobby noted with a touch of surprise. Gratifying and praiseworthy, of course, but not generally one of the most marked characteristics of the young people of to-day. Reaching the house, she called through the open window:

"Oh, Daddy, thanks ever so. I should have murdered Aunt Bella if she had gone on talking much longer."

"Don't talk nonsense," Lord Rone snapped, evidently a little disconcerted by this unexpected reference to murder. "Come in. I want you for a moment."

Presumably there was a door near, giving admission from the garden to the house. Both the lady of the wrap and her little fat emissary with the big head had followed a path leading directly to the building. But Maureen made no movement towards this path. The study window was not of the variety known as 'french,' but it was large, wide open—Lord Rone, when calling, had pushed the sash up as far as it would go—and the sill was not more than four feet from the ground. Maureen leaped. She was on the sill, the next instant in the room itself.

"Oh," she said. "I didn't know there was any one here. Sorry." She bestowed a flashing smile, first on Ford, the younger man, and then on Bobby, and next, less effective, another on her father. "You saved my life, Daddy," she announced. "I can't think what's come over Aunt Bella. She seems as if she can't stop talking. And it can't be cocktails this time," she added meditatively, apparently with some past incident in her mind.

She was small, dark, her best features, her large, bright, expressive eyes, showing a dark depth of intensity not often to be seen. Her mouth was a little too large, but when open it displayed two rows of what can only be called 'film star' teeth—unfortunately beneath a nose of the variety described as 'snub,' even 'very snub.' Even in the few words she had spoken her voice had revealed an extraordinary range and depth of tone. A vivid and striking personality, impressive by reason of the hidden powers suggested in some odd way in every gesture, every movement. An impression enhanced possibly at the moment by her unusual method of entering the room. But that this had not appealed to her father was evident for now he was saying coldly:

"It would be as well, Maureen, if you would be so good—"

"—As to look before I leap," she completed his sentence for him. "Won't you introduce me?" she asked, again bestowing that swift, flashing smile of hers upon the two visitors.

"Commander Owen, of the C.I.D., Scotland Yard, has called on official police business," Lord Rone informed her; and if he had hoped to impress her by this announcement, he failed entirely.

"Oo-oo," she cried. "Scotland Yard?" She had a way, small though she was, of holding herself upright in such a manner, when she so pleased, as to seem to add inches to her height, and she could apparently alter the range and tone of her voice at will. It was deep and thrilling now as, turning to Bobby, she commanded: "Tell me about the most dreadful horrible murder you ever had to do with."

"I have not called to chat about murders," Bobby said shortly, himself a little vexed by this performance.

Instantaneously she changed and turned into a pathetic little girl, cruelly misunderstood. She didn't actually put her thumb in her mouth, but she managed to convey the impression that there it was. In a voice now soft and low and full of tears, she said: "Oh, please, I am sorry. I am really."

Bobby felt he was being laughed at and tried to look severe and dignified. Lord Rone said very crossly indeed:

"That's enough playing the fool, Maureen. Stop showing off, please."

"Not me," replied the irrepressible Maureen. "All great acting is showing off. Now Henry, don't lose your temper." Lord Rone glared, choked. So many times had he forbidden his daughter to call him 'Henry,' and never had she taken any notice of the prohibition.

She went on: "Did you really want me for anything or was it just to save me from an early death from boredom, listening to Aunt Bella?"

Lord Rone, apparently glad of this change in the conversation, went across to a wall safe Bobby had already noticed. He opened it, opened an inner door, took out a small bunch of keys, and handed them to his daughter.

"Get me the Cellini golden dagger from the Long Gallery," he said. "This is the key to the glass case."

"It's what I've been longing for all afternoon," Maureen cried. "The only way to stop her. She's told us three times already what she said to the Paris gendarme and what he said to her. Now at last I can do something about it. Hey-ho for the golden dagger."

She was off—one might say she flashed away—before her father could speak again. He sat down at his desk again, looking slightly dishevelled, as people often did after an encounter with Maureen.

"A lively young lady," Bobby remarked.

The comment brought no response and indeed did not seem to be approved. Only too clear that Lord Rone would have used a different adjective and that at the same time he thought it slightly presumptuous for Bobby to use any adjective at all. Bobby said;

"I wonder if I may look at your 'Young Stallion'? Critics call it Paul Potter's masterpiece, don't they? A finer thing even than his 'Young Bull.' "

Lord Rone, though he seemed a little surprised by the request, as if he had hardly expected that the painting would be recognized or the artist known, made a careless gesture with one hand. Bobby interpreted it as consent. He went across to the mantelpiece above which it hung, and stood for some minutes, looking at it closely and thoughtfully. Something in his attitude attracted Lord Rone's attention. He said sharply:

"Well? Well?"

"Well," Bobby repeated, "I suppose as a mere layman, I oughtn't to say so, but it doesn't strike me as coming anywhere near the 'Young Bull.' I can't see why it's thought better. To my mind, it hasn't—I hardly know how to put it—well, life, power. There's not the sense of drama. At least, if it's there, I can't feel it. And the texture of the paint—I can still remember the treatment of the 'Young Bull's' flank."

He went back to his seat, wondering a little if this criticism of an acknowledged masterpiece had seemed intolerably naif. Lord Rone made no comment, and he had an air of being a little disconcerted or disturbed. Though why a casual expression of opinion by a passing visitor should trouble the owner of a picture of world-wide reputation it was hard to imagine. The door opened. There was a pause. They all three looked towards it. Maureen appeared. An 'entrance,' in fact. Only a spot of limelight was needed.

She stood there, quite still, and once again she astonishingly succeeded in making her small, slight body give the strangest possible impression of being so much taller and larger than it was. Somehow she contrived to make it seem as if it filled the whole doorway in which she stood.

"Is this a dagger that I see before mine eyes?" she boomed out startingly. With a sudden change of manner, while the three men stared, she went on: "No, it jolly well isn't. It's an empty glass case. I say, Dad, is that what it's all about? Someone pinched it?"

"What do you mean?" her father asked sharply. "Isn't the Cellini dagger there?"

"Not a sign of it," Maureen assured him. "The glass case is locked all right, but no Cellini dagger. Vanished without trace. Nothing to show how or why. And what's the matter with Linda? She's dodging about like a white mouse in a panic. When I asked her what was up, she just mumbled something and cleared off—speed top priority. You don't think she can have pinched it, do you? She doesn't strike me as that sort. No guts."

"We had better go and see for ourselves," Lord Rone said. "I don't understand this."

He led the way back into the inner hall, that of the glass dome, up a double stair in marble and gilt, and along a wide corridor in which stood several pieces of sculpture, and then into a gallery that seemed to run the whole length of the house. Here stood more sculpture, several suits of armour of superb fifteenth- and sixteenth-century workmanship, Italian and German. There was a fine collection of weapons to rival those in the Wallace Collection and the Tower. There were a number of oil paintings, too, chiefly portraits, and ranged down the centre of the gallery was a series of glass cases. To one of these Lord Rone went at once, followed by the others. A glance showed that one place in it was vacant.

"Seeing believing, Dad?" demanded Maureen's voice from behind.

Bobby was bending down, examining the lock closely. Lord Rone took the keys from Maureen and was about to open the case. Bobby stopped him with a gesture that, a little to his surprise, Lord

Rone found himself instinctively obeying. It was Bobby now who was speaking with the sharp authority of a man accustomed to being obeyed. He said:

"Is there any other key to the case?"

"Duplicates of all keys are deposited in the bank," Lord Rone told him. "These are kept in the safe. You saw me take them out. They are not often used. No one could have got hold of them. The safe has a combination lock. No one knows the number of the combination except myself, though I always carry it with me."

"The number of your watch?" Bobby asked.

"How do you know?" demanded Lord Rone, very much taken aback.

"Oh, it's often done," Bobby explained. "Quite common. Useful idea. Or a 'phone number or that of a typewriter or something of the sort. Only you said you always had it on you."

He had been closely examining the lock as he talked. He said now:

"There's what looks to me like a trace of wax. I shall have to ask you to allow our experts to make an examination. My own idea is that an impression of the lock has been made and a duplicate key manufactured."

"What for?" Maureen asked. "The golden dagger is too well known for anyone to try to sell it. Nothing else has been touched. Those gold snuffboxes and the gold christening spoons made for Catherine Howard's baby that was never born are still there. Why should anyone want to pinch the dagger—except to do somebody in?"

No one answered this question.

CHAPTER IV

REFLECTED GLORY

NO ONE SEEMED to know quite what to say in the uneasy embarrassed silence that followed this unanswered question. Bobby was deep in thought and at the same time willing to wait to hear any spontaneous comment either father or daughter might make. Spontaneous comment is often enlightening and there were points about both of them that seemed interesting. Maureen had a little the air now of wishing she had not spoken—a state of mind very unusual with her. Lord Rone was frowning heavily and occasionally throwing unfriendly glances at Bobby, as if holding him in some degree responsible. In a rather dogged sort of way, as if resolutely thrusting out of his mind an unwelcome thought, he said presently:

"In any event, there's been no murder here. I think we are entitled to assume that I should have heard of anything of the kind. Death can't be hidden."

"I think sometimes it can," Maureen said, and suddenly she looked older.

"Can you tell me," Bobby asked, "when you saw the Cellini dagger last?"

"I can hardly say," Lord Rone answered. "Difficult to be sure."

"The servants might know," Maureen said. "I suppose it's Linda's job to do the dusting every morning."

"Is that the young woman who opened the door?" Bobby asked.

"I expect so. I'll ask her, shall I?" Maureen said. "She's about somewhere."

"Would you please simply tell her that I should like to speak to her?" Bobby said a little sharply.

Maureen, already halfway to the door, turned.

"For fear the witness might be suborned?" she inquired, and, though her tone had grown light again, there was still an undertone of unease apparent in the most expressive voice Bobby had ever heard. "Downy bird, aren't you? Henry, you'll have to watch your step."

Her father glared at this fresh use of his first name. But Maureen was already out of the room and they could hear her voice pealing through the passages. Without seeming to shout, she could use it, as now, like a trumpet, to send her summons rolling through the end-

less rooms and corridors of this enormous building. To Lord Rone
Bobby said:

"Do you think you could give me a list of all the inmates of the
house?"

Maureen was back again in the gallery now. She said: "Linda's
coming. She was just round the corner, hanging about most likely,
wondering what was up."

Linda appeared—the same young woman who had admitted
Bobby and Ford. But now she showed no trace of the alarm, even
panic, she had betrayed before. Either whatever had caused it had
somehow been removed or she had conquered it so completely that
no sign of it remained. Bobby wondered which. He said:

"I am inquiring into the disappearance of an article of some
value from this case."

He indicated it as he spoke and Linda came forward to look.
"The golden dagger," she exclaimed at once. "Oh, has it gone? That
lovely, lovely thing."

"Can you say when you saw it last?" Bobby asked.

"It was there last time I did the dusting," she answered. "I should
have missed it if it hadn't been, I'm sure. You couldn't have
helped."

"When was last time?"

"Monday morning," she answered. "I only do in here twice a
week; it's really enough. Monday and Thursday mornings."

"It must have been in its place all right Monday afternoon, too,"
Maureen interposed. "It's the pet particular of Uncle Bill; he says
the lady talks if you like to listen. I don't," she added with just a
touch of bravado, as if once she had tried the experiment and had
not liked it. "He would have noticed at once if it had gone and he
was up here all afternoon and evening nearly. About that article in
'Arms and Armour' trying to make out that that old suit of tin
reach-me-downs in the corner"—for such was the young woman's
irreverent description of a really magnificent suit of early sixteenth-century armour of Italian manufacture—"had been done up
at Brummagem. Uncle Bill was awfully peeved."

"This is Tuesday afternoon," Bobby remarked. "We must try to
get it nearer than that. What is your name?" he asked the housemaid.

"Belinda Blythe," she answered.

"And your home address?"

"I haven't one," she explained, looking pathetic. "I'm an or-
phan—a foundling, I suppose you would call it. I came straight here

from Mr. Tudor King's when he gave up his London flat. I had been there seven years. Mr. Tudor King, the celebrated novelist," she repeated, as if she thought the mention of that name should have made a greater impression.

"Who is he? Never heard of him," Lord Rone grunted.

"Oh, Henry," Maureen protested, her use again of his first name, producing automatically her father's accustomed frown. "You are so out of date. He sells by the bucketful. It's the most absolute tosh."

Miss Belinda Blythe, evidently deeply offended by this aspersion on the literary merits of her late employer, said stiffly:

"Tudor King's readers don't think so."

"They would if they could—think, I mean," Maureen retorted.

For the moment it seemed as if there were about to develop a literary debate—than which few can be more bitter. But Bobby intervened.

"We won't go into that," he said. "You have your identity card, Miss Blythe? I will ask you to let me see it presently. I think that will do for the present."

"I will ask the others about it if you like," Linda volunteered. "But I don't think any of them come in here very often."

"I think, Linda," Lord Rone said, "it would be as well for you to leave the matter in Mr. Owen's hands."

"Yes, my lord," Linda said. "I am sure your lordship knows best—and Miss Maureen, too."

She had laid a certain emphasis on Maureen's name as she turned away to depart. Lord Rone watched her go and then said indignantly:

"Insolence—deliberate insolence. I suppose her references were taken up. From this writing person?"

"It sounds as if he were very popular," Bobby remarked. "I think I've heard his name. The young woman had probably been basking in his reflected glory and didn't like hearing it called tosh."

"That would be why she was trying to get her own back," Maureen agreed. "I'm sure she was trying to hint I had done the pinching. What you would call a devoted reader. All the same, the stuff is soppy. The *Literary Weekly* tore it into little bits the other day and then did a hornpipe on them. Rather a shame, but you couldn't help laughing."

"She had better have a week's notice," declared Lord Rone. "There are some things one cannot and should not put up with."

Maureen reached up and patted him on the back. He at once had a fit of coughing.

"You old innocent," she said. "Giving notice to a maid is obsolete. It's simply not done, certainly not in the best circles."'

"If I may," Bobby said, "I would like to ask you not to send her away. I should much prefer no one here to leave until this business is cleared up."

"Coo," cried Maureen delightedly. "We're all under arrest."

"Maureen," thundered her father, and Maureen made a face at him.

Bobby didn't thunder. He was more subtle. He was getting a little tired of this noisy and self-assertive young woman. He said tolerantly:

"When you are just beginning to grow up, you like to say things of that sort."

Lord Rone had again an air of approving the remark but thinking it should not have been made. Maureen for once made no attempt to retort. She even had a slightly—very slightly—subdued air as she said:

"Anyhow, Linda did spot it had gone. I don't believe any of the others would have. It's a beautiful bit of work, but I shan't mind much if we never get it back. There's something about it—the handle, I mean. Sometimes you could think it was alive—watching, waiting."

"Nonsense," said her father. "It's valuable—heirloom as well."

"Cellini's favourite," Maureen said. "Whenever he had a specially juicy murder on hand, he always used it. Says so in his book. And we've kept up the tradition."

"That's only gossip," Lord Rone said. "Probably entirely untrue."

"One of our ancestors," Maureen explained to Bobby. "In the Golden Days of Good King Charles. See Bernard Shaw. The Lady Rone of the time got a dagger in her heart one day and it's always said to have been the Cellini one. Her loving husband didn't seem unduly disturbed and goodness knows why they didn't hang him. Silken ropes in short supply, probably."

"I wish, Maureen . . ." Lord Rone began, but got no further.

"O.K., Henry," she interrupted him, "only Mr. Owen might as well know. Murder in the family. Three hundred years ago, but it might crop up again. Not that anyone would ever suspect you, old dear," she added, giving her parent another thump on the back and so starting him off on another fit of coughing. "So there's only me.

Oh, and Our Mum, too. I do think that's such an awfully sweet expression, don't you? All England in two words."

"Do you think," Bobby, ignoring this, asked Lord Rone, "you, could give me a complete list of all the inmates of the house—guests and employees as well."

"There's one rather odd thing," Maureen said. "I expect it doesn't matter. It's the Mr. Tudor King Linda talked about who has taken the New Bungalow."

"Is that near here?" Bobby asked.

"A mile away," Maureen said. "More."

"Has Mr. King visited you at anytime—in connection with the letting?"

"No. It has nothing to do with me," Lord Rone said. "The New Bungalow is not on the estate."

"All the same, it is a bit queer," Maureen said thoughtfully. "I don't suppose there's anything in it really, but it is a bit odd when you think of it—Tudor King turns up here and rents a bungalow he never occupies—no one there except a woman who says she is his secretary and another woman who has vanished now."

"Vanished?" Bobby asked sharply.

Maureen regarded him with grave, startled eyes.

"Oh, I didn't mean that," she said. "I just meant she had gone away. I only thought it was funny, him coming and never being seen, and Linda taking a job with us after being with him, and then the golden dagger—well, vanishing. It really is funny. But then, authors are funny, aren't they?"

CHAPTER V

THE COBBLERS CATALOGUE

BOBBY DID NOT ATTEMPT to comment on an axiom so universally accepted. He had his notebook on the table. He said:

"I gather you have some guests staying with you at present. Could you let me have their names, if you please?"

"All of them alive and kicking," Maureen interposed.

"Be quiet, Maureen," said her father automatically. "Well, there are my old friends, Sir William and Lady Watson."

"It was Lady Watson I was saved from when Daddy called," Maureen explained. "She just simply doesn't seem able to stop talking."

"She is not the only one," Bobby said drily; and Maureen again looked a little—oh, very little, infinitesimally little—abashed.

"You are probably unaware," Lord Rone was continuing, either unaware of this little bit of byplay or ignoring it, "that Sir William Watson is one of the best-known historians and archæologists in the country. A very great authority, everywhere so recognized. One of his major works is the Cobblers catalogue, a work of the highest value, known the world over. That is my own copy," and as he spoke he pointed to three stately volumes on a shelf of the nearest bookcase.

"Published price sixty guineas," said Maureen, "and when guineas were guineas, too, and not just meaningless symbols. Not exactly a best-seller. Doesn't include the Cobblers pictures either, and there are some pretty swell ones here—not counting the fakes."

"Sir William would know all about the Cellini dagger?" Bobby remarked.

"Two photos, one a special plate, and a page of letterpress," Maureen informed him. "The thing really is a fine bit of work. Nasty, all the same."

"I shall be glad to receive it back," Lord Rone said. "I hope every precaution will be taken to see that it is safe?"

"I accept full responsibility for its custody," Bobby assured him. "It will, of course, be returned to you as soon as possible. Is Sir William the gentleman I saw crossing the lawn and then returning again to join the ladies who were sitting out there?"

"The poor man couldn't find the wrap Aunt Bella wanted, so she packed him off to look again," Maureen explained. "He's the ideal hubby. The more Aunt Bella bullies him, the more devoted he grows. A dog's life, but he loves it."

"Aunt Bella?" Bobby repeated. "Is that Lady Watson? They are relatives, then?"

"Not really," answered Maureen. "Honorary rank only. But I've always called them uncle and aunt. I was only a kiddy when Uncle William was doing that catalogue—it really is a one-er, you know. He may be a doormat to Aunt Bella and like it, but he knows his onions all right."

"Sir William," Lord Rone interposed, either to explain expressions he apparently thought Bobby might fail to understand or else that he thought should be clothed in more appropriate language, "is one of the greatest living authorities on his own subjects, and he happens to be devoted to his wife. Young people today find devotion in a married couple to be extremely comic."

"Now, Daddy, play fair," Maureen protested. "Everyone knows you are devoted to Mum, and so you jolly well ought to be, and it isn't comic. What is comic is the way Aunt Bella gives Uncle Bill hell all day and, I expect, all night, and the way he laps it up and asks for more."

"He happens to owe his life twice over to her devoted and tireless nursing," Lord Rone reminded her severely.

"She'll be able to have another go soon," Maureen said cheerfully, "if the way he keeps sneezing is anything to go by. I heard Aunt Bella giving him fits for getting his feet wet in that awful rain yesterday afternoon. She really has an extra special turn for nursing. It might even stop her talking."

"I wonder if you have an extra special gift for nursing, too, Miss Maureen?" Bobby asked innocently.

"Me? Good gracious, no," Maureen answered, as if at first slightly surprised by the suggestion; and then, with a sudden cocking of a doubtful eye at Bobby, she said: "Another left hook straight from the shoulder?" To her father, she explained: "He means that if I had it, it might stop me talking, too." She gave what can only be described as a hollow laugh, worthy of the best days of Surrey-side melodrama. "Little he knows," she declared in her most thrilling tone.

But Bobby was thinking that what he had just learned showed that both the Watsons had full knowledge of the golden Cellini dagger, of where it was kept, of its value, and would also have ample opportunity to visit the Long Gallery without arousing attention or suspicion. But then could any suspicion of any sort possibly attach to an elderly, henpecked gentleman of such eminence, or to an elderly lady who talked so much and bullied her husband? A vision came into Bobby's mind of a fat little man with an outsize head trotting amiably and anxiously across the lawn, and he decided he had never come across anyone less likely to rob an old acquaintance of a valuable work of art or to be mixed up in anything else in the nature of a criminal activity. Of course, one never knew. The most unlikely people do the most unlikely things for the most unlikely motives. Nor did Lady Watson—Maureen's Aunt Bella—seem an any more likely candidate for guilt.

"There are other guests in the house, I think you said," he remarked to Lord Rone.

"There are two young men staying here at present," Lord Rone admitted, but with a certain reluctance, or so Bobby thought.

He grew attentive. He saw Ford looking at him and knew the same thought was in both their minds—two larky young men trying to amuse themselves at the expense of their host and the police. If it was like that, Bobby decided, he would take care to see they were soon very sorry for themselves.

"Might I inquire their names?" he asked. "I shall probably have to ask to see them."

"Mr. Richard Moyse and Mr. Norman Oxendale," Lord Rone answered. "I am in need of a secretary," he went on, "and I suggested to Mr. Moyse that he should come down here for a day or two, so that I might consider him for the post."

"I take it, then," Bobby said, slightly disappointed, since a candidate for a situation would hardly be likely to start by trying to play practical jokes on his prospective employer, "you had satisfactory references?"

"Well, it has hardly seemed necessary so far," Lord Rone answered, though again with a touch of hesitation. "Nothing very much has been said up to the present."

"Dick Moyse," interposed Maureen, "more or less saved Daddy's life the other day, and he's being most awfully modest about it. A man did a snatch of Daddy's dispatch case and sent him sprawling into the road. As near as possible, he would have been run over, only Dick happened to be passing and he dashed into the road, stopped a car just in time, helped Daddy up, and dashed away again after the dispatch case. Got it back, too. Jolly good show."

"It certainly sounds so," agreed Bobby. "Suggests very considerable presence of mind."

"I should have been greatly inconvenienced," Lord Rone said, "if the dispatch case hadn't been recovered. There were some very important papers in it. Not much value to anyone else. Nor, Maureen, is the word 'sprawling' entirely appropriate. I merely went down on one knee, though certainly in front of a car that was going at a very high rate of speed."

"I would like a word with the young man later on," Bobby said. "You have another guest?"

"Mr. Oxendale," Lord Rone said. "He wrote to ask if he might see the Cobblers pictures and miniatures. He gave Sir William as a reference to his qualifications. Sir William thinks very highly of him as an art critic, especially as regards miniatures. They are his chief interest, apparently."

"He is interested in other things as well as miniatures," Maureen observed complacently.

"You knew him previously?" Bobby asked her.

"Oh, yes," Maureen said. "I heard talking about miniatures at the Bay Tree, so I told him about ours and he seemed awfully interested. Then he wrote to Dad, so I said why not ask him down for a few days, and Mother did. It meant a bit of a change for her, she can't get about much, poor dear."

Bobby had never visited the Bay Tree, but he knew the name as that of a restaurant off Piccadilly where the cream—sometimes the sour cream—of the intellect of the town was wont to assemble for lunch and dinner.

"Would it be possible," he asked, "for me to see these two young gentlemen? They may be able to tell us something."

"Maureen," Lord Rone said, "see if you can find them? Oxendale was asking if he might make a sketch of the old stables. He may be there. Moyse was talking about going for a walk. I don't know where."

"He asked me about the path through the west plantation," Maureen said. "I told him it stopped at the New Bungalow, and he would either have to come back the same way or else by a much longer way through the village. Which he won't do; not him. He hasn't the feet for country walks."

She went off then and Bobby asked if he might see Lady Rone.

"It's the mistress of the house," he remarked, "who is most likely to know better than anyone else what's going on and if there's been anything out of the way happening."

So Lord Rone took him out across the lawn to where the little group he had seen before was still sitting quietly under the trees. There Lady Watson seemed to be still talking energetically, her husband still listening with rapt attention, and Lady Rone, in an invalid chair, still busying herself with some light needlework and apparently allowing the flood of discourse to pass tranquilly by to the accompaniment of an occasional faint 'Dear me' or some such exclamation from herself. She was an elderly woman, frail-looking and worn, and must once have been very good-looking till the passing of the years and much experience of pain had taken their inevitable toll. She greeted Bobby in a low, gentle tone in which appeared none of the querulousness that invalids sometimes develop. The news of the disappearance of the Cellini dagger from its accustomed place and its discovery in a 'phone box was received by her with equilibrium, her only remark being that, of course, it was a very wonderful piece of work, but for her part she wouldn't mind if they never saw it again. Lady Watson was much more voluble in her expressions of wonder and dismay. Sir William seemed both startled and angry, almost as if he had suffered a personal insult.

"Disgraceful, intolerable," he proclaimed. "What on earth can it mean? Why take it only to return it?" he demanded. "In a 'phone box of all places? Which one?"

He was even so far moved as to stop his wife's flow of comment with a curt decision that she, though she seemed surprised, obeyed instantly. He repeated his question, "Which 'phone box?" but then broke into a violent fit of sneezing, for which he apologized profusely on the ground that he had been out in Monday's rain, got wet through and caught a cold. This gave Bobby a chance to leave his question unanswered and for Lady Watson to tell him sharply that it was all due to his carelessness in forgetting to take his umbrella with him. All the same, Bobby was left with the impression that though Sir William might be the perfect henpecked husband, he could evidently assert his authority when he wanted to. For Lady Watson still showed no inclination to renew that flow of talk he had checked so abruptly. Indeed, something cold and hard and hostile had come into the fat little man's dark eyes, as if this treatment of so fine and treasured a relic of Renaissance art had aroused in him very deep-seated emotions and instincts. Bobby even wondered if his wife's show of bullying was not a kind of protective screen to conceal, even from herself, her fear, even awe, of her seemingly docile mate.

Bobby went on to put a few general questions, but without learning anything fresh. In reply to a third inquiry from Sir William, his sneezes happily over for the time, Lord Rone gave the position of the 'phone box, and Sir William considered it frowningly as if he thought it might in some way be significant.

CHAPTER VI

BLACK EYE

LORD RONE AND BOBBY returned to the house, where Ford had been left waiting in the study. On the way Bobby said again that he would like to interview as soon as might be convenient the members of the domestic staff. Lord Rone protested that they were all old and trustworthy servants, and Bobby had once again, as so often before, to explain that suspicion automatically attached to everyone who by any possibility could have had access to the Long Gallery.

"Including," Lord Rone asked with sarcastic intent, "myself and my family and guests?"

"Well, I said 'all,' didn't I?" Bobby asked. "Of course, we consider probability and motive and all that. An owner of valuable property isn't likely to rob himself, but it does happen. Insurance generally. Draw your insurance money and keep the stuff."

Lord Rone made no comment, but Bobby had an idea that he found this remark somewhat disconcerting. Before anything more could be said, a good-looking young man presented himself, tall and fair, with that well-groomed look characteristic of the public school and university product, at least when it has not gone over to the corduroy trousers, sloppy, flowing ties, and the other customary indications of a high degree of intellectuality and sensibility. He had, too, the cheerfully self-confident air the same education generally gives to those to whom life so far has offered the smiling welcome due to their position.

"Sorry to trouble you, Mr. Oxendale," Lord Rone said as he came in. "Unfortunately—But perhaps Maureen has told you?"

"She said Scotland Yard chaps were here," the young man answered, glancing at Bobby and the silent Ford: "Something missing from the Long Gallery, isn't there? I do hope it's not one of these exquisite miniatures."

"The Cellini dagger," Lord Rone told him before Bobby could speak. "It has disappeared from the Long Gallery and been found again in a 'phone box near here."

Oxendale looked as if he were finding it rather difficult to take this in.

"But—well, what for?" he asked. "I mean to say—"

"Exactly," interposed Bobby. "When an object of very high artistic and money value disappears from where it's kept and then is found again not far off, an explanation does seem to be needed."

"Oh, yes, quite so," Oxendale agreed. "Doesn't seem to make sense, does it? Still, if it's been got back, that's something."

"There's another complication," Bobby went on. "A 'phone message was received at the Yard. I needn't go into details at present, but we would very much like to know who sent it."

"Not me," Oxendale said promptly. "I never use the thing. Hate it. Haven't got one. What's the good of locking your door and settling down to work when, if you're on the 'phone, anyone with twopence to spare can walk in on you any moment? I count my time worth more than twopence."

There was not much more he seemed to have to say. He agreed he had been in the Long Gallery several times since Monday to examine again the collection of miniatures.

"I may be writing a monograph on miniatures," he explained. "The elder Oliver especially. There's one of his up there—very fine. Shows a young man against a background of the flames of love. Not identified as yet, apparently. I've an idea about that I want to try out."

The miniatures were, however, all at the further end of the Long Gallery from that where stood the glass case in which had been kept the Cellini golden dagger. He had never noticed whether it was still there or missing.

"I remember it, of course," he said. "Wonderful bit of work. But it's painting I'm chiefly interested in. A chap has to make a living somehow," he explained apologetically, as if regretting so vulgar a necessity, "and it may as well be something interesting like being an art critic."

"Well, there are certainly some magnificent things, here," Bobby remarked. "That Paul Potter, for instance," he added, glancing at it where it hung above the mantelpiece.

" 'The Young Stallion,' " Oxendale said, turning to look. "Yes, rather. The best thing Potter ever did. A masterpiece if ever there was one. I should rank 'The Young Stallion' as one of the forty or fifty finest pictures ever painted."

He had spoken with enthusiasm, and Lord Rone looked very pleased; even, Bobby thought, relieved, as if the criticism Bobby had passed upon it shortly before had been troubling him. Odd, Bobby thought again, that casual criticism by a passing visitor with no very special qualification should seem to have been taken so seriously.

Oxendale withdrew then and was succeeded by Mr. Richard Moyse. He was a small, rather dandified young man with wide, innocent blue eyes, a well-shaped if somewhat small mouth and nose, and a very pleasant, smiling, friendly manner. His hands were small and well-kept and of them he seemed a little proud, so carefully did he keep them in view. He had correspondingly small feet, clad in shining, well-cut, expensive-looking shoes. A glance at them made Bobby understand at once what Maureen had meant by her remark that Moyse had not the feet for a long country walk. He, too, had nothing of much interest to tell. He had not used the telephone since his arrival at Cobblers. He had had no occasion to. He had only been in the Long Gallery once, on the day of his arrival, when he had made the customary tour of the Cobblers art treasures that was incumbent on all visitors. With a slightly shamefaced air, he confessed he was not much interested in the visual arts. With him it was—music. He gave a little ecstatic sigh. "Music," he repeated, and let the word linger on the air like Shakespeare's 'dying fall'. As for the, golden dagger—yes, he had seen it. No one could help noticing it. "A frightening thing," he said, and he turned a little pale, as if he found terror even in the memory.

"A superb work of art," he repeated, and then, as in a burst of confidence, he added: "To tell the truth, I would give half the other works of art in the world for one movement by Popolivinski."

So he, too, had to be dismissed. Nor did the questioning of such of the domestic staff as were at the moment available produce anything more. How the golden dagger had vanished from its place in the Long Gallery, to appear again in the 'phone box on Road X79, remained as great a mystery as before.

"None of all this seems to be getting us much further forward," Lord Rone commented with some severity when the last of the available staff had been dismissed. "After all, it has been recovered. Is it necessary to pursue the matter further?"

"That will depend," Bobby answered, "on what the report says of the stains on the handle. If they do prove to be human blood, I am afraid we shall have to go into it very thoroughly indeed."

Lord Rone did not look as if this prospect pleased him. Maureen reappeared. After a certain show of hesitation, which Bobby thought, from his experience of her so far, to be a somewhat unusual phase with the young lady, she said:

"Oh, by the way, Daddy, does Mr. Owen know about Mr. Baldwin Jones? Have you said anything about him?"

"No, why?" her father asked in a surprised tone. "He could hardly have anything to do with it. He left Monday afternoon."

"Who is Mr. Baldwin Jones?" Bobby inquired.

"I met him in Town—at the Bay Tree," explained Maureen.

"You meet everyone there. I believe they used to let him run his face for a meal—goodness knows why. He said he had seen me at an R.D.A. show."

"He left last Monday?"

"Yes. In a hurry."

"Why?"

"Well, I suppose it might be because of the black eye I had given him," Maureen explained once more.

CHAPTER VII

THEATRICAL PRODUCER

BOBBY GLANCED UP QUICKLY, not quite sure what this remark meant or whether it was intended to be taken seriously. Maureen had now, however, a distinctly sulky air, and he thought that probably this time she had spoken neither from bravado nor from what her father had called 'showing off,' but because she felt she had better mention herself an incident that in any case Bobby was sure to hear of.

"Really, Maureen," Lord Rone protested and looked as baffled as he so often did before his daughter. "Was it necessary to mention that? Mr. Owen will hardly be interested."

"May I ask," inquired Bobby, in fact very much interested, more especially as he felt Lord Rone's remark was meant as an indication that it was no business of his and consequently he thought it might well be so, "may I ask how did that happen? Young ladies don't usually give young gentlemen black eyes."

"Oh, well, you see," Maureen explained, smiling now, for indeed her mood changed with a most bewildering rapidity, and with her mood it almost seemed as if her personality changed as well, "it's not so much that I mind awfully about being kissed, only—" And there she paused, her head a little to one side, as if waiting to see what would be the effect on her two listeners of this pronouncement.

Lord Rone said, as he seemed to be in the habit of saying: "Maureen! Really!"

Bobby said:

"Only you believe the occasion should be adequate and the actuality rare?"

"Did you make all that up yourself?" Maureen asked, evidently much impressed.

"A quotation," Bobby told her. "Alexander Bain. A Scotsman."

"He would be," declared Maureen with conviction.

"And the black eye?" Bobby asked.

"I never heard anything about this before," protested Lord Rone.

"Darling," Maureen said, "I can't help your having a daughter, but I do try to spare you all I can." To Bobby she said: "At any rate, when I'm the kissed I do like to choose my kissor. So when Baldy tried it on his own, I took a swing at him with my umbrella—one of those stumpies you get in Switzerland." She produced her sweetest, most childlike smile, and she could look very sweet and innocent and childlike when she chose. She went on: "You just ought to have seen him go flop. Jack Longton says the black eye wasn't me at all, but I'm sure it was, even if Baldy did go over whack against a gate-post. Jack's an awful beast. He always tries to take you down. I told him he was just jealous, and I expect he was."

"Who is Jack Longton?" Bobby asked, interested by this introduction of a new name.

"Jack Longton? Oh, everybody knows him," Maureen declared. "He's a jolly good producer, though nothing like as good as he thinks he is. He writes, too. He had a play on at the Central last year."

"Had he, though?" said Bobby, impressed as everyone is on hearing of that remarkable feat.

"Ran nineteen nights," Maureen told him. "He groused a lot. I told him it was a jolly good run, considering what the play was like."

"I am sure Mr. Longton must have felt it very nice of you to say that," remarked Bobby, unable to resist the comment. "Has he ever stayed here?"

"Not him," Maureen replied. "He offered to stand me a lunch at the Bay Leaf if I would ask him down for a week-end, but I told him nothing doing. And then he had the cheek and impudence to turn up as a Saturdayer."

"What's that?" Bobby asked.

"The house and grounds are open to the public on Saturdays," Lord Rone explained. "Most inconvenient. But it was put to me that the public should be allowed an opportunity of seeing the Cobblers collection. I agreed."

"It's to improve their little minds," Maureen put in. "Quite a lot come along. Half a crown a head. Catalogue, abridged by Uncle Bill himself from his big one, five bob. With reproductions, including a frontispiece of the 'Young Stallion,' seventeen and six. Jolly dear if you ask me, but they pay up like lambs. Or did. More sales resistance now with less money about."

"The money received," Lord Rone said stiffly, "only just covers expenses. It is necessary to have an attendant in every room. There was one most unpleasant incident. A man was seen apparently trying to open one of the cases in which part of my stamp collection was shown—including the eighteen-seventy stamp, which you probably know is extremely valuable."

"The one," explained Maureen, seeing that Bobby did not much look as if he did know, "on which the old Queen's head was printed upside down. Only six of them got into circulation and no one knows what became of the other five. So this is unique; and every other collector goes green whenever he remembers that Henry's got it and he hasn't."

"I have had high offers," Lord Rone admitted. "It was a great find. I was called at the time of the incident I mentioned. The person concerned was full of apologies. I did not accept them. I had him removed from the house and I gave instructions that he was not to be admitted again on any account. Fortunately, he had a distinct cast in one eye, so he could easily be recognized."

"I act as guide sometimes when I'm on tap," Maureen interposed. "It's rather fun. I've had tips sometimes, but not often. People are getting jolly close with their money."

"Mr. Longton would know all about the Cellini dagger, then, and where it was kept?"

"Well, he ought to," answered Maureen, "considering he's had the cheek to come two Saturdays running and asked all the fool questions he could think of, trying to stump me. He doesn't miss, much; not him."

"Can you give me his address and that of Mr. Baldwin Jones?"

"They might know at the Bay Tree. Baldy hangs around there a good deal," Maureen said doubtfully. "He keeps it rather dark. I expect it's in some awful slum when it's not the Superb or some other swell hotel. He alternates."

"And Mr. Longton?"

"Oh, he has a flat in Town somewhere. Anyhow, he's in the 'phone directory. Just now he's staying at the Cobblers Oaks Hotel. He is studying a new play he's to produce—and probably writing a new one himself he hopes will run twenty nights instead of nineteen."

"That's not very far, is it?" asked Bobby, knowing that Cobblers Oaks, a famous beauty spot, was only a few miles away.

"Oh, no; half an hour's drive. He had the impudence to say he would be over every Saturday morning till further notice."

The thought crossed Bobby's mind that if Mr. Longton could get over every Saturday morning, he could equally easily get over every night. It would be as well, he decided, to have a chat with Mr. Longton and probably with Mr. Baldwin Jones, too. Mr. Longton could be seen on the way home, but presumably the other young man would have to wait till his address was known. In the meantime, as no more information was likely to be obtained and as it was growing late, Bobby decided it was time to depart.

It was an announcement received with few signs of regret, and Bobby and Ford were hardly out of the house before Ford said:

"That young lady, sir. Do you think she's all there?"

"Why? What makes you say that?" Bobby asked.

"Well, the way she talks, never the same two minutes together," Ford replied. "And then giving people black eyes! Not what you expect."

"She's in with a stage and arty lot in Town," Bobby said. "Apt to go to the head with young people. At present she is seeing everything in terms of the theatre. She hasn't realized yet that it's life that often holds up a mirror to the stage."

Ford pondered this. Then he pronounced his verdict.

"Not what you expect from a young lady," he said.

"Well," Bobby admitted, "I did rather think at first all her chatter and the way she kept putting her oar in might mean there was something she was trying to keep back. I don't know. May have been the black eye incident. Most likely it was just a way she's got into and hasn't learned to tone it down yet. I think myself, we were lucky she didn't start calling us 'darling' and wanting to kiss us goodbye—especially you as the younger."

Ford looked alarmed at this and then gradually let his features relax into a faint smile.

"Oh, well," he said—contentedly.

"Now, Ford," said Bobby—sternly.

A cryptic exchange both seemed to understand, and then they had arrived at the Cobblers Oaks Hotel.

The receptionist's desk was closed, but a porter appeared. To him Bobby said:

"I think Mr. John Longton is staying here. He will be expecting us. There's been a 'phone message, hasn't there?"

"Yes, sir, a few minutes ago," the man answered. "I'll let Mr. Longton know. He'll have finished dinner by now."

The porter went off accordingly, leaving both Bobby and Ford consumed with envy, for they had had no chance even to begin their dinner. Ford said in rather a hesitating voice:

" 'Phone message, sir? Were you expecting there'd be one?"

"First thing that young woman did was to warn Longton about us, most likely," Bobby answered. "Or at any rate, as soon as she thought her father wasn't looking."

A young man was coming towards them. He was sturdy and well built, with broad face and high cheekbones, his most noticeable features his eyes, large, bright, and quick, under heavy, overhanging brows, and his chin, which stuck out defiantly, as if challenging all the world to try to hit it and then see what happened. There was, too, a certain quick agility in all his movements, as of one who knew he had to hasten, if there were to be time for him to do all he had to accomplish; and Bobby was soon thinking that these movements he made could easily degenerate into a nervous fidgeting. What is called 'highly strung,' indeed, in spite of the rather contradictory solidity there seemed to show in his manner and physique.

"Mr. Longton, isn't it?" Bobby said. "I think Miss Maureen Carton has 'phoned to tell you to expect us?"

"Yes. Did she tell you she was going to?" Longton said, evidently surprised. "She asked me not to let on."

"A misunderstanding," Bobby answered, waving it aside. "You and she are friends, I think?"

"Well, we are more or less on terms of mutual insult," explained the young man. "What's it all about?"

Bobby asked if there was somewhere where they could talk for a few minutes, and Longton led the way to an alcove sheltered by an enormous palm. When they were settled, Bobby said:

"Didn't the young lady explain?"

"Only that two blokes from Scotland Yard were on my track and I had better mind my p's and q's. And something about the golden dagger they think is a Cellini piece turning up in a 'phone box I couldn't make head or tail of. Then she rang off. I think her father came along and she thought she had better dry up. I thought at first it must be about Baldy Jones. He was threatening blue murder."

"Oh, yes. Why was that?"

"Well," Longton explained. "It was at the Bay Tree—Monday night, I think. I—well, I poured my coffee down his neck and when he seemed a bit peeved I said to come outside, and then the waiters came hovering round so we both did. Go outside, I mean."

"Anything happen?"

"Oh, no; there's no guts to Baldy. He said he was going to summons me. I didn't much expect him to. Is pouring coffee down a chap's neck a summonsable offence?"

"Well, really, I hardly know," Bobby admitted. "Might depend on how hot it was."

"Oh, just restaurant coffee," Longton explained.

"I take it Mr. Jones had been saying something about Miss Maureen and—"

"Oh, no," Longton interrupted with every appearance of extreme surprise. "Her name was never mentioned. Why should it be? It was my production of that new play from the U.S., *Desire Up Under*. I welcome criticism, of course, but mere vulgar abuse and an idiotic trying to be funny, I do draw the line at. Hence the coffee. Where does the Cellini dagger come in?"

Bobby answered this sudden change of subject by explaining what had happened. Longton said he was sure he had seen the dagger in its place on the Saturday. He had asked Maureen, acting as guide, some questions about it.

"Ragging her," he explained. "She doesn't know the first thing about Renaissance art, or anything else much for that matter. But she played up jolly well, invented like one o'clock, made a great impression. I heard two of the party telling each other she must have made a profound study of Italian art."

Bobby asked a few more questions. Longton had little more to say. Nor did he know—or for that matter want to know—Mr. Baldwin Jones's address. If you wanted him—Heaven alone knew why anyone ever should—you could generally find him hanging round one of the West End pubs.

There seemed nothing more to be learned; and so Bobby and his companion were soon on their way back to Town and to the suppers they so ardently hoped they would find waiting for them.

CHAPTER VIII

BLOODSTAINS

LATER ON THAT NIGHT, Bobby, smoking a meditative cigarette after a home-produced supper that had left within him no room for any more envy of Jack Longton's hotel-produced dinner, began to let his thoughts dwell again on his Cobblers visit.

"Of course," he told Olive, his wife, who was already looking at the clock and hinting at bed, "it all depends on the result of the analysis of these stains on the golden dagger."

"Well, then," Olive suggested, "why not wait till you get the result before worrying about it?"

"Don't be so painfully commonsensical," Bobby ordered.

"There's no such word," retorted Olive. "So I can't be, can ?"

"There are a lot of worrying little things," Bobby went on, ignoring this most justifiable protest. "They may not amount to much, only why are they? Lord Rone, for example. Why was he bothered because I wasn't so awfully impressed by the 'Young Stallion'?"

"Well, if you had a picture worth thousands and thousands of pounds and someone came along and hinted it wasn't, you would look bothered fast enough. I know I should."

"More to it than that," Bobby said. "At least I think so, but I've no idea what. There's the girl, too. She didn't at all like telling me about the Jones young man's black eye and she wouldn't if she hadn't felt she had got to before someone else did."

"No really nice girl would want to talk about a thing like that," Olive assured him. "Be your age, Bobby. Would any eligible young man be attracted by the prospect of a black-eye-dealing wife?"

"Well, there's that," Bobby conceded. "Sir William Watson, too. Interesting case. Henpecked door-mat and all that, and yet somehow you get the idea that at bottom she's a bit scared of him. She closed down double quick when he told her to."

"He may have given her a scare some time," Olive suggested. "Men are so unaccountable, aren't they? Some silly little trifle or another set him off, perhaps, and now she's trying to forget it by asserting herself. And he may be trying to forget it, too."

"Now you're going all psychological and Freudian, and Lord knows what," Bobby protested. He went on: "Then there's that young man, Richard Moyse. He didn't look to me at all the sort of person to dash about rescuing people from under motorcars and recovering stolen dispatch cases. A bit unfair, I suppose. You can't go by looks, but there is a lot of very valuable stuff lying about at Cobblers—including a stamp collection there seems to have been one attempt on already. A gentleman with a cast in his eye found meddling with one of the cases. Stamps are about the most valuable loot you can get hold of in these days. Easily negotiable. Prices rising. Current everywhere. Almost impossible to identify. Give me stamps or diamonds and it's stamps for me every time."

"What's the golden dagger got to do with it, if it's stamps?" Olive asked.

"May be some sort of red herring," Bobby suggested. "I don't know, but then I don't know anything."

"Well, then, why talk?" Olive asked simply.

"There's the Oxendale young man, too," Bobby went on, again ignoring a question to which he knew he had no reply. "He seemed the most ordinary of the lot and, of course, that makes him the most open to suspicion."

"That's being subtle," Olive rebuked him, "and you're always saying in those lectures you give recruits and people that fifty cases are solved by the simple approach to one that's solved by being subtle."

"I ought," declared Bobby firmly, "to put the ratio at a hundred to one, but this may be the one exception."

"Maybe," agreed Olive. "And it may not, and, anyhow, what is there to solve as yet?"

"Well, I do rather want to know," Bobby explained, "what the golden dagger, as they call it, was doing in a 'phone box? All very curious. The parlourmaid, too. Belinda something—Blythe, I think. Belinda Blythe. An improbable name. And why was she so flurried at first seeing us and then perfectly calm and collected again? Takes a bit of explaining. Bad conscience?"

"She was nervous most likely. That's all," Olive said. "A name like that," she pointed out. "Well, it would, wouldn't it?"

"What about her former employer, Mr. Tudor King?" Bobby went on. "Is it only a coincidence that he has rented a bungalow nearby, but hasn't shown up yet? Tudor King seems quite well known. Miss Maureen called him sloppy. I seem to know his name somehow."

"Well, I don't see how you could help, the way it's splashed about," Olive said, and cast an uneasy eye at a cushion near under which she was uneasily conscious there was coyly sheltering at the moment the latest Tudor King—nor were by any means all the tear-stains on its pages those shed by previous readers alone. "I've read one or two books of his," her conscience forced her to admit, and her artistic sensibility forced her also to add: "I dare say he is a bit sloppy, and why shouldn't he be? So was Dickens, and worse, too."

"Dickens is Dickens," Bobby told her, "and that is all that here below we know or need to know. Try to get one of Tudor King's books from the library, will you? I would rather like to have a look at one of them."

"I'll try," Olive promised, one guilty eye still on that concealing cushion close by. "Or I'll get you a copy of *The Teen-Ager*. He has a story running in it. What about bed?"

Bobby yawned and got to his feet.

"To-morrow," he announced, "I'll see if I can get hold of this Baldwin Jones chap. I would like to have his version, both of the black eye business and of the coffee at the Bay Tree. When people start talking about murder and the whole set-up seems so screwy, you've got to sit up and take notice. There's Jack Longton, too. He was on the spot like the others and he knew about the Cellini dagger. Add it all up and what do you get?"

"Precious little," Olive said as she gently but firmly propelled him out of the room and bedward.

Next morning, as soon as he arrived, Bobby found waiting for him on his desk the analyst's report. His face was grave and troubled as he went to consult a senior colleague.

" 'Undoubtedly human blood'," he quoted. "Means we've got to go into it more closely."

"No corpse," commented the other.

"No corpse known," Bobby corrected him.

"No report of anyone missing," came the prompt retort.

"Tudor King," said Bobby.

"Oh, the author bloke," said the colleague doubtfully, and he said it as if it were the sort of thing you would expect from an author, and nothing to worry about anyhow.

"I think," Bobby said, "it would be as well to try to get what information we can about Mr. Baldwin Jones and about Tudor King as well."

"Better be careful," said the colleague warningly. "Authors are devils to talk."

"Oh, if he starts to talk, I've got him," declared Bobby with complete confidence.

"Yes, but they don't talk," came another swift retort. "They write letters. In the Press. Much worse."

Bobby looked thoughtful at this, but none the less determined. He went away, and the first thing he did was to ring up the famous Bay Tree Restaurant and ask if he could be given the address of Mr. Baldwin Jones, who was, Bobby understood, a customer of theirs.

"Nothing to do with him personally, of course," Bobby explained carefully. "But he might be able to give us some information about a case of bag-snatching he may have seen."

The Bay Tree people were sorry they couldn't help. They would like to know Mr. Baldwin Jones's address themselves. There was an account outstanding and Mr. Baldwin Jones had not been seen in any of his usual haunts for two or three days. Oh, yes, they said, in reply to a further question, they knew Mr. Longton as an occasional customer. A theatrical gentleman. But they knew nothing about any fracas between him and Mr. Baldwin Jones. Most certainly not at the Bay Tree. At the Bay Tree such things did not occur. It was not consonant with the dignity of the Bay Tree or with the standing of its customers, and Bobby realized that no admission to the contrary would ever be extorted from the Bay Tree—the use of rack and thumbscrew being barred by modern usage.

So he hung up and sent for Ford, whom he had warned to be in readiness, and sent him out to wander round West End bars, especially those frequented by the hangers-on of the theatrical world. He was to see what information he could there pick up.

On this errand therefore Ford departed while Bobby himself went on to the palatial offices of *The Teen-ager*, and of some ten or twenty other periodicals, all of them only to be distinguished from all the others by a difference in the poise and persons of the various members of the Royal Family, whose photographs appeared on their covers.

The Editor of *The Teen-ager*, in private life the holder of one of the amateur boxing championships, offered Bobby a drink from a well-stocked cupboard and said if Bobby could tell him anything about Mr. Tudor King, he, the Editor, would be awfully pleased to hear it.

"Nobody seems to know anything about him," the Editor explained. "His copy comes in regularly. Same old stuff, every time, and it goes down the same old way. Different names, different setting. Characters and plot exactly the same. Our readers love it like that."

"He has to be paid, though," Bobby said.

"Oh, yes—and how," said the Editor enviously. "We send his cheque to his agent and his agent pays it into the bank and his lawyers draw it out and hand it over, I suppose. Bank and lawyers close as oysters. Some of the smartest boys in Fleet Street have been out on his trail, but none of them had any luck. All sorts of stories, of course. Sometimes it's a duke or a Cabinet Minister. Once it was an elderly invalid lady living in the Orkneys, and there was a war-time top-rank General had a good run. You can take your choice."

"What's the idea?" Bobby asked.

"Publicity, of course," the Editor replied, a little pained at having to give so obvious an answer. "There's two dodges. Get in the limelight and stick there. Or conceal yourself in a cloud of darkness. That's much the most difficult bring off, but very effective if you can. Tudor King has all right. What's he been doing?"

"Nothing," Bobby answered. "Can't we want to get in touch with a man without it being assumed he's committed a murder?" and when he had said this he paused abruptly, for he felt as if thus he had betrayed a secret fear of which he himself had not been aware. "Or something," he concluded lamely.

But the Editor had not noticed.

"Sorry I can't help you," he was saying. "Sure you won't have a drink? No? Too bad. Means I can't either. Rule I've made. Never take a drink alone. Not safe. I say, be a good chap, and if you do turn up anything about Tudor King, tip me off."

"I shall do nothing of the kind," Bobby told him.

"I thought that's what you would say," the Editor sighed. "Blue lamp incorruptibles, aren't you—the whole lot of you? Enough to drive a chap to drink." He cast a longing eye at that well-stocked cupboard, but nevertheless went firmly across to shut and lock it. "Well, thanks for calling," he said as he saw Bobby preparing to depart. "Nice break. It's my morning for doing my 'Mother of Nine' column. Hell of a job, but it goes like hot cakes. By the way, there is something I can tell you. Tudor King is the son of a small tradesman in a small provincial town, and was educated at a small private academy for the sons of gentlemen."

"How do you know?" Bobby asked, and the Editor gave him a triumphant grin.

"Deduction, my dear man, pure deduction," he said. "If King had come from a working-class family, there would have been a touch of real honest to goodness vulgarity in his work instead of that awful mincing refinement of his. Only a small provincial town could produce his particular brand of snobbishness. If he had come from anything like educated people, he wouldn't have made the awful bloomers he did in his last book. *Upper Circles*, he called it. Every blessed character with a title and all of them outdoing Ouida at her most Ouidaesque. The *Literary Weekly* had a special article. Dukes addressing their wives as 'your Grace,' and breakfasting off solid gold plates. That sort of thing. Really funny, and the *Lit. Weekly* made the best of it. What about offering me a job in the C.I.D.?"

"I'll think about it," Bobby promised. "I suppose you don't happen to know anything about a Mr. Baldwin Jones?"

"He comes in here sometimes," the Editor answered. "Brings in odd pars—about actresses' legs chiefly. Don't know anything about him personally. Why? Haven't seen him for a week or two. You don't think he is Tudor King, do you?"

Bobby laughed, and said he had no views on the subject and so departed, the Editor's farewell remark being that there would be no trouble about finding Baldwin Jones. All Bobby had to do was to pop into the nearest pub, and if he wasn't there, try the next.

CHAPTER IX

MISSING MEN

AFTER LUNCH, FORD appeared to report the result of his West End wayfarings. He was a little depressed, for he was still in that sanguine stage of youth which has not yet learned that success is generally bought at the price of many failures. He had discovered little, and that little of small value, and he was afraid that it might be thought he had been remiss in some way.

"No one seems to have seen Baldwin Jones for a day or two," he told Bobby, "and no one seemed to know much about him. In one place they told me to try the Superb Hotel in Mayfair Square, and they all seemed to think that was some sort of joke, though they wouldn't say why. And everyone always took it for granted I was looking for him because he owed me money. Two or three said they would like to know what had become of him for the same reason."

"The Superb Hotel?" Bobby repeated thoughtfully. "Miss Maureen said something about the Superb, too. You may have got something there, Ford."

Bobby did not really think this very likely, but he said it because he guessed that Ford feared he might be blamed for the scanty store of information he had brought back, and it was Bobby's belief that there is no sharper spur for a willing horse than an occasional word of praise. Indeed, Ford at once looked more cheerful and became fiercely determined that next time he would be really brilliant. Bobby picked up the 'phone and put through a call to the Superb asking if he could have a word with one of their staff, a man who had previously been in the Force till enticed away by the offer of much better pay.

The man asked for was fortunately available. In reply, he said he thought he remembered the name—Baldwin Jones, was it?—and he would call back as soon as he had made sure. This Bobby took to indicate a prudent desire to consult his chiefs before saying anything. So he sent off Ford to inquire in the appropriate quarters if anything was on record about a gentleman with a cast in one eye, interested in stamps, and with a penchant for acquiring them by other than the humdrum method of purchase.

"Don't be long," he said as Ford was leaving on this errand. "I think we may have to take another run out to Cobblers. It rather looks now as if we had heard of one man missing."

"Yes, sir. That's what I was thinking," Ford said, and departed.

Meanwhile Bobby applied himself to the consideration of some of the papers in his 'In' tray till before long the 'phone rang. The call was from the Superb.

"I thought I remembered the name," the distant voice said. "It's on our 'Full Up' list."

"What's that?" Bobby asked.

"List of people to be told how much the management regrets that no accommodation is available. For one reason or another. Nothing very serious sometimes. Mr. Jones had been here two or three times. Rather noisy and threw his weight about a good deal, but there are plenty try to make a splash that way—especially when young and not brought up to it. But last time there was a row between him and a young American gentleman. The American gentleman was busy irking Mr. Jones up just to knock him down again. Our people had to interfere. We cleared them both out.

"What was the row about?" Bobby inquired.

"We didn't ask; nothing to do with us," came the answer. "Something about a woman. It generally is. They were both put on the 'Full Up' list, but the American gentleman has been taken off again."

"Dollars?" Bobby suggested.

"Oh, no," said a voice that sounded suitably shocked. "But we heard that he and his mother stay at the Ritz regularly every year and no complaints. If they are good enough for the Ritz, they are good enough for us. The mother is a wealthy widow from the Middle West somewhere. Likes to get in with British society folk because she says there isn't any society in New York."

"Probably means," Bobby suggested, "that she isn't accepted there. Not in the Four Hundred or whatever they call it. Much more exclusive than ours, New York society, I believe, and money no passport at all—because they've all got such a lot it's taken for granted. Why is the dollar drive like charity? Because it is? Because it covers a multitude of sins? Choose your own answer. Well, thanks for what you've told us. If you do happen by any chance to hear any more of Mr. Baldwin Jones, give us a ring, will you? Nothing against him personally, but he may be able to tell us something about someone we are interested in. Goodbye."

He rang off then, and very soon Ford appeared.

There was nothing in the Yard records, he reported, about anyone with a cast in one eye and interested in the acquisition of stamps. But he had been advised to try a firm supposed to know all there was to know about stamps and stamp-collectors. Their reply to Ford's inquiry was interesting. They had never themselves come in contact with anyone answering to the description given. Crooks knew better, it was implied, than to try to play tricks on a firm of such knowledge and repute. But lately they had had a complaint from a well-known collector and customer of their own. It seemed that a young man claiming to be a representative of theirs had called on this gentleman and had offered a very high price for some of the specimens shown him. He had then departed to ask the firm, he said, to confirm his offer. He had, however, not returned and had not been heard of since. Nor had some of the stamps he had been examining. No proof he had taken them, but inquiry showed that he had been staying at a local hotel where there was also staying an older man with a cast in one eye. In the hotel they had appeared to be strangers to each other, but it so happened that one of the staff had noticed them in apparently earnest conversation on the outskirts of the town. They might, of course, simply have recognized each other as fellow guests at the same hotel and been discussing the weather or the scenery, and there the matter had to be dropped: A similar story had come from another quarter, again the chief actor being a young man, with another older man hovering in the background.

Bobby said he thought all this interesting and suggestive, but nothing they could follow up at present. So that, too, had to be left, at any rate for the time, and would Ford arrange for a police car, complete with driver, to take them to Lower High Hill?

"Might be as well this time," Bobby said, "to have a uniform man with us. The more we stir things up, the more likely we may be to hear something to give us a lead instead of groping about in the dark as we are now."

Ford went off accordingly on this errand and the 'phone rang again. This time it was the Editor of *The Teen-ager*.

"I thought I would tip you off, though you wouldn't me," he explained. "Tudor King's agent is in a devil of a stew. Got a swell contract from Hollywood—umpty-umph dollars. Commission enough for the agent to buy that new Rolls Royce he has his eye on. But he can't get in touch with King for him to sign the contract. Says he seems to have vanished from the face of the earth, and if the contract isn't signed at once, Hollywood may fall back on Bernard Shaw stuff or something like that. Well, can I expect any gratitude? What about a hard and fast contract for your reminiscences when you retire?"

"I'm not thinking of retiring just yet," Bobby retorted, "but you can have all the gratitude you like. Of course, you realize you have only done your duty as a good citizen bound by common law to give all possible aid and comfort to the police in the execution of their duty?"

"Oh, hell," said the Editor and rang off, and to Ford, who had returned in time to hear this conversation, Bobby said:

"Two missing men?"

"Yes, sir," said Ford. "I wonder which? Or both? One did it and one hopped it?"

Bobby said he thought it was too early even to start guessing, and soon he and Ford were on their way. Constable Yates had been warned to expect them and was waiting at his cottage, which served also as the local police station. He had nothing to report. The village was humming with all kinds of rumours, but none that seemed to have any substantial grounds. The lady occupying the New Bungalow had asked that a special watch should be kept on it, but that was probably only a nervous reaction to the many rumours in circulation.

"I had to tell her," Yates explained, "that I couldn't rightly—I mean watch special the New Bungalow, me having enough ground to cover already and then same being on private property and, near a quarter of a mile across from Higgles Lane. And that I don't come by in general. I told the lady, on receiving said request in writing, accompanying permission to enter on private property, I would forward same for instructions."

"How do you get to the place if it's on private property?" Bobby asked.

"You have to cross two fields," Yates explained. "It's in the lease. Occupiers and those with business with same have permission to cross the field in a direct line. But only for the time."

"Curious sort of arrangement," Bobby said.

"Yes, sir," agreed Yates. "There's been a deal of talk about it. It's mushrooms."

"Mushrooms?" repeated Bobby. "What on earth have they got to do with it?"

"Well, sir," Yates answered. "It's one field seems most out of the common favourable to mushrooms and some say as mushrooms is wild fruit, and common to all, same as game would be but for the game laws, so they can be picked by any, and all Mr. Gilson—it's his field—can do is to order trespassers to clear off. So Mr. Gilson took and sowed mushroom seed all over the field and says now it's cultivated mushrooms, not wild, and it's stealing to take 'em. Which a lawyer gent says maybe, but how is Mr. Gilson to prove what's taken is seed and not wild?"

"Better take it to the House of Lords for decision," Bobby suggested, smiling. "But why build a bungalow where there's no right of way?"

"Seems when Mr. Gilson built," Yates answered, "he reckoned on being allowed to join up with the path that runs from Cobblers by the west wood to the village. Not much now, being out-of-the-way. But him and Lord Rone and Saine fell out over wheeled traffic, and his lordship said if Mr. Gilson was going to stand on his rights about the mushrooms—they do say his lordship is partial to same when fresh picked—he would stand on his rights about the path. So there it is."

"Village politics," Bobby remarked. "Result a very much isolated bungalow. You have to cross two fields to get to it from Higgles Lane? How far is the lane from here?"

"About a mile. Seems there's a writing gentleman has took the bungalow for to be quiet when doing his books; and if quiet is what he wants, he's got it there all right."

"You said something about an occupant," Bobby remarked. "Is he there himself yet?"

"No, sir; not arrived. It's a secretary lady getting the place ready for him as spoke to me, and wanted a special watch kept. Claims she's heard things—what she says was a loud sort of cry Monday night and then a light moving and noises next night in the wood behind the house. Not but that she's a lady looks able to take care of herself. When I called she was chopping wood and using a hatchet like a good 'un. I don't wonder she's a bit nervous, though. In my humble opinion, it's more than the writing gentleman ought to ask of any female woman. Why, murder could be done there easy and no one know nothing about it for days."

"We'll hope that won't happen," Bobby said, though wincing once again at this introduction of the word 'murder' that seemed to hover continuously in the shadowy background of the case.

CHAPTER X

THE BUNGALOW

THE WAY TO HIGGLES LANE lay through the village, where naturally the appearance of a car driven by a policeman in uniform set tongues wagging ever more busily. That from gossip something of value can be obtained if we do but diligently distil it forth was one of Bobby's favourite theories, though he doubted whether the prospect of that happening was very bright on this occasion. Then, too, of course no one in the village knew as yet of the darker, more dreadful fears roused by the discovery that on the golden dagger were stains of human blood.

"Though, for that matter," Bobby remarked as they drove through the village, "blood may mean no more than a cut finger or a bloody nose."

But he did not believe for one moment that this was all that was meant by the stains on the golden dagger.

The car was left in Higgles Lane in charge of its driver while Bobby and Ford followed a faint track, only barely visible, across two fields to where, at the further end of the second field, against the green background of the West Plantation, stood the New Bungalow.

Still further behind it, like a dark distant cloud, lay the great plantation of fir and pine planted by Lord Rone and Sane under pressure from the Forestry Commission and now hanging there on the slope of the hill like an army of the night gathering to descend upon the valley.

At the moment, however, the bungalow was bathed in sunshine; it faced south, and looked a pleasant and inviting habitation, even though one that somehow had strayed from its fellows and not yet found a way to rejoin them. From behind it came the sound of hammering or knocking. Before it lay a small, not very well kept garden, and when Bobby pushed open the gate admitting to this garden, a bell jangled loudly. It had been hung on the inside of the gate, apparently so as to give early notice of the approach of visitors. Promptly from the back regions, presumably in response to the summons of the bell, issued a tall, gaunt, elderly woman, carrying a hatchet in one hand.

She looked at them unwelcomingly from heavy, deep-set eyes that yet seemed somehow to hint of hidden fires well capable of bursting into unexpected flame. Firm, even fierce lines, too, about the mouth. A vivid, unusual personality, Bobby thought, one it was a little surprising to find content with the generally rather quiet, suppressed life of the secretary and housekeeper. She said:

"Police, aren't you? About the dagger from the Cobblers collection someone found lying about somewhere? Well, nothing I can tell you. I know nothing about it."

She had a bitter and a hostile air as she stood there, swinging the hatchet in one hand. Into Bobby's mind there flashed memory of a performance of the *Agamemnon* he had once witnessed years before, and of Clytemnestra standing thus, axe in hand after the murder, just as this woman stood watching them darkly from her sombre, slightly bloodshot eyes.

"Not only about that," he answered, producing and offering his official card, of which, however, she took no notice. "I think you told the constable here that you have heard noises and seen lights in the woods nearby?"

"Something going on," she said. "At least I thought so. No business of mine, but I didn't like it. If you want to talk about it, you had better come inside. I don't suppose it has anything to do with this business of the lost dagger or whatever it is."

With long swift steps, she crossed to the bungalow, pushed open the door—it had apparently only been on the latch—and entered, leaving them to follow. The door opened directly into a long, low room, well lighted by three windows and somewhat scantily provided with furniture almost entirely of the bamboo type. A portable typewriter stood on a more substantial wooden table near one of the windows. On the walls were several cheap engravings—Landseer chiefly as well as, for the sake of variety probably, one or two of ships in full sail. For animals and ships in full sail make an irresistible appeal to the great British public. On some shelves, originally, Bobby suspected, meant for crockery, stood a number of books.

As Bobby and Ford followed her into this room, the woman indicated two of the basket chairs, took herself the chair standing before the wooden table, turning it so that she could face them. She still swung in one hand her hatchet from which she did not seem to wish to be parted and she stared at them with a sort of controlled malignancy, as if she hated the sight of them, but did not mean to let that influence her in any way. Bobby noticed that Ford was watching the swinging hatchet rather carefully, as if half expecting she might soon be using it on them. Apparently she too noticed his somewhat doubting expression, for now she produced some sort of harsh rumbling sound, probably intended for a chuckle.

"I've been chopping wood," she explained. "They wanted to make an absurd charge for bringing coal across the fields. I told them I didn't come here to be robbed. There's plenty of wood to be had for the gathering, but it has to be cut up."

"Oh, yes," Bobby said. "Are you the tenant? I understood it was Mr. Tudor King, an author."

"Don't let him hear you call him an author," she retorted with another of those harsh and little mirthful chuckles of hers. "The author, if you please. Tudor King, the author. Yes, he is the tenant. My name is Cato if you want to know—Charlotte Cato. I'm housekeeper and secretary and everything else. The domestic Pooh-Bah. Old enough to be his mother, so that's all right." She paused and stared at them challengingly, as defying them to deny it. She waved a hand towards the books on the shelves. "Those are his on the bottom shelf," she said. "He always has them by him. The trophies of his spirit, he says. Those on the upper shelf are mine."

"Yours?" Bobby repeated, not quite understanding.

"That's what I said. Nothing to make goggle eyes about," she snapped, and got up and crossed to the bookcase. This time she left her hatchet behind. She passed her hand slowly and lovingly over those on the upper shelf—nine in number. "Cynthia Cairn," she said. "That's me. 'An' author—never 'the' author. Charlotte Cato *née* Cato and married a Cato, a cousin, and wrote as Cynthia Cairn." She took down one of the books, seemed inclined to offer it to Bobby and then changed her mind and put it back again. "It wouldn't interest a policeman," she told him. "It's serious work, a study of social conditions as affecting the development of a writer of genius. Rather like George Gissing. You won't know his name. But it probes deeper, much deeper, and so, of course, it was even less popular." Now her hand was flicking lightly across the books on the lower shelf, rather as if she meant to flick them away into nothingness. "All about dukes and earls," she explained, "all the men brave and handsome, all the women lovely beyond compare, except one plain brave little thing who finally gets the duke and then, after a hair-do and a visit to a West End dressmaker or two, turns out the loveliest of the lot. The Cinderella story. It always works. I showed my readers life as it is, squalid, sunk in mud and dirt. Tudor King shows life as it isn't, but how nice it would be if it was." She snorted—the only possible word—with deep contempt, and added: "He makes money. Lots. I could have starved."

"Well, I'm glad that didn't happen," Bobby remarked.

"It nearly did," she told him "when the business went bankrupt. Customers began to stop away. They seemed to think it was getting above herself for a small grocer's wife in the filthy little out-of-the-way town where we lived to start writing books. Nobody ever read anything there, anyhow—except *Ally Sloper*. Some of them said my books were immoral, too. They always do if you face facts honestly. Luckily Tudor King doesn't or I should be out of a job and he would be doing something useful for a change."

"You don't think very highly of Mr. Tudor King's work, I gather," observed Bobby. "I'm told the critics don't either."

"That's what sent him off," she said moodily, but without explaining where to, and when Bobby asked she only stared at him and was silent for a time. Then she said: 'Abroad,' but Bobby felt sure that was not what she had meant at first.

Since now she did not seem to wish to say more about either her work or her employer's, Bobby asked if she could give him an address where Mr. King could be found. She shook her head.

"He's travelling," she said. "Gathering material. Getting experience. It'll probably ruin his work if he does. But he won't. Experience slips off him like water from a duck's back. I know. I've tried to tell him things. He'll return when he wants to. He hasn't said when."

"He has always been rather secretive about himself, hasn't he?" Bobby asked. "No one in London seems to know anything about him or even where he lives?"

"Rubbish," she retorted. "Newspaper talk, that's all. He has to do his work and you can't with newspaper reporters always on your doorstep and silly fool girls ringing you up to say they couldn't bear it if there wasn't to be a happy ending. Has life happy endings?" she demanded, giving Bobby another of those challenging stares of hers. She went on: "So he cut out all publicity—he hated it, anyhow—and then his agent saw his chance and worked it up. That's all."

"I see," Bobby said, though wondering if this were the true and complete explanation and if it were the agent alone who had 'worked it up.' He went on: "Could you tell us exactly what it was you heard? On Monday night?"

"It was after I had gone to bed. I was asleep and it woke me up. A cry. There was something about it. I don't know what. I'm not easily frightened. Only I had never heard anything like it. I got up to look, but I didn't hear anything more. Then it began to rain. Torrents. A cloudburst. I told the woman who comes to clean. She said there were often strange noises in the wood, and no one liked to go there after dark. There's an old story about some earlier Lord Rone and Saine discovering his wife there waiting for her lover, and killing her with the golden dagger all this talk's about. So, now her ghost haunts the wood. The village policeman heard and came to ask about it. I saw lights the next night, Tuesday, and I told him about that, too."

Bobby asked one or two more questions without learning much more, and then he and Ford walked back across the fields towards their waiting car. Bobby was silent, but halfway across the second field Ford ventured to ask:

"Lady talked quite a lot, sir, didn't she? Didn't amount to much, though."

"Oh, I think so," Bobby said, rousing himself from his thoughts. "Always listen, Ford, when anyone wants to talk. The more they talk, the more they tell. Partly reaction in this case, though. I dare say she doesn't get much chance to let off steam when Tudor King's about. Curious position. Highbrow novelist—dead failure—secretary and everything else to lowbrow novelist—howling success. Doesn't like it but sticks it. So does he. I wish we had been able to take a shorthand note, but it wouldn't have done to try. She would have dried up at once."

"Shorthand note, sir?" Ford repeated, much surprised. "You think it may be important, what she said?"

"Oh, yes," Bobby said. "But goodness only knows in what way and whether it's relevant. Background stuff very likely. As soon as possible, write out the best and most complete account you can of what she said. I'll do the same. Between us, we ought to get most of it down. Underline anything that strikes you as useful. If we both hit on the same thing as significant—then it probably is. There's a kind of odd, hungry look about her, too—a lean and hungry look."

"Well, sir," Ford said, puzzled, for he was not as familiar with Shakespeare as he should have been, "what with the rations an all, it's a wonder we all haven't."

"Oh, I didn't mean that sort of hunger," Bobby explained. "I meant hunger for life, experience, that sort of thing. And hunger, either sort, can explain a lot."

CHAPTER XI

TWO-LEGGED LAP-DOGS

IN THE VILLAGE, at the little half police station, half country cottage, Bobby left Ford, with renewed instructions to write out, while his memory was still fresh, all he could recollect of their talk with Mrs. Cato. He himself, he said; would go on to Cobblers, but return presently to pick Ford up again.

"Two people we can't get in touch with," he remarked in rather a worried way, "though it's too soon to call them missing. We've got a bit of a background view of one of them, Tudor King. The other one, Baldwin Jones, seems to have been a visitor at Cobblers, so they may know something about him."

He did not say, though it was in his mind, that at Cobblers there might be a greater readiness to talk if he were alone than if he were accompanied by Ford. Ford's presence might make the visit too obviously official, and what Bobby hoped was to get them at Cobblers chatting as freely as Mrs. Cato had done.

"In talk is my faith," he told himself, thought it a good motto, and on the way tried his hand at putting the words into Latin—with inconspicuous success, since he had forgotten almost all the Latin he had ever known.

Three-quarters of the way up the long Cobblers avenue he saw Maureen standing under one of the trees and looking rather lonely. Seeing him, she waved, and he stopped the car and got out, telling his policeman chauffeur to wait. Maureen, he saw now, had on what he was beginning to call her Lady Macbeth look.

"Have you seen Lady Watson?" she demanded without giving him time to speak.

"No," he answered. "I haven't noticed anyone. Are you looking for her?"

In her deepest, most tragic voice, Maureen answered, "She's pinched my man."

"Dear me," said Bobby, not knowing what else to say.

With one of her sudden, bewildering changes of mood, Maureen bestowed on him a broad grin.

"It's not much of a loss," she announced. "Norman—Mr. Oxendale, you know. But so humiliating. Such an awful let-down. Why, she must be fifty if she's a day—well, forty, anyhow. Besides, she's fat," and these last three words she rolled out with such denunciatory force that Bobby's chauffeur, though he had not been listening, though he was too far off to distinguish words, yet looked up with a startled air, evidently wondering what was happening.

"Oh, well, you know, fatness is sometimes rather reassuring," Bobby said, and it was in his mind that he would have felt more at ease after the interview with Mrs. Cato if she had been comfortably fat instead of being so tall and gaunt and grim. Who can imagine a fat Clytemnestra? He asked: "Does Lady Watson often—er—pinch young men?"

"As often as she gets the chance," Maureen said, returning to her former Lady Macbeth scowl. "My fault for giving her the chance. I let out I was going down to the village and Norman asked if he could come with me, and he was waiting, so off she went and bagged him. It wasn't even as if I had kept him waiting either—at least, not much."

"How much?" Bobby could not help asking.

"Practically punctual to a dot," Maureen assured him. "Not more than a quarter of an hour, anyhow. Or maybe twenty minutes. You can't complain of that, can you?"

"Well, at any rate, not until after you are married," Bobby answered.

She surveyed him with grave disapproval.

"What an awfully beastly thing to say," she complained. "So cynical. So disillusioning," and she managed to look as if all illusion had left her forever. "Just as I had been done out of a proposal, too."

"From Mr. Oxendale?"

"I'm practically certain he meant to," she lamented. "And I do so like being proposed to. Isn't it heartbreaking?"

"Another time, perhaps," he suggested.

"The first fine careless rapture has gone," she told him gravely. "It's boring when it becomes a habit, like Jack."

"Mr. Longton?" Bobby asked. "Does he very often?"

"Every time we meet. I've begun to tell him we might as well get it over, and if he'll pop I'll say 'No,' and then that'll be done with till next time."

"And does he always—er—pop?" Bobby inquired solemnly.

"Oh, well, sometimes he sulks," she admitted. "It's a bad fault of his. Still, I can generally wangle a proposal sooner or later."

"Well, I wouldn't say 'No' too often," Bobby warned her. "One day he might think you really meant it."

"Oh, I do," she cried; "and I do think that's a most awfully rude thing to say." With great dignity she said: "I think we had better talk about something else if you don't mind. Unless you would like to propose to me yourself," she added hopefully.

"I'm married already," Bobby confessed.

"I thought as much," she told him. "That's why you were so horrid and cynical just now. Have you brought back the golden dagger? Daddy's beginning to fuss. I expect he'll be starting pulling strings soon, if you don't look out. He can be jolly nasty when he starts doing that. I tell him it's the black market of the spirit, and a fat lot he cares."

"I'm afraid," Bobby answered, "it's going to be nastier than probably Lord Rone expects. The report says the stains on the blade are human blood."

"Oh," she said, startled; and stood still, staring at him, and there was that in his expression as he looked back at her that once again made her change. She seemed to grow more natural, all her affectations, her frivolity, seemed to fall away, leaving her stripped and bare, for once entirely herself, a rather frightened, rather lonely young woman, who saw in Bobby's eyes a stark reality she had never known before. "Oh," she repeated softly and then more loudly, but still very quietly: "What does that mean?"

"It is what I am here to find out," he answered.

"Not—not," she began, and he could see that her lips were framing the word 'murder.' But then she boggled at pronouncing it and said instead, and rather quickly: "Well, that needn't mean anyone has been killed? There isn't anyone could have been."

"There are two people we want to get in touch with," Bobby said: "One is Mr. Tudor King, who has taken a bungalow here, but who hasn't arrived yet and whose present address isn't known."

"Can't Mrs. Cato tell you?" Maureen asked quickly. "I've seen her in the village. She's rather grim. She would be splendid in a murder part. If ever I play one I shall build on her."

"I think we had better not talk too much about murder at present," Bobby told her. "This isn't acting, you know. This is real life."

"I've thought sometimes," Maureen told him, this new Maureen who had put aside so quickly all her bright, smart chatter in order to speak with such simple gravity, "that if acting isn't real, it's sometimes something more. Hadn't we better go back to the house? I think my father ought to know."

They began to walk towards the great, massive building, blocking, as it did, the long vista down the drive. Bobby called to his chauffeur to follow, and to Maureen, he said:

"We haven't been able to get in touch with Mr. Baldwin Jones either."

"He left here early Monday. I told you," Maureen said quickly, and with, or so it seemed to Bobby, a touch of uneasiness in her voice and manner, as if the introduction of this name were unwelcome.

"He could have come back," Bobby said. "It is not far. An hours' journey—less."

"Why should he?" Maureen asked. "If he wanted anything he could have 'phoned or written."

"He could have returned without doing either," Bobby remarked. "He seems a very illusive person. You knew him before?"

"Well, in a way—the way you do know people you don't really know from Adam. He said we had met at some cocktail party or another. Well, of course, I couldn't say we hadn't, could I? Because you never know who you have met at cocktail parties, do you? Or if you've really been there, for that matter."

"I'm afraid," Bobby confessed, "I'm not very well up in cocktail party procedure."

"Lucky you," Maureen said unexpectedly. "The limit; they bore you so stiff you have to drink too many so as to forget where you are."

"Then why go to them?" Bobby asked,

"My good man," she retorted, "you've simply got to show as often as you get the chance and never mind putting in an occasional gate-crash. Unless you want to be hopelessly left behind—one of the forgotten men."

"I see," Bobby said, reflecting that he was obtaining many unexpected side-lights on the artistic life. "Interesting. Did you know he was friendly with the Watsons?"

"Don't believe he was," declared Maureen. "I rather think he only got to know Aunt Bella by pretending he knew me. Introduction move. And once he got in with a respectable background—me,"—Maureen paused to explain in case Bobby had missed the reference—"he was jolly soon installed as her newest lap-dog. Aunt Bella rather likes lap-dogs—especially the two-legged sort. Now Baldy's taken himself off, she's got her eye on Norman. That's why I was so cross when she pinched him just now."

"What does Sir William think of all that?" Bobby asked.

"Oh, he doesn't mind," Maureen answered. "He knows it's only Aunt Bella's little way and he keeps his eyes open. He's a doormat, and he likes it, but he doesn't mean to have anyone else letting her wipe her shoes on them. He can get quite tough if he wants to."

"And now," Bobby remarked, "Mr. Oxendale is a candidate for the vacant lap-dog situation?"

"No; marked down for it, that's all," Maureen corrected him.

"You knew him, too, in Town, you said, didn't you?"

"Well, we used to run across each other pretty often. I told you I rather thought he wanted to come to Cobblers so as to get a chance to propose. I didn't mind. I rather specialize in proposals. I'm no Helen of Troy, but I do get proposals."

"Was he friendly with Mr. Baldwin Jones?"

"Not that I know of. Very likely they met sometimes. I don't know."

"How does Baldwin Jones get his living? Or has he private means?"

"I shouldn't think so," replied Maureen, evidently considering this a most improbable idea. "He calls himself a freelance of the arts. Writes a little. He's done a play, but, of course, everyone has. He talks a lot about the films, but I don't believe it amounts to much more than a job as an extra sometimes or walking on. And a little journalism and all that. If he's in funds he splashes, and if he isn't he borrows. He really has a sort of way with him somehow. I've heard him boast he's never met a man he couldn't borrow a fiver from or a woman he couldn't kiss," and Bobby saw, rather to his surprise, for he had not expected it of her, that she was crimson from brow to chin. It may have been because she saw him watching her that she went on hurriedly: "He really can jolly men and look at a girl as if all he asked for was to die at her feet. It fetches you when you are very young," and Maureen sighed a little sadly as she remembered her teens she knew would never come again now that she was twenty-one.

CHAPTER XII

SPREADING SUSPICIONS

IN THE HOUSE Maureen led the way at once to the study. The only occupant, however, was Mr. Richard Moyse, busy at the typewriter, so that Bobby wondered if he had already been installed as secretary. Maureen said:

"Oh, I thought Father was here. Do you know where he is?"

"No; he didn't say," Moyse answered. "Shall I try to find him for you? It's Mr. Owen, isn't it? About the lost dagger? I'll tell him."

He went off accordingly and Maureen said:

"The perfect secretary. Falls over himself trying to please." She added thoughtfully: "I think his flirting technique is most awfully vulgar."

"Has he tried it on?" Bobby asked.

"Well, of course," Maureen answered. "You can't know what anyone's really like till you've flirted with them, can you?"

"Well, it's not a technique generally encouraged in the Force," Bobby explained gravely.

"I call that rather a waste of a good-looking boy like the one you had with you before," Maureen told him. She added, looking gravely at Bobby: "I don't think I should like to flirt with you. I think you can be rather frightening."

"I'm here on a rather frightening errand," Bobby said, and then the door opened and Lord Rone came in.

"Got any further forward?" he asked. "I shan't be sorry when you feel able to return the dagger. It's valuable and it's an heirloom. I'm responsible for its safety."

"They go with the title to the heir male," Maureen explained. "Cousin George. He's a pig," she added simply.

"Now, Maureen," said her father in his usual tone of helpless rebuke.

"He wanted," Maureen explained to Bobby, "to send a lawyer to check them over and see if they were all right. Cheek. He thought we had been selling them on the q.t."

"I'm afraid," Bobby said, ignoring this apparent family dispute about heirlooms, "that it will be some time yet before it can be returned. Proper care will be taken of it. You remember it was being submitted for expert examination. The report has now been received. It states that the stains on the blade are of human blood."

Lord Rone had seated himself at his desk. Maureen had huddled herself in one of the deep armchairs, clasping her knees in her arms. Bobby was sitting near the table on which the typewriter stood. They were all three silent as Lord Rone seemed to be frowning over this piece of information he had just been given. He said presently:

"I can hardly believe it. It seems incredible. What do you propose to do?"

"To take all possible steps to get at the truth," Bobby said in his official tone. "It has to be considered in the light of the 'phone message that a murder had been committed here. And we have to remember that the names of two persons have been mentioned and with neither of them have we been able so far to get in touch—Mr. Tudor King and Mr. Baldwin Jones."

"I can't conceive that either of them can be concerned," Lord Rone answered. "Mr. King has apparently not arrived here yet and Jones left Monday morning. I saw him go myself."

"Mr. Jones may have returned and Mr. King's arrival may not have been noticed," Bobby said.

By now Lord Rone was looking a good deal more disturbed. He had been fidgeting with some of the things on his desk. He stopped doing this and Bobby had the idea that he was feeling the need for self-control.

"Well, you must take whatever steps you think necessary," he said finally. "I don't see that I can help you in any way. I can't help feeling there must be some perfectly simple explanation, but that's your affair, and the less I hear about it the better I shall be pleased. I am extremely busy and my time is fully occupied."

"I don't think you've quite got the idea, Dad," Maureen told him. "Mr. Owen has his eye on all of us and he'll be wanting to I dig up everything he can, and it's going to be beastly for us all— including you and me."

"Don't talk nonsense, Maureen," her father said, very angrily.

"I am afraid Miss Maureen is right," Bobby said. "We shall try to cause as little upset as possible, but we shall have to get to the bottom of the business."

"What he means," Maureen explained, "is that he doesn't intend to stop till he has. Digging up the garden for the dead body and all that sort of thing. Plain hell."

"Maureen," said Lord Rone, now so angry he could hardly get the words out. "Be quiet," he commanded.

"You are such an old innocent, darling," Maureen told him with a kind of affectionate tolerance that made him angrier still. "Mr.

Owen thinks he has reason to believe there's been a murder and we are all under suspicion."

"I think I've already explained," Bobby interposed. "Anyone in any way concerned must be considered."

"May I ask," inquired Lord Rone, "what possible motive we are supposed to have had for murdering our guests? It's so entirely preposterous," and now his tone had become almost pathetic.

"I know," Bobby agreed. "Only the preposterous does happen, though we can generally rule it out soon enough—as I am sure we shall in this case. The first thing is to establish facts. Then the motive may appear—or not. If it does it may be so trivial as to be incredible. One murderer said he killed his sister-in-law because she had such thick ankles."

"Well, it's a reason," Maureen said. "If it's Baldy, anyone might have a motive. He was a nasty bit of work. He wasn't above a bit of blackmail on the side."

"Oh, yes," Bobby said, interested at once, and still more interested when he saw Lord Rone's troubled air suddenly become more marked. "Can you give me any details? Names? Anything?"

"It may not be true," Maureen answered. "That's why I didn't say anything before. It's only what people used to say, but if you're going round asking questions you would be sure to hear. It was only in a petty sort of way. Everything he did was always like that—small and mean."

"How do you mean—a petty sort of way?" Bobby asked.

"Well, it was," Maureen answered. "If it's him been killed I shall feel rather awful telling you all this, but someone would be sure to sooner or later. What I mean is he would get to hear you had been having dinner at some small out-of-the-way restaurant with some man or you had been losing too much money at bridge, and he would drop little hints about telling your husband or your father, and then presently there would be something about his having forgotten his wallet and how awkward it was having to explain to a head waiter, and finally you found yourself lending him a pound note you knew you would never see again. I don't think it ever amounted to much more. Too afraid of the police or getting thrashed. I did hear that once he got such a thrashing he couldn't show up again for nearly a month till he had something more like a human face for people to see."

"I think, Maureen," Lord Rone said, "you could occupy your time more usefully than in picking up bits of gossip. Undignified. Vulgar."

"Darling," Maureen retorted, "you don't pick it up—more like forcible feeding."

"Even if it never amounted to much," Bobby said, "someone may have thought it did—or might."

As he spoke he moved and with his elbow knocked some papers off the table near which he was sitting. He stooped to pick them up. He had noticed that Lord Rone's apparent uneasiness showed no sign of diminishing. As he gathered together the papers he had scattered to the floor, he could see Lord Rone's feet and legs under the desk at which he was sitting. It was only a glimpse Bobby thus obtained, but enough to show him how those feet were restlessly crossing and recrossing each other, how nervously toes were working inside soft indoor slippers. He put back on the table the papers he had gathered together and reflected that often those who felt the necessity of exercising a strict self-control forgot to control also their feet. Maureen was saying now:

"We may as well face it, Dad. We are all going to be under the eye of the police, all in the same boat together. At least, unless Baldy and Tudor King turn up safe and sound, and unless Mr. Owen can't hear of anyone else to fuss about. All of us. Not Mother, luckily. The poor darling couldn't, even if she wanted to; but me and Aunt Bella. She's too fat really, but I expect Mr. Owen would say that didn't count, and anyhow she can look daggers even if she doesn't use them. And Uncle Bill and Jack—no, not Jack, luckily."

"Why not Mr. Longton?" Bobby asked. "He has visited the house and knew where the dagger was kept."

"He was away in Town all Monday," Maureen explained. "What you call an alibi, isn't it? He went to see the author of the next play Jack's to produce. When an author and a producer are talking, they may want to murder each other all right. Nothing more likely. But they are far too busy to bother about anyone else. So if you hear that Jack and Baldy had the most awful row you needn't think that means anything. Jack's rather fond of having awful rows. He does with me about nothing at all. There's Norman Oxendale, but no one could possibly think he has the guts to murder anyone. Lap-dogs don't bite. And Dick Moyse. I don't like him. Too swarmy. But it doesn't make sense to think he could come trotting down here just for the fun of committing a murder. I shouldn't be a bit surprised though if he wasn't listening at the keyhole now."

As she spoke there was a knock at the door. It opened and Mr. Richard Moyse himself appeared.

"Oh, I do hope I'm not interrupting," he said ingratiatingly. "I wouldn't have ventured only I saw Linda coming away, so I thought I might. I was wondering if I might have the typewriter, please? If I might, then could finish what I was doing in time for the post."

CHAPTER XIII

"CURTAIN UP"

LORD RONE NODDED AN impatient consent. Moyse advanced, murmuring excuses. He picked up the machine—it was one of the small portable kind—and retired, still apologetic, indeed almost as if oozing apologies from every pore of his body.

"He might have been retiring backward from the presence of royalty," Maureen commented when he had gone.

Bobby went across to the door which Moyse had closed behind him, and opened it an inch or two. He said to Maureen: "Did you hear something?"

"I thought I did. I wasn't sure," she answered. "He entered prompt to his cue, didn't he?"

"Hadn't we better have the door shut?" Lord Rone said. "Why leave it like that?"

"Eavesdroppers don't care to approach an open door," Bobby explained. "It may mean someone's leaving. If you are careful to speak fairly softly, they won't come near enough to hear anything." To Maureen he said: "Would the Linda girl be likely to have any-thing to do here at this time?"

"I shouldn't think so. I don't know." Maureen answered. "I suppose a maid can always think up something if she wants to put in a little keyhole work."

"Linda is the tall girl I saw when I was here before, isn't she?" Bobby asked.

Maureen nodded, and Lord Rone said discontentedly:

"This sort of thing is most unpleasant—unnecessary, too," and from his lordship's expression Bobby was inclined to think that both epithets were intended to apply to him. "There seems no rea-son to suppose that Moyse was listening. Very unlikely. A most offensive suggestion."

"We will hope unjustified also," Bobby said. "Quite possibly his appearance at that special moment was purely coincidence. I must thank you for what you have told me and I will ask you, if there are any further developments, to let me know immediately."

"I don't see that there are likely to be any," Lord Rone said. "Is it really necessary to carry the matter further?"

"I am afraid so," Bobby said. "I cannot possibly report that I am fully satisfied. It wouldn't be any good if I did. The case would certainly be held to require further investigation. There's not much to go on at present, of course. But it does seem probable that it was someone in this house who made the 'phone call. And if so, that someone must know a good deal and must somehow have been in possession of the golden dagger. The inference is, of course, that if murder has taken place it is almost certainly one of those whose names Miss Maureen mentioned just now."

"There you are, Dad," Maureen said gloomily. "What did I tell? All of us in it up to the eyes. You and me, Uncle Bill and Aunt Bella. Dick Moyse and Norman Oxendale. All the servants, I suppose, including specially Linda. I should push in that woman at the New Bungalow—Mrs. Cato. She looks the part. That's the lot, isn't it?"

"Mr. Longton," Bobby said.

"Jack's got an alibi, I told you," Maureen reminded him.

"It hasn't been checked yet," Bobby reminded her in his turn and did not add, though he thought it, that alibis were often the first refuge of the guilty. "Difficult to check, too. We have no idea yet when the murder happened—if it ever did happen, which hasn't been proved yet."

"Exactly," exclaimed Lord Rone, brightening up at once. "It seems so futile to talk like this about something that perhaps never happened."

"But Mr. Owen thinks it has," Maureen said. "You can tell he has precious little doubt—'phone call, missing dagger, bloodstains. Curtain up. Two people more or less missing as well. Mr. Tudor King for one and they are talking about him in the village already. Only why should anybody want to murder a perfectly harmless, unnecessary author like him? There's poor Baldy, of course. But you don't murder rats. Or do you? It's a hell of a mess, anyhow."

She went over to the window and stood there with her back to them. Bobby thought she was trying to keep back her tears. Over her shoulder, in an odd little voice, she said:

"It all looks so peaceful."

A gong sounded. Lord Rone got up in a relieved sort of way and said briskly that that was lunch, and less briskly, would Bobby care to join them. Bobby said that was very kind, but he thought he must get back to the village. Without turning round, Maureen said:

"Mr. Owen means he can't lunch with people he may be having to arrest soon. Not the thing."

Neither of the other two said anything. Lord Rone was too depressed and worried even to utter his accustomed rebuke. Bobby had no wish to dissipate any aura of suspicion that there might be. It might result in someone coming forward with helpful information. Maureen came away from the window and went with him to the front door. From the study window the view had been chiefly of the lawn and the trees beyond, but from here, the front of the house, there was a long view over green and pleasant fields, a small brook meandering across them, down to where the old village lay half hidden in a fold of the ground. Maureen stood still to look at it and somehow her mobile, expressive features gave the idea that she was bidding it farewell.

"It's so lovely," she breathed. "Hundreds like it everywhere in England. But this one is ours."

Bobby understood what she meant. He had always liked to spend his leave abroad when possible, but for all the grandeur of the Alps, the warmth of Mediterranean sunshine, the romance of the Rhine, the long flow of the Danube or the quiet of the Finnish lakes, there was for him an appeal in the soft, sweet English countryside that nothing else could rival. He did not answer her, telling himself he was there on a grimmer errand than admiring landscapes. Maureen spoke again.

"You can't look at it and think of murder or things like that," she said, half to herself and then, to Bobby, she said, pointing at the same time to the dark mass of the newly planted pines hanging sombre and menacing on the higher ground behind the New Bungalow: "You might think of murder there perhaps, you might look for it there, but not down here."

She went back into the house, leaving him standing there. He walked on slowly, thoughtfully, to where his car was waiting. He did not really think Maureen had meant anything, but—well, had she?

To his policeman chauffeur he said as he was taking his seat:

"It's an odd case—difficult. You expect to start a murder investigation with a dead body. No sign of one at present."

"Easy to hide, sir," said the chauffeur cheerfully. "You never know." He, too, was looking up at the dark, close-growing pines. "Up there," he said. "Bit of a job digging all that up, though," a memory in his mind of long, laborious hours spent in digging up a suburban garden—all to no purpose.

"Too soon to think of that," Bobby said as he settled himself in his seat. "Besides, I expect the Forestry Commission's men cover it pretty thoroughly. They would notice anything most likely."

He liked to drive himself as a rule, but he left that job this time to his companion. His thoughts were in a turmoil and he wanted to try to get them into order. He felt that Maureen, probably without intending it, had told him a good deal. So had her father for that matter. But exactly where that 'good deal' led, he was not at all sure. As they turned into the avenue they saw Lady Watson and Norman Oxendale hurrying towards them, evidently feeling that they were late for lunch. Lady Watson stopped, however, and made a beckoning gesture. Bobby stopped the car and got out. Lady Watson said:

"They are all saying the most extraordinary things in the Village. Is it true you've found a dead body?"

"No; it isn't," Bobby answered.

"Norman," Lady Watson said to her companion, "be a dear and run on and tell them not to wait lunch for me. I shan't be long." Obediently Norman went off, not without alacrity, though whether in deference to Lady Watson or because he wanted to get away from Bobby's vicinity as fast as possible may be an open question. Lady Watson continued: "They're saying you've come to arrest someone at Cobblers."

"I wouldn't pay any attention to what people say," Bobby advised her. "It's generally nonsense. What I am trying to do, what has got to be done, is to find out why the golden dagger, as they call it, was taken from the case in the Long Gallery where it was kept, why it was returned, and who it was rang up from the call-box here."

"No one has ever had a glimpse of Mr. Tudor King, have they?" Lady Watson asked. "Isn't that very peculiar? Don't you think that extraordinary woman at the New Bungalow ought to be asked about it? That's what they are all saying in the village."

"I've no doubt they are saying quite a lot in the village," Bobby said. "They generally are."

"Well, it's all so funny, isn't it?" Lady Watson persisted, though a trifle dampened by Bobby's unenthusiastic response to her suggestions. "You know that new girl at Cobblers used to be at Mr. Tudor King's flat? She's slipping out late at night without anyone knowing and going off by that path through the wood? It goes to the bungalow."

"Well, both she and Mrs. Cato were in Mr. Tudor King's employ, so they know each other," Bobby remarked. "But what makes you say the girl goes out late without anyone knowing?"

"I saw her myself—Monday night and last night. I was sitting at my window because I couldn't sleep—and then Sir William does snore so. Monday night it was terrible. I never closed an eye listening. I saw her distinctly."

"Wasn't it dark?"

"Well, of course. I said it was late. She came out from the garden door just under my window and the light from the passage showed plainly who it was."

"At the moment," Bobby said, "I don't see much connection between Linda's late visits to Mrs. Cato at the bungalow and all this other business. She may be merely feeling lonely at Cobblers and want to have a chat with someone she knew before."

"It's all so very odd," said Lady Watson impressively, and went away, presumably in search of her lunch, and Bobby looked after her thoughtfully.

He was asking himself if there was anything behind her intervention, if, for example, she were trying to divert suspicion from someone at Cobblers. Or if it were only that she found it difficult not to be always talking. Not unnatural if she had been excited by the gossip and the rumours which the village was busy circulating. To his chauffeur he said:

"We'll pick Ford up and then get back to Town as quickly as we can."

"Yes, sir," said the man mournfully; so mournfully indeed that Bobby could not help noticing—and being thereby reminded of lunch.

So he said that perhaps they had better see if they could get something to eat first, and the chauffeur immediately smiled again.

CHAPTER XIV

"THE PERFECT SPIV"

BACK IN TOWN, Bobby first jotted down a rough outline of plans for further investigation he had tried to think out during the return journey. He made arrangements, too, for other work he had on hand to be carried on by colleagues, since he felt he must give his full attention to what had now crept into the papers under the headings 'Golden Dagger Puzzle,' 'Valuable Mediaeval Dagger Lost and Found.' All this satisfactorily disposed of, he returned home to warn his wife, Olive, that he would have to be out late, possibly all night, indeed; information Olive received in the small, sad, lonely little voice she reserved for an announcement all too frequent.

"I shouldn't be a bit surprised if the 'phone call doesn't turn out a fake," she declared as she started that so familiar task of cutting sandwiches, and preparing, for the vacuum flask, coffee that made her, as a poor weak woman, fairly tremble before its strength. "Isn't it just the sort of silly trick all those boys would think awfully funny?"

"I've rather given up that idea," Bobby told her. "And they are not boys exactly. And then you know it is human blood the golden dagger shows. It's fairly certain all the four of them are there for private reasons of their own, different from what they pretend."

"Four?" Olive asked. "Why four?"

"Dick Moyse, Norman Oxendale, Jack Longton, Baldwin Jones," Bobby recited. "Dick Moyse, for instance. I don't like that story of the recovered dispatch case and all the rest of it. Smells. He strikes me as the perfect spiv, and perfect spivs don't go in for humdrum everyday jobs like a private secretary's, even if they could hold it down, which as a rule they couldn't."

"Perfect spivs don't go in for murder, either, do they?" Olive asked.

"They might if cornered," Bobby said. "Even a cornered rat is dangerous. Anyhow, Moyse is certainly on some game of his own. Then there's Norman Oxendale, the budding art critic, ostensibly there to study miniatures, but most likely with an eye on Maureen Carton."

"Do you mean he is in love with her?" Olive asked, interested at once.

"She's a catch, I suppose," Bobby said. "Only daughter of a very rich man."

"Well, you don't go committing murders because you're in love," Olive protested.

"It's been known to lead to jealousy," Bobby reminded her. "And jealousy to murder. Next, Jack Longton, man of the theatre, on terms of what he calls mutual insult with Maureen, not invited to Cobblers, but turns up there when it's open to the public on Satur-days. No reason given why he has to come to an hotel nearby in order to study the play he's to produce. Then the last of the four, Baldwin Jones, arriving with the Watson, as established 'lap-dog,' to quote Maureen, but almost certainly something else as well."

"But he's not there," Olive exclaimed; "not now."

"No; he isn't, but he was," Bobby said.

"Oh, well," Olive said uneasily.

"Of course, it's not only the four young men we have to think about," Bobby went on. "Lord Rone, for instance. Take him next. He got very worried when Maureen started talking about blackmail, rather as if the word meant something to him. Maureen let out that there's some family feeling over heirlooms, and are they all safe? Does that link up with her father not liking it when I said I didn't think his 'Young Stallion' picture lived up to its reputation and with his looking relieved when Norman Oxendale praised it? Does that suggest the thing may be a copy and that the original has been sold? He does seem to be living rather beyond the six thousand a year said to be all anyone can have clear after income tax and super-tax. Plenty of people are spending capital because they think it will only go in death duties, so they may as well have the benefit while they're alive. And is selling heirlooms his way of raising capital?"

"But that wouldn't make anyone want to murder anyone else—except the tax-collector," Olive remarked.

"It might lead to quarrelling," Bobby answered. "And quarrels have nasty results sometimes. All very vague. Matter for suspicion, but only the bare outline of a case. Till filled in."

"If he's really been selling heirlooms," asked Olive, "could he have been employing an agent—Baldwin Jones?"

"It's possible," Bobby agreed. "Or Jones might even have had the idea of trying to steal the thing—or one of the other heirlooms, perhaps. You can't rule out the idea that attempts at theft—of the golden dagger or the stamp collection possibly—come into it somehow. There's the vague sort of hint that Moyse may have been concerned in attempts on other stamp collections. There has even been one such attempt already at Cobblers. But Baldwin Jones has vanished for the time and theft may have nothing to do with it. Tudor King seems to be missing too. Anyhow, he isn't at the bungalow he's rented, and the present occupant is a rather grim sort of person who appears to be linked up with one of the inmates at Cobblers—Belinda Blythe; the new maid there, who did seem a bit scared when she knew we were police. Didn't seem to like us at all."

"You don't think," Olive asked, though with some hesitation, "I mean—you don't think the two of them could be the same—I mean Mr. Tudor King and Baldwin Jones? Under different names?"

"Well; there again, it's possible. Have to be remembered," Bobby agreed. "It'll have to be kept in mind. But Jones seems to be generally on his beam ends. Tudor King is said to be making pots of money."

"Do authors ever?" Olive asked incredulously. "I mean unless they are Bernard Shaw and that sort of thing."

"I'm told it does happen," Bobby answered, though his tone, too, was a little doubtful. "The idea seems to be that Tudor King is a kind of Bernard Shaw of the literary underworld. Baldwin Jones turns up now and then at swell West End hotels, and that might be when, as Tudor King, he's just got a cheque from his publishers and he's blowing it in. You can spend an awful lot in the West End if you try—a hundred a night without any trouble."

"How nice," said Olive. "I'm having to give you marg for your sandwiches because there's no butter left," and she added that she didn't suppose he would mind because he wouldn't know the difference any more than if he were a Cabinet Minister. "Any favourite suspect?" she asked as Bobby seemed inclined to ignore this excursion into high politics and to drop instead into one of his profound and silent meditations, occasionally known as the 'Owen trance.'

However, this time he roused himself to answer her question.

"No," he said; "not yet. I've been told quite a lot, but more than I can sort out at present. Still, it does look as if a faint suggestion of the outline of a pattern were beginning to show. Something like a hint of an underlying connection, a thread of cause and effect, so to speak. Anyhow, there's not one of the lot of them at Cobblers who strikes me as quite at ease."

"Well, would anyone?" Olive asked, tying up one packet of sandwiches and thinking that he had better have another as well, margarine and all, "when perhaps there's been a murder and a dagger worth hundreds and thousands getting lost and turning up again? I know I wouldn't."

"The girl worries me as much as anyone," Bobby went on. "Maureen, I mean. I can't quite place her. She never seems to know herself when she's play-acting and when she's being serious."

"Well, of course, both at once," Olive said. "But you can't suspect her. You always say women never use knives, and I'm sure I shouldn't. I don't know how you can ever tell which is the right place—and so messy," she added with distaste.

"I've a pretty good idea she knows something," Bobby said. "She's told me a lot, but I'm not sure whether she's trying to help trying to put me off. One thing I am fairly clear about. She engineered Norman Oxendale's visit chiefly in order to show Jack Longton where he got off. She went out of her way to insist. Longton had an alibi and to tell me there was nothing in it if I heard he and Baldwin Jones had had a row. She may have told Longton about Baldwin Jones's attempt to kiss her and he may have thought he had to do something about it. It might be that she is trying to take the credit for the black eye Jones got, though it really belongs to Longton."

"Isn't that rather a side issue?" Olive asked, thoughtfully surveying her two packets of sandwiches, deciding that it ought to be enough even for Bobby's nocturnal appetite, and, anyhow, now there was left as little margarine as butter and no more of either to be had till next week.

"The whole thing is lousy with side issues," declared Bobby impatiently. "You've got to try to dovetail things together to make them fit, and up to now they jolly well won't. All dead ends."

"Miss Carton and Mr. Longton are both theatre people," Olive reminded him. "You've got to remember that. Theatre people are never quite normal, are they?"

"Oh, well, I don't know that you can say that exactly," Bobby protested. "Some of them are a little mad, but that's only because they live in a different world. The Watsons aren't theatre."

"Do you think they come in?" Olive asked. "I mean, seriously. Not just because they were there on the spot. That is, if there is a spot to be on at all."

"Lady Watson went rather out of her way to give her husband an alibi," Bobby said. "Complained his snoring kept her awake all night. Implications there, if she happened to know Baldwin Jones intended to return. She's fond of collecting what Maureen calls 'lap-dogs.' Has she gone too far with one of them? There's the story of the row at an hotel when Baldwin Jones got rather badly knocked about. Was that a case of a lap-dog turned nasty and trying a little blackmail that didn't come off? If we could trace the people concerned, it might be a help, but they've gone back to America. Take too long, anyhow. Time is always of the essence of the contract when it's murder. Besides, they might not want to talk. But if, instead of a young, vigorous man, an elderly man like Sir William were concerned, might he use not his fists, but a dagger—even a golden one?"

"You said," Olive reminded him, "that he was most awfully bullied and henpecked and all that. It doesn't sound as if he would ever take to killing?"

"Henpecked *in excelsis*," agreed Bobby. "But Maureen seems to think he rather likes it and is quite able to assert himself when he wants to. I've noticed myself how quickly he can shut his wife up when he wants to. I thought at the time that at bottom she was really a little frightened of him. It might be that at one time or another he did something he is thoroughly ashamed of and is trying to make up for it by letting her bully him. She has forgiven but they neither of them forget."

"Isn't that rather far-fetched?" Olive asked doubtfully.

"Real life so often is—nothing so improbable as what happens," Bobby answered. "I heard something of the sort about a very well-known writer—dead now a good many years. I feel myself that Watson is a man of very strong emotions, feelings, all very strongly suppressed, but still liable to break loose. Then there's Lady Watson herself to be considered."

"Oh, surely," Olive protested.

"Well, the alibi she was so careful to give her husband covers her, too," Bobby pointed out. "She collects Maureen's lap-dogs. Now apparently she is after young Oxendale. That may be because she can't do without one. Or she might want to show one's as good as another, so why should she mind about losing one of them? As a theory, suppose that lap-dog Baldwin Jones was trying the same game that earned him what he got at the Superb Hotel and that he came back Monday night to keep an assignation with her? Developments might have followed. She is not an unattractive woman, even if Maureen calls her fat, which might mean that she's put Maureen's nose out of joint once or twice. Jones may have tried to go too far, she may have taken the golden dagger as a precaution, and there you are."

"Sounds," said Olive discontentedly, "as if you thought all of them did it, and they can't all."

"No; but one of them did," Bobby answered. "At least, that's how I feel, though there's no proof yet, and for that matter it might be either of the two we can't get in touch with—Tudor King or Baldwin Jones; either of them. Or even both."

"Oh," Olive exclaimed, really startled this time by such development of her own suggestion.

"Anyhow," Bobby continued, "that's the set-up. And that's the lot we have to keep in mind. Jack Longton, the theatre man; Norman Oxendale, the budding art critic; Baldwin Jones, who isn't there; and Dick Moyse, the perfect spiv, with one eye, I am inclined to think, on the stamp collection, which includes one stamp worth goodness knows how much because Queen Victoria's head on it is upside down."

"Why does that make it valuable?" Olive asked. "It sounds silly."

"There is no why," Bobby explained. "It's just the way it is. When it's stamps, the value of a bloomer is above rubies. Then I've to remember Lord Rone and his background of heirlooms that, like Baldwin Jones, may not be there any more; and Maureen, whom I don't pretend to be sure about yet. She's a woman and an actress, and I've always heard that if women are hard to understand, then she's doubly hard to understand if she's an actress, too."

"Fiddlesticks," said Olive contemptuously. "Now, if you said men were hard to understand—" And she sighed and became lost in contemplation of a task she felt beyond all mortal powers.

"Not to mention," Bobby went on, his voice getting more and more depressed as he pronounced each name, "the two Watsons, Sir William and Lady Watson, the first suppressed but liable to break out, the second fat but comely—ask Maureen. And hovering on the outskirts of the case Mrs. Cato, grim and hatchet-swinging, and Linda Blythe, liable to be scared when police come on the scene, and the spiritual, but not physical, presence of Tudor King. Sort it out for yourself."

"Not me," Olive declared. "I wouldn't know where to start. Do you?"

"Asking questions," Bobby said. "The right questions. All detection is there. The right questions. No murderer can take it."

CHAPTER XV

A HAT

LATER THAT NIGHT, Bobby brought his car to a standstill in Higgles Lane, a lane leading nowhere in particular, and more than a mile or so from the village of Lower High Hill, where he had no wish, by this nocturnal visit, to add to the number of the rumours already in such wild and whirling circulation. He and Ford, who was accompanying him, alighted. By arrangement, a sergeant, his Alsatian dog, two uniform men, were waiting. One uniform man was left with the car and its varied contents, including the sandwiches, the coffee, a pick and shovel, and what is known, but not officially, as the murder bag. The instructions given to this man were that if he saw a light flashed from the borders of the wood behind the bungalow, he was to come at a run, bearing the pick and shovel with him.

These arrangements made, Bobby, Ford, the sergeant with his Alsatian dog on the lead, and the second uniform man, all under the guidance of the sergeant, made their cautious and silent way across two or three fields, and then into the wood through a gap in the fence marking the boundary of the Cobblers property. ("Where the poachers get in," explained the sergeant in a cautious whisper, "though there's not so much of that now with game not preserved the way it used to be. Geese and turkeys is what they want these days.") Further on, skirting at a safe distance the bungalow, where, Bobby noticed, no light showed, they reached the little-used path that led from Cobblers close by the bungalow and on to the village by way of a distant farm, now better served by another recently opened road.

About halfway along this path, where the wood was thickest, the undergrowth most dense, Bobby divided his forces. He sent Ford on to take up his post at the point where the path entered the wood, with instructions to give warning if he saw or heard anyone approaching, but to be careful not to alarm whoever it might be. To the sergeant and his Alsatian he assigned the part of the wood lying to the north of the path coming from Cobblers. He himself, he said, together with the second uniform man, would take that portion of the wood lying south. It was the smaller half, the least overgrown, and therefore much the easier to examine.

"If there is anything to be found, except a mare's-nest," he explained, "it'll almost certainly lie to the north. It's furthest from the farmland, so we will give you and your Alsatian the first chance. Dog better than man sometimes."

"'That's right," agreed the sergeant. "Almost human they are, and nose and eyes a sight better than ours. Aren't they, Boy?"

The dog, hearing its name, gave a low whimper, and pricked up its ears, and Bobby said:

"Ford is going to give two hoots like an owl to warn us if he spots anyone coming. He heard it given in a B.B.C. broadcast, and he has practised it up and says he can do it O.K. I hope he can— good Lord, what's that?"

For at this moment they were startled by a strange, weird noise resembling nothing else ever heard on land or sea, by day or by night. It was repeated.

"That's twice," Bobby said doubtfully, for though he was not quite sure what an owl's hoot sounded like, he could not think that any self-respecting bird of any kind had ever produced a cry like that.

"Can that be him warning us, do you think, sir?" the sergeant asked wonderingly, and even a little awestruck.

"More like," said the uniform man judicially, "the dying squeal of an elderly pig what's been stuck in the middle of a sneeze."

"Luckily, if it's who I think it may be," Bobby said, "she isn't country and probably doesn't know much about owls."

"Wood said to be haunted," observed the sergeant. "It might be taken for a ghost and then they'll be scared off."

Fortunately, this fear, which rather worried Bobby for the moment, proved unfounded. Approaching footsteps became audible, and there showed the gleam of a strong electric torch, which evidently the newcomer was using to show the way. The little party of watchers, sank into the obscurity of the surrounding darkness, the sergeant conveying to the Alsatian a warning to make no sound. The footsteps were quite near now. The light of the torch she carried showed the newcomer to be a woman whom Bobby recognized as the maid, Belinda Blythe. She passed by quickly, and then, a little further on, paused and seemed to be searching the ground as if looking for something. To and fro she flashed the light of her torch, keeping it low. Once or twice she even took a step or two away from the path into the shadows of the surrounding trees and bushes, but soon came back again. Then she went on her way and Bobby followed cautiously, at a safe distance, till he had seen her enter the bungalow. He noticed that the door opened to her approach, so that evidently she had been expected and waited for. Bobby went back to join his assistants.

"She was expected," he remarked. "I wonder if someone else is there, or only Mrs. Cato?"

"Did you notice, sir," asked the sergeant, "how she stopped a few yards up the path as if she thought someone might be waiting, and then hurried on?"

"It may be someone is waiting there," Bobby said, "someone she knows is not likely to go away."

"Yes, sir," agreed the sergeant, but in a puzzled voice, for he did not understand the sudden gravity in Bobby's voice and then the dog, perhaps concluding the injunction to silence no longer held, now its human companions were talking together, lifted its head and sent a long, sad howl echoing through the silent trees. A moment later Ford appeared, looking rather pleased with himself.

"Heard me all right?" he asked. "Not so bad, was it? But I'll practise it a bit more till I get it more natural like."

"Well, you're young," said the sergeant. "By retirement age you may have got it something like something, though I can't think what."

"Never mind that," Bobby interposed hurriedly, for now Ford was looking deeply offended. "Ford, you push on and watch the bungalow. If anyone comes out, follow them. If it's Miss Blythe and she comes back this way, we shall see her, so you stay by the bungalow and watch. If she goes in any other direction, follow, of course." Ford went off obediently, though not without a final, hostile glance at the sergeant; and to that unappreciative person Bobby said: "We'll see if we can find anything to account for Miss Blythe stopping where she did. It did rather seem as if she were looking for something."

They walked on together a few yards to the spot where Miss Blythe had paused, and once again the dog sent its long, mournful howl echoing through the trees.

"Now, Boy, what's the matter with you?" the sergeant asked rebukingly, and the dog looked up, rather with the air of asking in return if such a question were really necessary.

"See that?" Bobby asked, flashing his torch to show where on a bush by the side of the path, some twigs had recently been broken off.

"Shall I let Boy go?" asked the sergeant, and when Bobby nodded an assent, he slipped the leash. "Search, Boy, search," he said.

The Alsatian bounded away. A moment or two later the dog's cry sounded once more, like a long-drawn lamentation wailing through the loneliness of the wood. No one spoke. By the light of his torch Bobby hurried in the direction of the sound. The sergeant and the uniform man followed in single file. The dog was scratching with its paws at a kind of natural hollow that had been roughly and hurriedly filled in with brushwood, debris of one sort or another, collected hurriedly from the vicinity, but that only imperfectly concealed the body of a dead man. Bobby stood staring grimly, thoughtfully, at that still form. The sergeant said:

"No leg-pull about the 'phone call."

They were still silent about that rough, improvised grave when once again there came that sound, so little resembling an owl's hoot, they had heard before.

"Go back to the path," Bobby said to the uniform man. "If anyone comes along, stop him. Blow your whistle to let us know."

The man departed. Bobby and the sergeant began cautiously to release the body from the rough concealment it had been given. It was that of a youngish man, and the cause of death was evident—a deep wound in the body, over the heart. Death must have been instantaneous or nearly so.

"We must wait for daylight," Bobby said. "Can't do much in this darkness and we may destroy evidence if we aren't careful. The poor chap won't mind waiting a little longer."

"Might never have been found, not for years," the sergeant said. "No one uses this path much and no call for anyone to go poking round. Do you think it'll be the author gentleman, sir? Him as took the bungalow and never been seen since."

"Never been seen of all," Bobby corrected him, and then they heard the constable's whistle that told them he had seen and stopped someone on the path from the bungalow.

It was Miss Blythe they found there, indignantly demanding what right the constable had to interfere with her free movements. When Bobby and his companion appeared, she turned on them the wrath and indignation that had left the constable so entirely unmoved.

"What's all this about?" she demanded. "I must get back to Cobblers—they'll be locking up soon."

"There is a dead man," Bobby said. "We have only just this moment found the body. You were in Mr. Tudor King's employ. Now you are here—I had not meant to ask you, it will not be pleasant—but now you are here, will you see if you can identify him? Mr. Tudor King is said to be missing."

"A dead man," she repeated, and looked more bewildered than shocked. "You don't mean—not about the golden dagger? I thought . . . I mean to say, I thought all that had come to nothing."

"It has come to a dead man," Bobby said. "If it is Mr. Tudor King—"

"Of course it isn't," she interrupted. "He isn't missing either. He's only gone away for a holiday. It's so silly. He'll be very angry." She paused, her first bewilderment and doubt giving way now, Bobby thought, to unease, dismay, even fear. "I don't know what you mean," she said. "You said—" And then she paused. "Didn't you?"

"Yes," Bobby answered.

"Oh," she said, and it was as if only now did she fully realize the meaning of his words. "Oh," she repeated, and then in a voice no longer angry but shaken, she said, "Do you mean it's true—what the 'phone said?"

"Yes," Bobby repeated.

"It can't be anyone I know," she said slowly. "I've only been here a week or two. I don't know anyone." Once more she paused and then went on: "It couldn't be Mr. Baldwin Jones, could it? He was staying at Cobblers, only he left on Monday. He might have come back."

"Have you any reason to think he did?" Bobby asked.

"Well, no," she answered. "No, only—well, there was a hat Monday night and I picked it up and put it on the bush there out of the wet. I meant to take it to Cobblers, only it was gone when I came back. It was like one I had seen him wearing, so I thought it might be his, but I don't know, and besides I met him just about here one night when I was going to Mrs. Cato's at the Bungalow."

CHAPTER XVI

THE TURK'S TAIL

DELAY CAUSED BY THE lateness of the hour and the consequent darkness was replaced by an intense activity as soon as daylight permitted. Nor was it long before the news of the discovery spread through the village and beyond, so that presently it was necessary to draw a cordon round the wood to prevent a rush of sightseers that would have seriously hampered the work going on. Journalists, too, soon began to make an appearance, not, at this stage of the proceedings, entirely welcome.

Identity of the dead man as Baldwin Jones had been quickly established, but not as yet publicly announced, and now Bobby, content to leave routine work to the various specialists who had been hurried to the spot, was back at the Yard, concentrating on planning the future course of the investigation.

To the various C.I.D. men he had summoned for a talk and to receive their instructions, he explained that the first thing necessary was to find out everything possible about the somewhat illusive personality known in life as Baldwin Jones.

"I want," he said, "to have as complete a picture as possible of his background, his friends and relations if any, his means of livelihood, so on. That ought to give us a starting-point. At present it does look as if one of the Cobblers people must be guilty, but there seems no very adequate motive and no explanation of why a weapon was used that certainly links up with Cobblers. And no hint of who made the 'phone call or why, or what became of the hat Miss Blythe sticks to it she found on her way to the bungalow, but was gone when she came back later on."

"Is it right, sir," one of the men asked, "that he may turn out to be the writer gentleman there's talk of being missing?"

"I wouldn't pay any attention to that," Bobby said, a trifle vexed, for he felt this meant that Ford had been talking; and his own pet aversion was for his men to start work with the least suggestion of any preconceived idea in their minds, which, he held, should always be entirely blank until knowledge of facts made impact. He went on: "There's nothing we know of that in any way links up Baldwin Jones with Tudor King, except, of course, that he was in the neighbourhood of a bungalow, which Tudor King has rented but never visited as far as is known. Besides, authors are a harmless race and seldom murdered—except, of course, by critics. And I suppose," he added, considering the point thoughtfully, "they would plead justifiable homicide in self-defence. Well, you understand what I want you to do. See what you can pick up about Baldwin Jones's background, his friends and habits, where he came from, what he did for a living. Above all, if he seems to have had any criminal connections—black market or in any other way."

The men went off then to play their part in weaving the meshes of the net in which it was hoped a murderer might soon be taken. Ford stayed behind, for Bobby had made him a sign to do so. First Ford had to listen to a brief lecture on the necessity of keeping his theories and ideas to himself till he could present facts in support. Then he was given more precise instructions. He was to visit literary and theatrical agents and more especially those agencies which specialize in supplying 'extras' to film companies. Maureen had said that she believed Baldwin Jones was sometimes so employed, and, if that were the case, his address might be known by one or other of such agencies.

"Apparently," Bobby went on, "he did a certain amount of stray journalism, if only by way of selling odd paragraphs to papers like *The 'Teen-ager*. Tudor King seems to have been a contributor as well. Only he was well paid, so it doesn't seem likely he would bother about selling them bits and scraps for occasional half guineas. We've got to remember, though, that Miss Blythe was at one time in Tudor King's employ, and she does appear to be in the habit of visiting Mrs. Cato rather late at night. But that may be only because Mrs. Cato feels lonely in her rather isolated bungalow and to Miss Blythe feeling lonely in her new job at Cobblers. All rest of the Cobblers staff have been there pretty well from birth apparently, and they may be inclined to treat her as an outsider. By the way, taking her story at face value, she may have had a narrow escape herself. The murderer may have been there, watching, and very likely he may have come back for the hat she talks about. It's a bit risky coming between a murderer and his crime."

"If she's not the murderer herself," Ford suggested. "Her and Mrs. Cato together."

He went off then on his assignment. From it he returned soon after lunch—or, rather, lunchtime, for he had been too busy and was now too excited to bother about eating.

"I've got Jones's 'phone number," he reported. "It was quite right, sir, what you said about him being likely to be on the films.

The second agent I went to had a list of extras, and his name was on it with his 'phone number where he could be reached."

"Good," said Bobby, very pleased. "That ought to be a big help. We had his name before and now we've got his local habitation as well."

"Yes, sir," said Ford, very pleased, too, for if it had been Bobby's suggestion in the first place, it had been he who carried it out successfully. "Another thing, sir. A barman in Collinton Street off Greek Street says Jones told him he made a big income writing under another name, but had to pay off heavy business debts. The barman said he didn't believe him; he had heard stories like that before, and Jones had to pay cash the same."

Bobby did not much believe the story either, but he supposed it might just possibly be true. He reflected that practically anything is possible in the strange literary, art, stage worlds where the irresponsible Bohemian and the staid City clerk mentality of the Anthony Trollope variety exist side by side, sometimes in the same personality, and the talent may be with either—or neither.

"Well, what about the 'phone number you've got?" he asked.

"It's a public-house, 'The Turk's Tail,' in Hoxton," Ford said. "I rang up our people to ask for particulars. They say it's a most respectable place, free house, owned by a Mrs. Abbott. It does a very good trade and there's never been anything against it. Mrs. Abbott is elderly, a widow, and very well thought of. It belonged to her father before her."

"Elderly widow," Bobby repeated. "Seems to fit. Elderly widow in the Superb Hotel story; elderly lady, though not a widow, at Cobblers. And where that take us? We must pay this Mrs. Abbott a visit. She may be able to tell us something. Be ready in half an hour. There are one or two things I must attend to first."

"Car, sir?" Ford asked hopefully.

"We'll go by 'bus," Bobby decided. "People don't always like police cars hanging about and a 'bus is almost as quick, anyhow —they both get held up just as long in the same traffic jam. Only snag is we shall have to pay our own fares and chance getting them back through our expense sheets, while, of course, no one would query the car. Had your lunch?" he added, for he had experience of young and zealous officers. "No? Well, get it. Never neglect lunch. You mayn't get another chance."

"No sir," said Ford and retired, appearing again, full of content, roast beef and apple tart, at the end of the appointed half-hour.

At the moment when Ford reported, Bobby was just taking a 'phone call. He put down the receiver and said:

"From Lower High Hill. Miss Maureen has left by train for London. I think, instead of coming with me, you had better meet her. Ask for a good man to be with you, point her out to him when she gets here and have her tailed. Keep me informed. I don't think it'll be only shopping or a matinée has brought her to Town to-day."

"No, sir. I shouldn't think so," Ford said, and retired, while Bobby set off alone on his visit to 'The Turk's Tail.' He found it in a turning off the main street, a quiet prosperous-looking little place. He went in, explained he was a police officer, though without giving his name or rank, and asked if he could see Mrs. Abbott. He noticed that his visit created no show of uneasiness or excitement, and concluded that in 'The Turk's Tail' consciences were fairly tranquil—as far at least as the conscience of any licence-holder can be easy under our complicated licensing laws. He was shown into a comfortable room, well furnished, half-sitting-room, half office, and there was soon joined by a pleasant-looking woman, stout and comely, of what seemed a well-preserved middle age.

"Nothing wrong, is there?" she asked cheerfully, and with no appearance of being afraid of anything of the sort. She went on without waiting for any reassurance: "I don't think I've seen you before. New to the district, aren't you?"

"Well, I'm from Central," Bobby explained. "We are making inquiries about Mr. Jones—Baldwin Jones. He was a customer of yours, wasn't he?"

"Oh, dear, has the poor boy been getting into trouble?" she asked at once and with every appearance of concern. "There's no harm in him, only he's so kept down and it makes him bitter and reckless. Is it anything money can put right? Anything in reason," she added hastily, her evidently sound business instincts asserting themselves.

"I'm afraid not," Bobby answered. "It is serious, very serious indeed, though not quite in the way you meant, perhaps. Was Mr. Jones any relation of yours?"

"No," she said, and, for she had been quick to notice that Bobby had again used the past tense and that he had spoken gravely, she asked: "How do you mean—was?"

"He has been found dead," Bobby told her then. "In the country. It must have happened last Monday. The body has only just been found. An inquiry has had to be opened."

She was staring at him open-mouthed. She seemed a little dazed and she had become very pale. Bobby began to think that the emotional relation between her and the dead man must have been much stronger than he had expected. She stammered:

"Baldwin . . . you mean . . . not Baldwin, not dead . . . he couldn't be, he was so young and strong." She paused, she had almost the air of expecting him to deny or to question what he had just said. She read in his expression that there was no hope of that. Suddenly she began to cry, very quietly. Bobby waited, wondering again what there had been about the dead man, of whom the accounts he had received had given him no very favourable impression, that seemed to have made him a favourite with women so different as this landlady of a Hoxton pub, a rich, American widow, the wife of an eminent English archæologist. Mrs. Abbott was wiping her eyes now and she managed to ask in a voice still unsteady:

"How did it happen? Was it an accident? Was it a car?" When Bobby shook his head, she asked, and with a growing unease, as if already she had a glimmering of the truth: "He can't have been taken ill, he was always so strong and well."

"No, it wasn't illness," Bobby answered. "It will be in all the papers—in the evening papers already, most likely, though I don't expect they've got the name yet. He had been stabbed. Death must have been instantaneous."

Mrs. Abbott quietly fainted away.

CHAPTER XVII

BURNING PAPER

THE ELDERLY WOMAN Bobby had spoken to in the bar came running in response to his call for help. Smelling salts were produced. There was much rubbing of hands, loosening of neck-bands. Brandy would have been administered had not Bobby protested that there was risk in administering any liquid to an unconscious person.

Clearly the news he had brought had been a very severe shock. Indeed, when Mrs. Abbott recovered she still seemed to find it hard to believe. A paragraph in an evening paper that had just been delivered helped to make her realize it was indeed the truth, and that no error or misunderstanding was possible, but also brought a fresh outburst of tears.

"I know the poor boy had wicked enemies," she sobbed, "but I never thought anything like this would happen."

"What enemies were they?" Bobby asked at once.

"Them as kept him down," she explained. "It was like a conspiracy, and he felt it bitter hard. Jealous they were. Jealous."

"Could you tell me more?" Bobby asked. "It may be a great help."

"It was all over his books," she told him. "Kept down he was. Kept down and all out of jealousy."

"Books," Bobby repeated quickly. "Do you mean he wrote—an author?"

She nodded with a kind of melancholy pride and again wiped away her tears.

"I have them all," she said. "He wrote my name in every one and something nice as well and always different."

This reminiscence was too much for the poor woman. She broke into fresh and noisy sobs. The elderly barmaid interfered. She prescribed more brandy. She protested that Mrs. Abbott was not in a fit state to answer any more questions. Bobby was inclined to agree, so he said he would come back in an hour or two, and then as he was going the 'phone rang, this time with a message for him. It was from the Yard and to the effect that Maureen had been met and identified at the railway station on the arrival of her train, had been traced to an address in Hoxton, and that Constable Ford had been picked up by a flying squad car to be deposited at the corner of the street in which was situated 'The Turk's Tail.'

Bobby said that was fine; made inquiries of 'The Turk's Tail's' staff and was told that the address given over the 'phone was only two or three hundred yards distant in a street that had a somewhat unsavoury reputation; learned in addition from the elderly barmaid, returned from persuading her employer to lie down and apparently a sort of under-manager for her, that no one, neither Mrs. Abbott nor anyone else, staff or customer, had ever known exactly where Baldwin Jones lived.

"I'm not one," said the elderly barmaid, "to breathe a word against the dead, such not being able to answer back, but I will say if ever there was a nasty, sly, underhand, sneaking snooping"—she sought for a word sufficiently expressive of her feelings and yet sufficiently respectful to the dead, and remembered it from frequent headlines in her favourite picture paper—"planner," she said fiercely, "it was him."

"Mrs. Abbott seems to have taken a great liking to him," Bobby remarked. "She is very distressed."

"No fool like an old fool, especially when female," came the swift retort, and then, with some reluctance: "He had a way with him, talk the hind leg off a donkey, he could, and talk most round as couldn't see through his cleverness."

"Mrs. Abbott has some books he wrote, I believe," Bobby said. "Do you think I could see one?"

This time the answer was a sniff, a veritable outsize in sniffs indeed.

"Got 'em all locked up and put away, she has," he was told, "like as they was that precious they might be run off with."

"Ever read one?" Bobby asked, and this time received a look of mingled surprise and disdain.

"I've no time for reading," declared the elderly barmaid. "If I do get a minute to myself, there's plenty to do not such a waste of time as that," and therewith all the world's literature seemed to vanish into limbo for ever more.

"I dare say you're right," said Bobby meekly, and retired to find Ford, who was already waiting at the indicated corner in a doorway, for a light rain was beginning to fall. Bobby joined him and asked:

"Any trouble tailing her?"

"No, sir. Easy as shelling peas," Ford answered. "I kept out of sight, but Sergeant Marks came with me himself, as I said it was important and you wanted a good man on the job. Marks said he didn't know anyone better, so he came along, and when the young lady got a taxi he made an excuse about having lost his umbrella so as to speak to the taximan and tell him to drive slow so we could follow easy. Marks will wait to make sure she doesn't leave."

"Good. That ought to cover it," Bobby said, putting on his raincoat. "We'll push on, shall we?"

Arriving, they were assured by Marks that Maureen had not left. He nodded to the door of a house opposite. On the step, ignoring the rain which, however, had nearly stopped again, a small cripple girl was sitting.

"See that kid?" he asked. "Cripple. I've been talking to her. Lost a leg when a flying bomb dropped. Her mother was trying to get her to come in out of the rain. She didn't want; said her Uncle Baldy might be coming. Not her real uncle, her mother said, when we got chatting, but the gentleman lodger on the top floor. He had made a bit of a pet of her and paid for some special treatment for her before the Health Service came in. Cost a deal, she said, and he was still giving her little treats. Took her to the pictures sometimes, so she thought there was nobody like him, and when he was away she was always sitting there, waiting."

"I'm afraid the poor kid will have to wait a long time," Bobby said. He thanked Marks for what he had done and dismissed him back to Central. He and Ford went into the house, and to Ford he said: "Baldwin Jones in a new character—philanthropist and child-lover. I wonder how many characters he has—how many we all have, for that matter."

They began to ascend the rickety and unwashed stairs. The houses here were all marked for demolition. Most of the tenants were under notice to leave. Nothing was being done, either by them or anyone else, to keep them clean or habitable. A woman came out of one of the rooms and watched them, but did not speak. Bobby had a feeling that possibly she was not without experience and had recognized them for police—or possibly she thought they were two more of the various sorts of inspectors with whom the street had been populous of late. On the top floor there were two rooms. They knocked at each in turn without reply. They knocked more loudly. Another woman called up the stairs to know what they wanted.

"Which is Mr. Baldwin Jones's room?" Bobby asked.

"Don't know," the woman answered promptly. "He's away been away weeks. Didn't say when he would be back."

She went back into her room then, and Bobby suspected that that was the stock reply given to all strangers making inquiries in this street.

Ford had been putting his ear to the cracks of the two doors. He was listening carefully.

"I think I can hear someone in here, sir," he said, showing one of the doors. "And I think I can smell burning paper."

"That may be what she came for," Bobby said.

He went up to the door and shouted, through the keyhole.

"Please open at once, Miss Maureen. We know you are there, and I don't want to have to break the door down."

He emphasized the threat by giving the door a push that showed the task would be one of no great difficulty, so old and infirm was it on its shaky hinges. A moment or two of delay and then the door opened and Maureen stood angry upon the threshold.

"Have you been following me?" she demanded, her voice a splendid compound of wrath, rebuke, and menace, so that one expected next to hear: 'Away with them to the deepest dungeon now unoccupied.'

But Bobby this time was much too angry himself to let his thoughts wander into such pleasant fancies. He pushed past her. Ford followed. Maureen went to stand by the window, watching them now in the manner of the tragedy queen watching the first and second murderers at work. Inside the grate was a heap of ashes over which, to Bobby's further annoyance, a jug of water had been poured. Afterwards the resulting mess had been stirred together so that not one legible scrap remained. Bobby turned to the girl.

"You little fool," he said with simple emphasis.

Maureen tried to stare back, but the tragedy queen attitude began to wilt under Bobby's grim contempt. She turned sulky instead and began to pout like a defiant child.

"You needn't be—Rude," she said.

"What have you been burning?" he asked.

"Never you mind," she retorted. "Nothing to do with you. And I am not going to answer any questions," she announced, and then added, with much less effect: "So there."

"Aren't you?" Bobby said, even more grimly than before. "In that case, you will be taken to Scotland Yard and detained for inquiries. A serious view must be taken of what seems the wilful destruction of evidence. You will be allowed to communicate with your father and to send for your solicitor if you wish."

Maureen looked at first as if she could hardly believe he was serious, and then began to look extremely uncomfortable, though trying hard not to let that be seen.

"I haven't destroyed any evidence," she declared. "It was only some old letters of mine. Can't I burn my own letters?"

"No," Bobby answered. "Above all, not when they belonged to a man who has been murdered. They might have been of value. How do I know they were your letters?"

"Do you mean to accuse me of telling lies?" she demanded with a return to her haughtiest 'down on your knees, varlet' manner.

"I don't think you would have the least hesitation if it happened to suit you," Bobby told her, for he was still very angry. "You've managed to make it almost certain you will be called as a witness at the inquest."

Maureen gasped and looked very dismayed indeed. It was a totally unexpected blow, and Bobby watched its effect with all the satisfaction of a boxer watching his opponent taking the count. But she rallied—metaphorically at 'nine.'

"They were only letters and I don't know anything else and you can't make me say anything else," she protested. "I wasn't going to have anybody else reading them, a lot of nasty lawyers and policemen"—and with what vicious emphasis did not that last word come out! "There wasn't anything in them really, only I suppose they were a bit silly. It's ever so long ago. I was only nineteen."

"Was he trying to blackmail you?" Bobby asked.

Once again Maureen gasped and this time there was no 'come-back.'

"How did you know?" she asked in the very smallest voice he had ever heard her use.

"Did you pay?" he asked in return.

She shook her head.

"I told him I would tell Jack Longton and if he didn't look out Jack would half kill him," and then quite suddenly she seemed to realize the full import of what she had said and for the first time she looked really frightened.

CHAPTER XVIII

POST-MORTEM CHEQUES

HER FEAR—HER SUDDEN dismay, indeed—when she realized what might be read into what she had just said were so evident that, in spite of all the girl's youthful folly, Bobby was beginning to feel a little sorry for her. All the same, he had no intention of forgetting the remark. He said:

"You will have to be asked to make a full and formal statement in writing. I shall have to ask you to go to the Yard to do that. You can ring up Lord Rone and Saine and ask him to be present if you wish."

"Oh, no," Maureen exclaimed, looking now, with one of her remarkable changes of personality, much more like a frightened child and much less like the tragic muse even than before. "I don't want him to know anything. He would be so awfully upset."

"Or your lawyer?" Bobby asked.

"Well, that would be just the same, wouldn't it?" she replied. "Lawyers are so stuffy. He would go rushing off first thing to tell Daddy all about it, and make the very worst of it as well. He thinks I'm just awful."

"Are you twenty-one yet?" Bobby asked next.

"Last month," she replied. "Why?"

"It means you are of age," Bobby explained, and could not help adding: "And by a fantastic legal fiction supposed to be grown up and fully responsible for your own actions. In your case, that's a wholly absurd assumption, of course."

"I say," Maureen murmured, "you can rub it in, can't you?"

"If you had happened to be born next month instead of last," Bobby continued relentlessly, "I could treat you as the naughty child you are, and I should communicate at once with your parents or guardian. I suppose we can do that still. Nothing against it."

"It'll be rather beastly of you if you do," protested Maureen. "I don't think you really want to be beastly, do you?" She looked up at him pleadingly, still in her role of little frightened child asking for protection, and Bobby was not free from an uncomfortable suspicion that she was beginning even to enjoy playing a role she thought she was doing rather well. "It would only upset Daddy for nothing, because I'll tell you anything you want to know. Just anything."

"Well, then, how did you first come to meet Mr. Jones?"

"I don't know exactly. A cocktail party, I expect," she answered. "You are always meeting people somewhere. He could be—well, rather fascinating. Somehow he made you feel—" She hesitated for a word and then wound up rather lamely: "I don't know exactly."

"Grown up?" Bobby suggested.'

The shaft struck home. She began to go slowly red, and still redder, till there was no high church dignitary or learned professor in all the land so red as she—or any rose in June either.

"I was such a kid," she explained defensively.

"And are still," Bobby retorted, rather brutally, as Olive was at some pains to point out to him later on. But he was still extremely angry, even if at times he did feel it rather hard to go on being angry with someone he was mentally classifying as the most hopeless little idiot he had ever known. "How did you come to know Jones's address? He seems to have managed to keep it dark generally."

"Oh, one or two people knew. I don't know if he told them or if they found out. I think he didn't like to say because of it's not being very grand or like the stories he told people. Or he may have had other reasons. I don't know. I don't quite remember who told me. Unless it was Norman Oxendale."

"How did you get in here?"

"The woman downstairs gave me a key."

"How much?"

"Well, I gave her a ten-shilling note, if that's what you mean."

"It is," Bobby agreed drily. "Was Mr. Oxendale a friend of his?"

"I don't think so. Not specially. You see, everyone rather sucks up to Norman in a kind of way. Anyhow, they all feel he's worth being civil to. Miniatures are only a sort of sideline with him. He reads for Bury's."

"Reads what? Who is Bury?" Bobby asked, puzzled.

"Don't you know Bury's?" Maureen asked in her turn and in her turn puzzled by such ignorance. "The big theatrical managers. They have seven plays running in the West End at this moment."

"Have they?" asked Bobby, less affected by so portentous an announcement than Maureen seemed to have expected.

"I think it's seven," she was saying now, counting on her fingers. "Yes, seven. Three American, three revivals, and one translation from the French. Bury," she repeated, "commonly known as the Author's Graveyard, because if you send them a play to read, it's generally buried for good."

"Why does that make Mr. Oxendale a person worth being civil to?"

"Oh, authors always hope, poor dears," Maureen explained. "You can never tell. There might be a miracle, and they all feel their own special script ought to have one. They all feel Norman must give it a good report. He often does. Bury's never read them, of course—the reports, I mean."

"It all sounds rather complicated," Bobby said, giving up all hope of understanding these matters, but interested to know that Norman Oxendale had been regarded as a person worth cultivating. Even the smallest piece of information might, he felt, be useful as a clue to a fuller comprehension of this strange make-believe world of the theatre, into which the grim shape of murder seemed to have thrust its way with such incongruous reality.

"Besides," Maureen was saying, "he always pretends he has a lot to do with casting. No one believes him, but everyone thinks, 'Suppose it's true,' and, if it is, just as well to keep on good terms with him. And, of course," she added, "he has a desk at Bury's and he might put in a word sometimes. I don't like him much, but I do try to be civil."

"He would have a good position there, I suppose?"

"I don't expect Bury's pay much," Maureen said doubtfully. "I don't know. He always seems jolly hard up, anyhow. But then," she added brightly, "everyone is, aren't they?"

Bobby agreed wholeheartedly—especially from the personal and private point of view. He said:

"Will you tell me what was in these letters Baldwin Jones thought he could get money out of you for?"

"It wasn't so much what I wrote," Maureen said. "There were only about half a dozen. Just notes really. Promising to meet him somewhere. Things like that. Sometimes he would stand me a dinner and we would go on to a dance. You see, he found out about Father being a peer, and he had an idea that was important, and, of course, it isn't a bit nowadays. So he wanted to be friends and I was feeling awfully out of it at first and I was jolly glad to pick up a man who seemed to know everything about everyone."

"But surely you have many family friends and relatives? I don't see why you should feel awfully out of it," Bobby said.

"Oh, they weren't any good for the people I wanted to meet—people who mattered, I mean," Maureen explained. "The top-rankers in the theatre. I kept away from relations as much as I could—a stuffy lot, all of them. When I went to the Dramatic

School I put down my name as Jones, and that gave Baldwin Jones a chance to pretend he thought we must be relatives."

"Why not use your own name?" Bobby asked.

"Dad was so dead against it. He said the stage was top-heavy with gilded youth, and I did so awfully hate being called gilded youth. I wanted to show him I wasn't, and then I got rather a nice letter from the School—it said I did show some signs of being possibly worth training. I was awfully bucked because generally they say, 'N.B.G.' and please don't call again."

"Well, then," Bobby said, still feeling rather lost with all these revelations thus thrust upon him, "if there were only a few letters and nothing much in them—why did he think you would pay to get them back?"

"I dare say," Maureen admitted reluctantly, "there might have been one or two things he could have twisted. I don't know. Besides—did you know he was awfully good at forging?"

"Baldwin Jones? No. Was he?" Bobby exclaimed, and he told himself that all this rather desultory talk seemed as if it might pay rich dividends. "Did he do much in that line?"

"He did when he got the chance," Maureen answered. "He had a way of coming along with small *post-mortem* cheques after you were dead."

"*Post-mortem* cheques," Bobby repeated. "How did he manage that? Cheques aren't valid if the drawer is dead."

"That was why," Maureen explained. "If you're dead, you can't say it isn't yours, can you? And if the relatives are really nice people, they don't want not to pay on what seems a perfectly good claim—especially if it's a cheque on a bit of paper and supposed to be because of playing poker or something and you've always been awfully respectable. Baldy was always careful to have a good story to tell and only for small sums."

"Had he a cheque of yours?" Bobby asked.

"Oh, no, nothing like that," Maureen answered, and suddenly looked older, more responsible, much more angry, too. "He was a foul beast," she said, "and I don't care if he is dead, he just was. He put in disgusting postscripts, horrid things. Forged so you couldn't tell they had been added. To frighten you out of your life. Well, so it did, but I wasn't going to let him get away with that." Her lips set into hard lines and her eyes were fierce and bright. "I said Jack Longton—" She stopped abruptly as she remembered what she had said previously and she did not repeat it. She said instead: "When I heard he had been killed, I made up my mind no one else was ever going to get hold of the things, and now no one ever will. You can call me a fool as much as you like, but you can't do anything about it. No one can."

CHAPTER XIX

A PHOTOGRAPH

MAUREEN WAS ALLOWED to go then—a very, though probably only temporarily, subdued Maureen. She was warned, however, that a much fuller and more detailed statement would be required later on. She was also given the good advice to tell her father everything and to consult that lawyer whom she had described as thinking her 'just awful.'

"She has managed," Bobby said crossly after her departure, "to muddle it all up even worse than before. Makes it look much worse for three of our suspects. Young Longton is evidently in love with her, and he may have thought it his bounden duty to play the knight errant and rescue her from the blackmail threat. Then her father may have felt her reputation was in danger and gone to extremes to save it. Both had easy access to the dagger and either might have taken it, perhaps as a kind of measure of precaution."

"Wouldn't you say that pointed to the father rather than to Mr. Longton?" Ford asked. "Longton looks to me as if he would feel quite up to handling Baldwin Jones without bothering about golden daggers. Only you said it made it worse for three suspects, didn't you, sir?"

"The Maureen girl," Bobby explained. "She may have worked herself into a state of hysteria. We've only her word for it that what she called the beastly parts were forgeries. If the little idiot hadn't burnt the things, that could easily have been established. Now there will never be any positive proof. She may have made up her mind to get them back at any cost and taken the golden dagger with her to back her up. Or even as a bit of play-acting for that matter. It all has to be taken into account."

"Seems to be getting more and more of an open field," Ford commented ruefully. "Plenty of trails, but which is the right one? And Mr. Tudor King no one seems to know anything about, except that he isn't there any more. I don't get Miss Maureen somehow. Is she—well, responsible, if you see what I mean?"

"Oh, yes," Bobby answered. "As much so as any of these theatre people is likely to be—not that that's saying much," he added.

Therewith Bobby departed, leaving Ford in charge till a relief could be procured and arrangements made for the safe custody and expert examination of the dead man's belongings. He himself went back to 'The Turk's Tail,' where he found Mrs. Abbott, though still very distressed, in a more composed mood.

At his request she showed him the series of presentation volumes Baldwin Jones had given her. But, to Bobby's disappointment, they proved not to be the works of Tudor King. They were, in fact, the collected edition, recently put on the market, and now remaindered, of a writer of whom Bobby knew as little as he had done of Tudor King until these recent events. He made a note of titles, and of the names of the author and publisher, and then went on to ask a few more questions. He learned very little.

Baldwin Jones had been at first just a chance, casual customer like many others who visited 'The Turk's Tail' from time to time. Gradually his visits had grown more frequent till he had come to occupy a privileged position. He began to be an occasional, and then more frequent, guest in the intimacy of the comfortable apartment, half office, half sitting-room, in which Bobby and Mrs. Abbott were now talking. But it soon appeared from what Mrs. Abbott said that there had been a certain reserve on both sides. Baldwin Jones had preserved his air of mystery as of a man of genius moving aloof and alone among common folk. On the other hand, Mrs. Abbott's common sense and business sense had alike prevented her, at least so far, from yielding completely to the odd fascination Baldwin Jones seemed able to exercise over women—whether the landlady of a Hoxton pub or the daughter of a wealthy peer or indeed almost any of the sex. When Bobby approached delicately the subject of money, Mrs. Abbott was emphatic that 'the poor boy' had no feeling for money at all. He had certainly come to be treated as a guest rather than as a customer and after a time had never been asked to pay for the food or drink he was supplied with. Occasionally he would confess to being hard up and Mrs. Abbott admitted that occasionally she had slipped a few notes into his coat pocket when he wasn't looking. He had always been very surprised to find them there and would tell Mrs. Abbott, as a joke against himself, that this money had been in his pocket all the time he had thought he had hardly enough to pay for his 'bus fares.

"Playing his fish carefully," was Bobby's unspoken comment on this.

Possibly also Baldwin Jones had realized that Mrs. Abbott was a woman of considerable strength of character and that he had better not tie himself up to her too completely until he was sure no easier game was in sight. All the same, Bobby told himself on his way back to the Yard that Mrs. Abbott had had a very narrow escape. It was an opinion that was strengthened when, as a result of a few inquiries and 'phone calls he made after his return, he learned that the books he had seen, presented to Mrs. Abbott by Baldwin Jones and claimed by him as his own work, were in fact by a gentleman who occupied a very important and influential—and, highly paid—post in journalism, and entirely unable to understand why his prestige in the literary world was not on the same level. Even this collected edition of his books, produced at his own expense, had attracted little attention—except from a few critics with a proper respect for the hand that fed them or might do so in the future.

Bobby's first impression was that here was another complete dead end. Then he began to wonder. It might be that Jones, unable to present Mrs. Abbott with his own books, since that would disclose the pen name under which he wrote, had hit on this idea of giving her another writer's books, confident, as he would be, that for her one book was much like another, as indeed for many of the great British public one book is much the same as another. All a part possibly of the mist of mystification in which 'Tudor King' seemed to like to move. But no kind of proof that Jones was in fact a professional writer at all or in any way to be identified with the elusive Tudor King. Except of course, that Tudor King was a kind of mystery man and so was Baldwin Jones, and that Baldwin Jones claimed to be a writer, while Tudor King was certainly one.

It had grown too late by now for much more to be done, and Bobby wanted as well to give Maureen full opportunity to take any action she wished. To give her such opportunity was indeed one of the reasons why he had let her go. It seemed to him specially important to know how close was her intimacy with Jack Longton, and whether it was to him that she would turn for help. Just a chance, he thought, or even more than a chance, that between them was the link—the dreadful link—of a guilty knowledge. But that was for the morrow, and now he went home for supper and bed.

He was early in his room at the Yard next day, and there he found, amid the usual mass of material waiting for him, one small and very interesting item. One of his men had managed to dig up a photograph of Tudor King published in a woman's paper several years previously. It was a bad photograph, badly printed on cheap paper, and from it recognition would not be easy. It showed a young man with a moustache and short, curly beard, wearing cricketing flannels and a loose blazer. Not a striking face by any means—indeed, with something rather soft and effeminate about it, Bobby thought, in spite of the moustache and curly beard. There was no photographer's name. Very likely an amateur's effort, Bobby decided. Oddly enough, he had a feeling that there was about it an impression of someone he knew, someone he had seen recently. Who this could be he entirely failed even to imagine. Certainly not Baldwin Jones, whom the photograph did not seem to resemble in the least, though, of course, it had to be remembered that the subject of the photograph was wearing beard and moustache, while Baldwin Jones, like most men to-day, had been clean-shaven. And the wearing of beard and moustache can make a vast difference in personal appearance.

"Take all that hair away and it might almost be a woman's face," he told himself, and he tried to make a sketch, reproducing the face in the photograph as he thought it might be without those appendages.

The effort was no great success. Nor was he much more successful when he first made a sketch of Baldwin Jones and then tried to add beard and moustache.

He threw these attempts into the waste-paper basket as useless, put the photograph in his pocket, made sure by a 'phone call that Longton was at his hotel and would be there all morning. Then he went out to the car he had asked should be provided for him and in readiness and drove off, meaning to call at the hotel to have a talk with Longton before going on to Cobblers.

When he reached the hotel, however, some slight embarrassment seemed to result when he announced his wish to see Longton. The receptionist appeared uncertain as to Mr. Longton's whereabouts. She pressed the bell that summoned the manager in moments of stress or urgency. He also showed some hesitation. Mr. Longton was, he thought, engaged on important business. Bobby said his business was also important and indeed pressing, and the manager gave a hesitating glance down a short passage near the entrance to which they were standing. Up it was coming the sound of distant voices Bobby had at first attributed to a radio set going at full strength. The manager saw Bobby was listening with renewed attention. He said:

"Very lively gentlemen, theatre gentlemen—good Lord, what's that?"

It was a resounding crash they had heard. Along the passage a door burst open. A youngish man with tousled hair bounced out and turned to shake his fist furiously at the room from which he had just emerged.

"It's murder," he bawled. "Sheer murder—I refuse absolutely. Absolutely."

"Sir, sir, if you please—" wailed the manager, hurrying towards him.

Longton shot out of the room into the passage. He was clutching his tie with both hands, as if preparing to strangle himself, but he spoke more quietly:

"Can't you get into your thick head," he demanded, "that my job is to translate this lousy tripe of yours into terms of the—theatre?" and on this last word his voice rose to a shout that out-shouted the best efforts of them all.

"Gentlemen, gentlemen," implored the manager, while the receptionist rang for the porter in case more help was needed.

"What's it all about?" Bobby asked, coming up.

"Hullo, you're the Scotland Yard chap, aren't you?" inquired Longton amiably. "I wasn't expecting you yet awhile." To the young man with the tousled hair, he said: "Have another chat after lunch, shall we?"

"O.K.," said the young man. "Of course, I'll rewrite it if you really think it would go better."

"Well, dear boy," Longton purred, "I do really think it's most awfully jolly good the way it stands, and of course I would keep it like that if you publish in book form, but you have to consider the mechanics of the stage, haven't you?"

"I suppose so, I suppose so," said the young man, and went off whistling with his hands in his pockets. "See you after lunch," he called as he disappeared.

To Bobby, Longton said beamingly:

"You can nearly always choke 'em off when they start meddling with their stuff by talking about the mechanics of the stage. Good tip to remember."

"I'll try," Bobby promised. "But who are they?"

"Oh, authors," Longton explained. "Irresponsible sort of John-nies." He shook his head. "Never know where to have 'em," he said. "You wanted to see me about poor old Baldwin Jones, didn't you? Shocking affair. I don't know there's much I can tell you, though."

CHAPTER XX

CERTAIN EXPLANATIONS

LONGTON LED THE WAY back into the room he had just left.

On the floor lay an overturned chair which had apparently in falling knocked over the large Chinese vase, now in fragments on the floor. The cause and origin, Bobby supposed, of that thunderous crash which a few moments before had startled both him and the hotel manager. Longton kicked the pieces together, shaking his head disapprovingly as he did so.

"All that," he said, "merely because I told him he would have to cut three or four pages of what he called the best dialogue he had ever written and turn his old Oxford don into a retired pig-dealer—and I know a man who is top hole as a retired pig-dealer. Impossible," lamented Longton, still busy collecting the more scattered bits of the disintegrated vase, "impossible to make these author chaps understand that the theatre has to be anchored to the facts. Facts, that's the essential. Seem to live in a world of their own, authors, I mean." He completed his task and again shook a grieved head over the heap of fragments that once had been a vase. "Bury's will have to pay up," he announced firmly. "No reason why I should, and I don't suppose the other bloke can. Not a bean probably; authors never have."

"Bury's?" repeated Bobby. "That's a big theatrical firm, isn't it? Seven productions—three American, three revivals, and one translation?"

"Interested in the theatre?" Longton asked, very pleased as he began to hope Bobby might be a kindred spirit.

"Oh, very," Bobby replied, and indeed he went sometimes when he felt he could afford it, which was seldom. "But, of course, only from the outside, which is really why I'm here. What counts in our work is getting the background right. If the perspective is wrong, then the whole picture we try to build up gets out of focus. As you are both connected with Bury's, I take it you know Mr. Oxendale?"

"Well, in a way I do," Longton answered. "I know he reads for Bury's. He has a desk there, but I don't suppose I've spoken to him half a dozen times. You're not thinking he has anything to do with this Baldwin Jones business, are you?"

"He was on the spot," Bobby replied, and added: "Like you."

"Me?" exclaimed Longton, and looked both startled and uneasy. "Good Lord," he exclaimed. "What the devil—in heaven's name— what the hell does that mean?"

"What it says," Bobby retorted, filled inwardly with admiration for so nice an assortment of phrases. "Everyone who had knowl- edge of and possible access to the weapon used—the Golden Dagger, as they call it—or who had anything to do with the dead man, has naturally to be interviewed. Which," Bobby added wea- rily, "does not mean they are going to be arrested next minute. It simply means that every possible scrap of information is required. For instance, is there any special reason why both you and Mr. Oxendale should be here in this neighbourhood at this particular moment?"

"Well, what about it?" demanded Longton. "Why shouldn't we be? Free country, isn't it?"

"I've tried to explain," Bobby answered patiently, "that in these cases background is all important. I believe one bit of background in your case is that you are in the habit of proposing marriage to Miss Maureen Carton at frequent intervals?"

"Who told you?" Longton grumbled, and without waiting for the answer, which showed no sign of coming, he went on: "I suppose a good many people knew—some silly fools tried to make a joke of it." He was again grabbing at his tie with both hands, still as if taking the necessary preliminary steps towards strangling himself. "Well, it's handy here for that author bloke and then she's a damn little vixen."

"Oh come," protested Bobby, slightly shocked. "That's not the way to talk about a young lady."

"Young lady," growled Longton. "Anyone can be a young lady. She wants to be an actress—a lot more difficult. She never will, though, unless I can get hold of her and put her nose to the grind- stone and keep it there. If I've got to marry her to do it, I don't mind," he added carelessly. "She knows it, and out of sheer devilry she gives me the go-by and instead she asks that Oxendale cub to stay at Cobblers."

"Does he want to marry her, too?" Bobby asked.

"Well, of course," Longton said gloomily. "Anyone would. Like his damn cheek, though."

"Perhaps," suggested Bobby, "he is like you and thinks he might be able to help her in her career?"

"Who? Him?" demanded Longton. "What on earth gave you that idea? Why, he knows no more about acting than he does about—" But there he paused, unable to think of anything on earth, above it or below, about which the ignorance of Mr. Oxendale could be more abysmal.

"Well," Bobby explained mildly, "I understood his job was to read the plays submitted to Bury's and report on them—though I was told, too, that his reports are never read."

"Wouldn't be any good if they were," Longton pointed out. "Impossible to tell from reading the script how a play will pan out. You might as well try to guess what the weather will be like by listening to a B.B.C. forecast. All you want from a script," he went on to explain, "is a foundation for producer and actor to work on. The theatre would be a lot healthier if we could do without plays altogether—and authors," he added with a yearning, far-away look in his eyes.

"Well, then, in that case," Bobby asked, "why do Bury's pay Mr. Oxendale to read manuscripts?"

"Oh, well," Longton said, and looked as if this were a problem he had never before considered and now found puzzling. Then he brightened up. *"Noblesse oblige,"* he said simply.

"I don't think I quite follow," Bobby remarked, feeling more and more at a loss.

"Oh, well," Longton repeated patiently, obviously trying to explain what he felt should require no explanation to anyone of' even normal intelligence, "Bury's are the leading managers and they do feel in a way responsible and that they must do their bit for the British drama."

"I see," Bobby said, giving it up. "Sorry to ask so many questions that don't seem to have much to do with what's happened, but I do feel rather lost with you literary and theatrical people. I had never even heard of Bury's till now. Nor, for that matter, very much about Mr. Tudor King. You know there are a lot of rumours about him in the village? He didn't write plays, did he?"

"If he didn't, he's about the only author bloke who doesn't," Longton answered. "I don't know. Never heard of him as a dramatist. Sort of disappeared or something, hasn't he? Well, there's a suspect ready to hand for you if you must cast someone round about here for the part."

"I don't think we can say he has disappeared," Bobby said. "He hasn't arrived at his bungalow yet, that's all. Do you know anything about Mr. Baldwin Jones?"

"Nothing much, poor devil," Longton replied. "I may have met him at some cocktail party. I don't remember. I knew of him. That's all. He had the name of trying to pick up bits of gossip to sell to the Press. I kept clear of him myself because of that, but I expect people tried to be civil, or bought him a drink now and then, on the chance of getting their names in the papers. I don't think anyone knew much about him. I did hear he had something to do with films, but I asked one producer. He hadn't heard of him."

"Did you know he was trying to blackmail Miss Maureen?" Bobby asked.

"Oh, Lord, you know about that?" Longton exclaimed. "Kept it up your sleeve all this time? Jolly good curtain," he continued with professional approval. "Hardly fair, though?"

"Mr. Longton," Bobby said, and now his voice had taken on a harder note. "I am investigating, murder and I am not doing it under any Queensberry Rules. Murder is outside the rules."

"Oh, well," Longton muttered sulkily, "you might have told me, all the same."

"Told you what?" asked Bobby. "That a man has been murdered? Perhaps, too, I wanted to be sure how far I could trust you to be wholly frank with me. You knew the dead man was a blackmailer and you must have realized that was important. Yet you never mentioned it. Miss Maureen rang you up to ask you to say nothing about it, didn't she?"

"No, she didn't; not like that, anyway," Longton retorted defiantly. "How do you know?" Bobby did not answer. He saw no reason to explain that it had been a simple deduction from what he knew of Maureen. Longton continued: "All she said was that you were nosing around and I had better not say anything more than I could help. I wasn't sure what she meant. She sounded upset. I was meaning to go over after lunch and ask what it was all about. I don't see where it comes in, anyhow. I mean, the filthy trick he was trying on. Unless you think Maureen did it herself?"

This was plainly meant as a purely rhetorical question—a kind of *reductio ad absurdum*. Bobby was not inclined to look at it wholly in that light. He said:

"My information is that Baldwin Jones was recently engaged in a scuffle of some sort. His face seems to have shown bruises inflicted some time before death. Do you care to say anything?"

"Trying to catch me out again?" Longton complained. "If you must know, Maureen told me what he was up to, so I hunted him up and told him he had better hand the letters over right away. There was a bit of an argument and very likely he did get a bit damaged. Nothing to speak of." Longton was tugging at his tie so fiercely that

Bobby was growing quite concerned lest he should really succeed in choking himself. He went on: "You know such a hell of a lot, you may as well know the rest if you want to. I said I would wring his neck if he worried Maureen any more. I think I meant it. Literally. I think he was a bit scared. It was all rather nasty. I mean, a girl's name, reputation—whatever you like to call it. A story like that at the beginning of her career might have put paid to all her chances. The theatre"—Longton always said that word all in capital letters, so to speak—"the theatre is getting jolly careful these days. Puritanical."

Bobby was slightly surprised by this statement, but did not attempt to dispute it. Instead he said:

"Then I may take it that if Miss Maureen says it was her umbrella was responsible and that it was because he tried to kiss her, that is what it would be polite to call an imaginary reconstruction?"

"You mean she told you it was her?" Longton asked. "Good Lord, of course it wasn't. She wouldn't know how, and if she did, she would have been so sorry she would probably have been busy ever since nursing him."

CHAPTER XXI

SPREADING SCANDAL

THAT ENDED THE INTERVIEW, and Bobby drove off towards Cobblers, telling himself that both Maureen and Longton were troubled and uneasy and that each was doing his or her best to protect the other.

But what conclusion was to be drawn? That each believed the other implicated in the murder? Or in one case was it not so much belief as knowledge? Or was it simply the not unnatural reaction of two high-spirited young people to unfounded and resented suspicion? Or again, did it mean no more than that Maureen had sought the help of a young man who had protested his devotion to her, and that there had resulted what Longton had described as a bit of a scrimmage neither of them wished should become generally known?

No way of resolving that problem at present. Cobblers came in sight and this time Bobby had no need to knock, for he had hardly alighted from his car when the Cobblers door opened and Maureen appeared.

She stood waiting for him in the open doorway, and when he approached she said in no welcoming voice:

"I thought you would be turning up again."

"I expect Mr. Longton rang up to tell you I've had a talk with him?" Bobby remarked. Maureen nodded, and Bobby went on: "Apparently he claims the credit for the Baldwin Jones black eye that you told me was your doing."

"Well, it was me practically," Maureen argued. "It was perfectly true really. If I hadn't told Jack it would never have happened, would it? So it was really, truly me, wasn't it?"

"But not your umbrella, stumpy or otherwise," Bobby suggested.

"I think that's rather a quibble," Maureen told him, her voice heavy with rebuke.

"It leaves me with the impression," Bobby said, "that you each want to protect the other—a kind of mutual cover-up. So I wonder why?"

"There is far too much gossip about the theatre as it is," Maureen answered, looking very wise and grown-up and evidently quoting something she had heard. "Even the smaller scandal does harm and we of the theatre can't be too careful."

"Very true, I'm sure," Bobby agreed. "Have you told Lord Rone and Saine about your letters to Baldwin Jones?"

Maureen nodded again, and, with one of her lightning changes, now took on the aspect of a hurt child.

"He was most awfully upset," she admitted ruefully. "I wouldn't have minded so much if he had rowed, but he hardly said a word, just sat there and worried. He seemed to think I had practically abolished the House of Lords all on my own. Not that I should have cared; stuffy old place. Talked about the family honour. In the last few centuries, we've had two murders, two trials for treason, three public executions, I think it is"—she was counting on her fingers—"one witch, one bigamy, one abduction, and I expect a whole heap of other things that got hushed up. So, I don't see why burning a few old letters"—these last words accompanied by a defiant nod at Bobby—"matters such an awful lot."

"Times change," Bobby said. "Do you think I could have a word with Lord Rone?"

"Wouldn't be much good saying 'No,' would it?" Maureen countered.

"None at all," Bobby agreed. "There's Mr. Oxendale, too. He might be able to help if I could see him as well for a few minutes."

"Well, you can't," retorted Maureen with considerable satisfaction. "He went to London this morning. I expect he'll be back some time to-day," she added. "Uncle Bill told him he had to be or else the police would think he was running away, and then they would be sure he did it."

"Oh, it's not quite so bad as all that," Bobby protested; and Maureen looked as if it were much worse, made a sound that if she had been a young man and not a young lady could have been described as a grunt, and led the way to her father's room. There Lord Rone was busy dictating letters to Dick Moyne, who had very much the air of being by now comfortably settled in as private secretary. On Bobby's entrance he got up to withdraw. Lord Rone suggested that he might go down to the village on an errand fairly obviously invented for the occasion. When he had gone, Bobby said:

"In cases like these, it is always wise to take every possible precaution."

"A most unfortunate affair," Lord Rone said. "Journalists have been calling here—'phone calls, too. Most embarrassing; most annoying. Most. My daughter tells me you are aware that he had possession of certain letters?"

"Letters that the young lady has very foolishly destroyed," Bobby interposed.

"Very naturally so," Lord Rone retorted, bristling at once in his daughter's defence. "An extreme step perhaps, but most understandable in the circumstances. After all, they were her property."

"No," Bobby said. "The copyright may have been hers—that is, she could have prevented publication. But the actual letters, the paper they were written on, that is, had become part of Baldwin Jones's estate and her action was legally indefensible."

"Mere hair-splitting," Lord Rone declared. "Such legal niceties are of no importance or interest. I agree that it was an extreme step, but I consider fully justifiable in the circumstances."

"You mean you feel the most extreme steps would be justified in such a case?" Bobby asked.

"Certainly, certainly; fully justified," Lord Rone declared firmly, even loudly. "I should undoubtedly have acted in the same way."

"But you would still feel—within limits?" Bobby asked.

"There could be no limits in such a matter," Lord Rone answered. "A father has a duty to protect his child."

"I can understand your feelings," Bobby said. "I have known of cases when a comparatively small act of youthful folly has wrecked a whole life. But you said, I think, no limits. None? Not even—murder?"

The word dropped like a stone in that quiet roam. Lord Rone rose from his chair and went to stand by the fireplace, beneath the great painting of 'The Young Stallion.' After a pause, while Bobby watched and waited, he said:

"You have led me on, Mr. Owen, to say more than I intended. I think I should prefer to continue this conversation in the presence of my solicitor."

"Very good," Bobby said. "Will you let me know when and where? Entirely to suit your convenience, of course. Our preliminary investigation is nothing like complete as yet. I was glad to notice you do not trust Mr. Moyse very far and made sure there was no chance of any eavesdropping this time. In confidence, I may say that I do not trust him very much myself."

"You don't mean you suspect him of . . . of . . . ?" Lord Rone asked, almost hopefully.

"I only mean that at present it would be better to trust no one, not even your oldest friend—no one. There is no evidence as yet against either your oldest friend or your new secretary or indeed against anyone else."

"I think you mean something, but I don't know what," Lord Rone said uneasily.

"All I mean," Bobby told him, "is that it seems certain that someone here at Cobblers killed Baldwin Jones and that someone else here knows who—or why the 'phone call?"

"I don't consider," Lord Rone said slowly, "that your deduction that the guilty person is or was a resident of this house is in any way justified. In fact, I consider it a most unjustifiable assumption. I shall take the opinion of my solicitor on the matter. It seems to me the murder may have been deliberately planned to throw suspicion on us. In the same way, I should think the 'phone call may very well have been made by the murderer himself. An act of defiance, so to say."

"What the vulgar call cocking a snook at us?" Bobby suggested. "It might be. But an attempt was made to hide the body, and but for the 'phone call nothing might have been known for long enough. Baldwin Jones seems to have been a very unattached person. No known relatives or close friends. His disappearance could easily have gone for months unreported. No one directly interested. And it seems difficult to suppose that anyone but an inmate of this house could have managed to get hold of the golden dagger."

"Its existence is well known," Lord Rone insisted. Bobby made no answer. It did not seem necessary. Lord Rone continued;

"There seem to be many rumours in circulation in the village. Particularly about Mr. Tudor King. I had never heard of him, but it seems his name is very well known."

"What sort of rumours?" Bobby asked cautiously.

"Well," Lord Rone answered, "one seems to be that he is the murderer and another is that he has been murdered himself. I rang up a literary friend in London to ask about him. Apparently he is a great favourite with the women's papers, and it seems, too, he has always been something of a mystery. My friend said he had avoided publicity so successfully that it has become a most successful form of publicity."

"Flee when no man pursueth," Bobby commented, "and all the world will soon join in the hunt. Who is supposed to have murdered the illusive Mr. King?"

"I understand some children were shouting after the woman at the New Bungalow yesterday afternoon—Mrs. Cato, I think her name is."

"That'll have to be stopped," Bobby declared. "I had better drop a few hints about slander being actionable. Do you know if anyone else is mentioned?"

"Well, one story seems to be that Baldwin Jones murdered Tudor King and then was murdered himself. Another is that Baldwin Jones and Tudor King were really one and the same."

"Well, that leaves an open field, doesn't it?" Bobby remarked. "Difficult to stop people talking. A few reminders about the slander laws may help. Of course, anything said to us would be privileged."

Bobby, who was becoming acutely conscious that it was now time for lunch, took his leave then. He was getting into his car when he saw Sir William Watson and Lady Watson hurrying up the drive towards the house as if afraid they were going to be late. Bobby got out of his car again and began to fiddle with his engine so that they might have an opportunity to speak to him if they wished—and as he hoped.

They were quite close now. Bobby finished what he had not been doing and made to get back into the car. Sir William announced his proximity by an enormous and air-shattering sneeze. Bobby looked round as if surprised, and Sir William said:

"Any fresh developments in this dreadful business? Or oughtn't I to ask?"

"Why not?" Bobby said. "I'm afraid the answer is 'No.' But the investigation has only just begun."

"Well, the sooner it's concluded, the happier we shall all feel," Sir William said, and he was indeed looking pale and worried. "I imagine you are still thinking it must be one of us here at Cobblers. Very disturbing indeed to think that we are all under suspicion."

"I'm sure no one can suspect you at any rate," declared Lady Watson indignantly.

"You notice, my dear," Sir William remarked, "that Mr. Owen does not confirm. He would have no right to until he is sure who it was. For my part, I'm quite at a loss. Who could it possibly be? What possible motive?"

"Those are the vital questions," Bobby agreed. "Together with the other puzzle of the 'phone call and why it was made? But for it, nothing might have been known for months, perhaps years. And having made it, why hasn't whoever it was come forward?"

"Probably afraid," Sir William said. "I remember when I was out East a whole family was killed because an assassin—" He paused to sneeze even more violently than before—twice over. "Because," he resumed, "he thought they might give evidence against him."

"I hope that didn't save him," Bobby said. "Probably only made his guilt more plain. I'm afraid you've caught cold, Sir William. Most people have just now, though. Anyhow, yours doesn't come from this new fad of going about without a hat. Responsible for much of it, I think."

"Oh, he never does that," Lady Watson declared. "I simply wouldn't let him."

"Wifely authority," smiled Sir William, and Bobby had not failed to notice that the hat he had on was a smart-looking Homburg, apparently fresh from the shop.

CHAPTER XXII

"JUST LIFE"

IT WAS ONLY A SHORT drive to the village. On the way Bobby kept a sharp look out for Dick Moyse, but saw nothing of him. There were footpaths though, as well as the road, so possibly Moyse might have returned by one of them. The first thing Bobby did, on the principle that what we have had even the jealous gods cannot take from us, was to visit the local pub in the hope of getting something to eat. They were able to provide bread and cheese, the latter having the advantage of being home-made and not of the variety known as 'mousetrap.'

This not unsatisfactory refreshment disposed of, Bobby went on to the small cottage that served both as village police station and as the residence of Constable Yates, sole representative of the law for a considerable distance around. Here were assembled three or four of the specialist officers engaged on the case. None of them had much of immediate interest to report, though, of course, such routine inquiries are of the highest value in avoiding waste of time and energy in following misleading trails. Nor did Bobby mention that he believed he had that morning gathered important information. Time enough to make that known if and when confirmatory evidence was obtained. On one thing all present were, however, fully agreed—that the spate of rumours now in full flood in the neighbourhood must somehow be stopped.

"Yates says," one man remarked, "that Mrs. Cato, the lady at the New Bungalow, has been complaining about the gossip that's going on. Says it's most unpleasant for her, the way people stare if she goes into the village."

Bobby said he would make a point of calling to see Mrs. Cato and assure her that everything possible was being done to stop such irresponsible talk. The little conference ended, Bobby drove on accordingly to the New Bungalow, where he found also Linda Blythe, whose afternoon off it happened to be. Both she and Mrs. Cato were very indignant.

"It's so silly, so utterly ridiculous," they kept saying in turn, and Linda said she supposed it was all because when she came to visit Mrs. Cato she used the generally unused path that led so near where the body of the murdered man had been discovered.

Bobby asked if they had had word recently from Mr. Tudor King, and Mrs. Cato explained that they didn't expect to. It was a motoring holiday. He might be anywhere on the Continent—Spain perhaps or Scandinavia.

"Filling his notebooks," Mrs. Cato explained. "Getting the facts right for the new novel he's writing. It's going to have a cosmopolitan background, and it's got to be right. Make the tiniest slip and the critics—pounce. Put the Bridge of Sighs in Florence instead of Venice and you would think that was all that mattered."

"Like that book," Linda Blythe agreed, "where the heroine was serving in the gloves and shoes department of a big London stores. Everybody knows gloves and shoes are never in one department, and then, to make it worse, promoted her to be first assistant in furs, so she could meet the rich girl who was buying a mink coat for goodness knows how much. As if a first assistant didn't need to know anything about what they were selling. Made you feel the author knew nothing about it. The critics never said a word. I don't expect they knew anything about it either."

"Oh, well, critics," said Mrs. Cato, and said it as if she had been a leading politician referring to the other side as 'vermin.'

"Readers noticed it, though," Linda said. "Letters by the dozen."

"Oh, readers," said Mrs. Cato, much as before, only more so. "I suppose you have to have them," she admitted reluctantly.

Bobby said politely that he could well understand how difficult readers and critics made things. Though for his part, he explained, he found one of the difficulties in this case to be the theatrical and literary atmosphere surrounding it, and to him so unfamiliar. Made it hard, he said, to estimate correctly the attitude and probable behaviour, past, present, and future, of those concerned.

"So easy," Bobby said, "to attach too much importance to one point and too little to another. Was there any special reason, by the way, for Mr. Tudor King choosing this neighbourhood?"

"He wouldn't if we had known there was going to be a murder," Mrs. Cato answered. "Mr. King is buying a villa in Capri. But it isn't ready yet, and his lease of the London flat ran out, so he had to find somewhere to go. Linda told us about this bungalow. It seemed suitable and Mr. King told me to take it. And sorry enough I am now, and what Mr. King will think with all this fuss and this disgusting gossip and crazy talk—well, I don't know."

"We are very sorry about that," Bobby assured her, "and we'll do all in our power to stop it. If we could get in touch with Mr. Tudor King, it would be much easier. I think you told me you are a novelist yourself?"

"Was one once," Mrs. Cato said with a kind of angry defiance, as though she threw a challenge in the face of neglectful fame. "Talked about. Discussed. Not now. Tudor King gets paid more for one short story than most of my books ever earned. But then I never pretended to give the public what it wanted."

"All the same," Linda interposed, "people do enjoy Tudor King, don't they?"

"My books," declared Mrs. Cato firmly, "were never meant to be enjoyed. I never tried to be a mere merchant of joy—like Tudor King." She was speaking now with great contempt and bitterness. "My works were studies of life as people really know it—a dreary repetition of a daily round without significance or purpose except to go on and on."

"Just life," Bobby suggested.

"Just life," Mrs. Cato repeated in a surprised and doubtful voice that in its turn surprised Bobby. "That's the title of one of my books. Did you know?" Bobby shook his head, and Mrs. Cato looked disappointed. "It was the one that was most discussed—took me two years to write and got long notices in all the important papers. But hardly any sales. I put all my irony and scorn into it, into the title even. *Just Life*," she repeated; "and life is never just as I showed."

"Could you lend me a copy?" Bobby asked. "I should really like to read it now I've met you."

Mrs. Cato, half flattered, half doubtful, gave him a suspicious glance, and hesitated.

"No," she said finally. "I never lend my books. If anyone wants one they can go to the trouble of getting a copy. In the remnant boxes of the second-hand shops," she added, more bitterly than ever. "If you lend your books, people think they are doing you a favour in reading them instead of receiving one."

"I shall make a point of getting hold of one," Bobby assured her, and was rewarded by another glare of mingled doubt and distrust, suspicion of his motives eloquent in every feature. "*Just Life*? I'll remember." He began to fumble in his pockets, produced his wallet, and from it the old photograph of Tudor King he had brought with him. He said: "I wonder if you would call this a good likeness?"

Mrs. Cato was plainly a good deal startled. She took the photograph and stared at it for some moments without speaking. Linda pressed forward to look at it over her shoulder and seemed equally surprised—even disturbed.

"How did you get hold of this?" Mrs. Cato demanded.

"One of our men sent it in," Bobby answered. "Good likeness?"

"No," Mrs. Cato snapped. "He hasn't got a beard now. What do you want it for?"

She crumpled it up angrily as she spoke and threw it on the floor, and Bobby picked it up again. He had for a moment the impression that she was going to try to snatch it from him. He said:

"Just one more thing. I believe Miss Blythe uses the path through the wood when she comes to see you. It's rather dark and lonely, isn't it?"

"Not now," Mrs. Cato answered. "There's police there all the time turning people back."

"They'll be withdrawn soon," Bobby said. "They were only searching for any further scraps of evidence. I think it might be better if both of you avoided using that path for the present. We still have no idea who the murderer is, but he probably knows a lot about us and what we are doing, and he may very well be afraid that Miss Blythe saw more than apparently she did and that she may have told you."

"Oh, but I didn't," Linda interrupted. "I didn't see anything except the hat I put on a bush out of the wet, only it was gone when I came back."

"All the same," Bobby persisted, "I think it would be much more prudent to run no risk of his trying to suppress the evidence he may be afraid Miss Blythe could give."

"I'll go with her," Mrs. Cato, said grimly. "I'll take the chopper."

Bobby thought she looked fully capable of using it to good advantage, and he remembered the first time he had seen her and, how she had come from behind the house, swinging it in one hand, like Clytemnestra coming to tell what she had done. Again he suggested mildly that it would be better to run no risks.

"Probably the murderer came back to get his hat," Bobby said. "He may even have been watching and have seen you pick it up. You are sure, Miss Blythe, there is nothing more you can tell me?'

"Only what I've said before," Linda answered. "It looked new and expensive. It came from Bailey and Bailey in Mock Street. I forget if I told you that."

"I don't think so," Bobby said. "Bailey and Bailey? They are rather fashionable people, aren't they?"

"Oh, yes," Linda agreed. "One of those small shops that have been there for centuries and charge the same way."

CHAPTER XXIII

A NEW HAT

BOBBY DROVE AWAY, perpending, doubtful. He had certainly learned a good deal, but of its relevance to the investigation he was engaged upon he was not sure. And then there were so many points that had to be cleared up. He felt indeed that Mrs. Cato's dislike, contempt—was hatred too strong a word?—for Mr. Tudor King, his work, and all that he stood for approached the pathological. He was inclined to think, too, that the younger woman, Linda, was very much on the side of Tudor King, and yet entirely under the influence, even control, of Mrs. Cato.

An odd situation, Bobby thought, and was it possible, even remotely possible, that Mrs. Cato's feeling towards her employer could have found issue in such violence as would account for Mr. Tudor King's rather curious and not very satisfactorily explained absence from the scene? Had Mrs. Cato really been able to bear no longer the constant contrast between the popular success of the Tudor King books and the unfortunate, unconsidered fate of her own novels in the twopenny boxes of the Charing Cross Road? And again, did the Linda girl know or suspect something, and did that explain the frequent visits daily or nightly apparently, that she paid to the New Bungalow?

He told himself that these were not questions to which he could devote much time at present. He could keep them in mind, but he must concentrate all his energies on the murder of the unlucky Baldwin Jones, all indeed that was officially before him. Only he found himself hoping, somewhat uneasily, that both Mrs. Cato and Linda would heed the warning given them. With an unknown murderer loose in the neighbourhood, every precaution was necessary—even though one of the women concerned had an air of being well able to look after herself and a trick of handling an axe as if she could use it very effectively should the need arise.

Turning these thoughts over in his mind and finding little profit in doing so, Bobby drove slowly back to Cobblers, where by good luck he arrived just in time to find Oxendale returned from his visit to Town. Bobby explained that he thought it might be helpful if Mr. Oxendale wouldn't mind answering a few questions, and Mr. Oxendale looked uncomfortable and said it was a sordid business and he wanted to have as little to do with it as possible, but he was, of course, entirely willing to do anything he could. Which was, he feared, very, very little. Of Baldwin Jones, he knew, for example, almost nothing.

"He called in at the office sometimes," Oxendale admitted. "I dodged him when I could. He was very persistent. Always trying to pull strings, and I hadn't any idea of pulling strings to please him. What influence I have—rather less than some people seem to imagine—I try to use to help talent, real talent. If I think a script is good, I say so. If I can give a hint about casting, I do. Where I see promise, that is. Jones was always trying to influence me. Annoying. One has to put up with that sort of thing in my position, but I shut down on it as much as I can."

"You have a position with a theatrical firm, I understand?" Bobby said.

"Bury's," said Oxendale; and if he did not say it with quite the almost religious fervour with which Jack Longton pronounced the word 'theatre,' he very clearly expected it to impress.

"I believe there were rather unfavourable rumours current about Jones, weren't there?" Bobby went on.

"Oh, there are unfavourable rumours about lots of people," Oxendale answered. "The theatre world is full of gossip—we are a self-contained community and we talk about each other. I make a point of never remembering what I can't help hearing."

"Very wise," Bobby agreed, and wondered if Mr. Oxendale were always as prudent and discreet as he claimed.

Clearly, however, he meant to say as little as possible, and Bobby decided that for the moment he would leave Baldwin Jones. He got out his notebook, glanced through it and then said:

"Oh, yes. Mr. Longton. Another theatrical gentleman. You know him professionally, I take it?"

"Can't help knowing Longton if you are with Bury's," Oxendale answered, and there was evident dislike in his voice. "A producer. I can't say I admire his work. Meretricious, I consider it. All for immediate effect. No depth. Of course, that's only my opinion, but if his theories are right, mine are wrong." Oxendale smiled as he said this, as if implying that to say this was a little like saying that if the Longton theories were right, then that two and two make four was wrong. "He is producing for Bury's at the moment. I fully agreed. Test before the footlight is the only test that counts—for informed opinion, that is. I don't mean the popular appeal, as with his *Arden of Faversham*. You remember that?" Bobby had never heard either of the production or the play, but he did not say so.

Taking his silence for acquiescence, Oxendale went on: "I don't deny the thing did attract some attention. I keep my own opinion, though, of course, I agreed he was entitled to his new hat."

"What for? What was that?" Bobby asked.

"Oh, I promised him a new hat if the thing went to the West End. Well, as it happened, it did. Not that it ran, but it was put on. Of course, I told him to go ahead and get his hat and send me the bill. Of course, he went to the most expensive shop he could think of."

"Bailey and Bailey?" Bobby asked.

"That's right," Oxendale said, surprised. "You know them?"

"I've heard of them," Bobby said without betraying that he found this piece of information of any interest. "You both know Miss Maureen Carton as well, I suppose, as I understand she intends to go on the stage?"

"In my considered opinion," Oxendale said impressively, "a genius—undeveloped as yet, but with all the marks. She should have started her training earlier, but Lord Rone made objections. Unless she is ruined by overwork, unless her native gift is forced into conventional orthodox channels, if she is allowed to develop as Nature intended—then a Siddons in the making."

"You have a very high opinion of her, then?" Bobby remarked.

"The highest," Oxendale said, "and my position at Bury's gives me exceptional opportunities for forming an opinion. The danger is that she may get into the hands of producers like Longton, who merely want to use her genius for their own glory. I shall try to save her from that fate."

Bobby was consulting his notebook again. It was beginning to seem to him that Maureen was rather in the position of the corpse of the Homeric hero for possession of which Greek and Trojan warriors fought so desperately. Not a very happy metaphor, perhaps, since Maureen was certainly a very lively kind of corpse indeed. Clearly, however, the rivalry between the two young men was keen. And had that any bearing on Baldwin Jones's fate? A possibility, Bobby supposed. And he could not help thinking that the odds in what might be called the Maureen stakes were clearly very much in Oxendale's favour, since Longton apparently was offering only hard work and lots of it and Oxendale was promising success through a trust in native genius that could trust itself alone. Pretty clear which road would seem most attractive. High stakes, too, since they probably included winning Maureen's hand, and marriage with the daughter of a wealthy peer has its advantages even in these days of perfervid equality when Procrustes and his bed have become the patron saints of the new society. Bobby closed his notebook and said:

"By the way, you knew Mr. Baldwin Jones's address, I think?"

"He gave it me once when he asked me to go to see him. I've entirely forgotten it. I never had the least intention of going."

"Why did he suggest it? I understand he made rather a mystery of where he lived."

"Well, it was in some slum or another; that was all," Oxendale explained. "He didn't like that known, but he had got hold of some play about the slums he wanted to read to me and then to take me round where he lived so I could see for myself how true to life it was. I expect he had written the thing himself. I told him to send it in in the usual way, and if I liked it, then we could think about going slumming together."

A plausible explanation, Bobby thought—even too plausible. "You told Miss Maureen, I think, didn't you?"

"Did I? I had quite forgotten. I may have. I don't know. Why? Does it matter?"

"Everything matters," Bobby told him. "Everything—in murder. Our information is that Jones was not above petty blackmail if he got a chance. Do you know anything about that?"

"Nothing," Oxendale answered. "I don't pay any attention to the sort of gossip that does go on. I'm always being blackmailed myself, for that matter. At least, that's what I call it. Authors, stage aspirants—all trying to bring pressure on me to say something about them to Bury's. It gets on one's nerves at times."

Bobby said he could well believe it, and how much obliged he was to Mr. Oxendale for answering his questions so frankly and fully, and Oxendale said he fully realized how important it was to give the police every possible assistance, and had the investigation made any real progress or oughtn't he to ask? There was that 'phone call, for instance? Was there anything yet to show who made it?

Bobby said nothing at all so far, but he still hoped whoever it was might yet come forward. Therewith he went to find Moyse, now busy again with his typewriter and Lord Rone's correspondence.

Moyse proved to be a good deal less communicative than had been the other two young men. He protested he knew nothing. Especially he knew nothing about anyone else at Cobblers. A complete stranger to all of them. He had wanted a job, and it had been a lucky break for him to get this one with Lord Rone. No, he had not been formally engaged, but it came to much the same thing. At any rate, he hoped so. It wouldn't be his fault if he lost what promised to be a very comfortable berth. And the less he had to do with the murder investigation the better he would be pleased. Murder was a nasty, rather frightening business. Moyse was a little pale as he said this. He didn't want to be mixed up in it in any way whatever.

Bobby assured him that no one would be mixed up in it unnecessarily, but there it was. Everyone on the spot at the time had to be considered, and Moyse said it was just his luck and went on with his typing.

So Bobby returned to the village police station, where he became immersed in all the routine work that was waiting his attention. But first he got a call put through to Olive to ask her to get hold of a copy of one of Tudor King's books and of one of those written by Mrs. Cato—Cynthia Cairn—before lack of public appreciation had driven her to accept whatever was the exact position she held with Mr. Tudor King. If possible, Bobby said, he would like it to be the one she had mentioned, entitled *Just Life*—a title apparently meant to convey a grim, ironic comment on human existence. Olive might be able to find a copy on the shelves of the local public library—even if only the shelves in the cellars. If not, would she make an excursion to Charing Cross Road in the morning and see what the twopenny boxes there could yield. Olive asked in return why this sudden interest in literature, and Bobby said he would explain when he got home—if she wasn't asleep, that is, for he would probably be late.

CHAPTER XXIV

MESSRS. BAILEY AND BAILEY

BOBBY, RETURNING HOME late, as he had anticipated, found this prognostication correct and Olive fast asleep. But on the floor by the bedside lay a copy of *Just Life*. So apparently the local library had risen successfully to the occasion.

He picked it up and turned over the leaves. Page after page of closely printed paragraphs. It gave him an uncomfortable feeling of being back at College, confronted with one of those learned pronouncements that had always seemed to him as remote as mountain peaks he had no desire to climb.

Putting the book down, he prepared for bed, and soon was as fast asleep as Olive herself. For her slumber was profound, and Bobby's last thought as he drifted into sleep was to wonder if this depth of slumber were a result of the attempted perusal of *Just Life*. At breakfast next morning he asked Olive how she had liked the book, and was answered by a prodigious yawn, as if the very thought of it nearly sent her to sleep again.

"It's all psychology," she explained. "Tremendously clever. If anyone does anything, there's always a complete analysis of heredity and environment and all the rest to account for it. That is, when anything does happen, because most of the time the characters never do anything; they just sit about and talk of their sorrows and disasters and how rotten everything inevitably is. And I must say they do rather get it rubbed in, poor dears. But it's awfully funny."

"Doesn't sound it," said Bobby as he made two mouthfuls of his share of the week's bacon ration.

"I don't mean funny," Olive told him. "I mean—funny. Because I got the feeling I had read it all before and I knew I hadn't. And then I discovered—what do you think?"

"I never think at breakfast," Bobby answered firmly. "One of the things definitely not done."

"It's all," Olive explained, "almost exactly the same as *Life at Manor Abbey Castle*."

"What's that?" Bobby asked. "Life at how much?"

"It's one of the Tudor King books," Olive answered. "Almost all the same thing—even down to the names of most of the characters. Not exactly, but very similar. Agatha instead of Angela. Like that.

And in *Just Life* there's a barrow-boy—Bill Veale—who works hard at deserting the girls he loves passionately—sometimes the brutal police have packed him off to prison, so he has to—and then they die in the gutter of hunger and T.B. Tudor King has a young, rising Cabinet Minister millionaire—William Vere—who spends all his time doing the same. Only with him it's affairs of State that take him away from the titled young ladies he loves so devotedly. In fact, it's all much the same, except there's a happy ending: the T.B. cures itself, and the scene is Mayfair and Monte Carlo instead of Shoreditch and Southend."

"How art thou translated, Bottom," Bobby said.

"That's a quotation, isn't it?" Olive asked suspiciously. "I suppose it does seem not so bad if it all happens in mink coats and pearl necklaces. Tudor King's heroine ends up yachting in the Mediterranean in the exclusive company of dukes and princes and the *Just Life* heroine ends in the Thames off Battersea Bridge—takes her two whole chapters, though. There's another thing. In *Just Life* the author does know what she's writing about. Tudor King doesn't."

"You know," Bobby said slowly, "all that does seem to add up to something rather fantastic that I've had in my mind. Only I don't see how it ties up with the Baldwin Jones affair."

"Suppose," Olive said, "Mrs. Cato found out Tudor King had using her books to write up, only differently, and had made a lot of money doing it?"

"It's an idea," Bobby agreed. "Something like that may have been happening. Only there again—I'm supposed to be investigating a murder and not whether author number two has been cribbing from author number one."

"Well, you think Baldwin Jones wasn't above a little blackmail when he got the chance?" Olive said, and before Bobby could reply the 'phone rang and he had to answer it.

The message was of no real importance, but it required attention, and even Bobby's attendance at his office as soon as possible. So he went off in rather a hurry. Later on, as soon as he had dispatched all on his desk of immediate importance he went to Mock Street, there to visit that well-known, very exclusive, and even more expensive establishment—Messrs. Bailey and Bailey, for some years now a subsidiary of Miram H. Haxton, Jnr., Inc., of New York, N.Y., and various other of the larger cities of the United States.

He was received with traditional suavity and gravity by an assistant who had less than a hundredth of Mr. Hiram H. Haxton's income and more than a hundred times his dignity. Learning Bobby's errand and profession, the suave assistant lost some of his suavity, looked pained, and passed him on to the last surviving Bailey, who might be placed as about halfway between the dignity of the assistant and the income of Hiram. He seemed more than a little puzzled when he understood the purpose of Bobby's visit.

"I don't know how we can help you," he said. "Certainly we have many credit customers. We have, for instance, pre-war accounts still outstanding, but we do a considerable cash trade as well. Not unusual for a customer to choose what he wants, pay for it, and take it away with him. Then we have no record, except, of course, in the ledgers."

"Have you any record of the sale of a black Homburg to a Mr. Longton? He is well known in theatrical circles, I think."

Mr. Bailey said they valued highly their connection with the stage, and he would make inquiries. He did so, but without result. If there had been such a sale, it had been for cash. But among the names of credit customers appeared those of Lord Rone and Saine and of Sir William Watson, the latter still owing for a black Homburg hat, price £5 5s., and for a golf cap, 12s. 6d.—both purchased during the week.

Bobby said he was much obliged, apologized for the trouble he had been giving, and asked that nothing should be said about his visit. This assurance he received with an alacrity which did not suggest that Messrs Bailey and Bailey considered that visits from the police added anything to the prestige of an establishment founded in the reign of Queen Elizabeth and claiming credit for having introduced the tall steeple-shaped Puritan hat from which in course of time the Victorian 'topper' evolved. All the same, when Bobby departed he left behind him a young C.I.D. man to keep observation that he was warned with severity must be as discreet as the shop itself—if indeed 'shop' is not too plebeian a word to apply to the Bailey establishment. As a result, there was presently a 'phone call to say that a man answering to the description of Mr. Dick Moyse had been seen there, had admitted his identity, and had agreed, though under protest and with many loud expressions of indignation, to visit the Yard.

Into Bobby's room he was in fact presently shown, still very indignant and even more sulky.

"What's it all about?" he demanded without giving Bobby time to speak. "Can't you think about buying a new hat without being picked up by dicks?"

"Oh, I wouldn't say 'picked up,' " Bobby protested, though noting with interest the use of the expressions 'picked up' and 'dicks,' underworld slang not very common in ordinary life. "The fact is, we think we have some reason to be interested in hats. Have you?"

"Well, it's all over the place that a hat was found in the plantation between Cobblers and the New Bungalow, if that's what you are getting at. Near where that poor devil of a Baldwin Jones was done in."

"I thought everyone would soon know all about it," Bobby said sadly. "I wanted it kept quiet. No such luck. But why Bailey's?"

"Oh, come off it," Moyse protested. "It's where Lord Rone goes, and it's him you're after, isn't it?"

"We are after the murderer," Bobby said, more than a little surprised, though, by this suggestion. "Do you mean you suspect Lord Rone is guilty?"

"Well, you do, don't you?" Moyse retorted.

"At the moment," Bobby told him, "we suspect everybody and nobody. The whole case is muddled up by a number of side issues that may mean nothing at all. You may be one of them. But now you are here I may as well tell you frankly that I am not satisfied by all that about Lord Rone's recovered dispatch case and his heroic rescue from under the wheels of a motor car. As the Americans are so fond of saying—it stinks. All the signs of a put-up job, don't you think?"

"Oh, well," Moyse answered, "anyhow, you can't deny it was a jolly good act." He permitted himself a self-satisfied smile. "Went like clockwork. Only you never can tell how things will turn out. No reason to expect any of you busies would be interested. Sheer bad luck."

"Yes, indeed," agreed Bobby sympathetically. "The best laid plans of mice and men, you know. But there it is. We are interested, and even very much so. But so far only if there's any tie-up with—murder. Mr. Moyse, I want you to get this. At present we have nothing against you. But I do ask you to remember that a man has been murdered. Murder—isn't that a thing apart?"

"I don't hold with murder," Moyse admitted, but still in his sulkiest tones. "There are limits."

"Isn't it because you felt that from the start that you put your 'phone call through to us?" Bobby asked.

"Me? What 'phone call?" Moyse asked with such starry-eyed innocence that Bobby was at once convinced his guess had been a good one. "Me?" Moyse repeated, still wide-eyed with surprise and innocence. "You mean the one telling you about it? What on earth put it into your head that was me? I knew nothing about it; not a thing."

"Well, if you don't very much mind," Bobby said, "and just for the sake of argument, shall we pretend that perhaps it was you—or someone very like you? You know this is a wholly private talk. It's not a statement. No one taking notes, and we don't go in for dictaphones or anything of that sort. Not a bad idea, but, Lord, what would the papers say? Why, they might even call it un-English. That wouldn't do, would it? So you can talk perfectly freely if you will. No one will ever know what you do say."

"Except you," Moyse interrupted.

"Not officially," Bobby answered; "and what a policeman doesn't know officially, he doesn't know at all. Mr. Moyse, I repeat, I am asking you for help and I promise you nothing you say now will be held against you or even remembered. Except," Bobby added gravely, "as regards anything that might in any way help a murderer to escape."

He was silent then and Moyse was silent, too, wriggling the while uncomfortably on his chair and throwing occasional glances towards the door, as if wishing very heartily that he was on the other side of it. Bobby waited. He had a curious way of waiting, patient and grave, that others besides Moyse had found carried with it a strange compelling force of its own, as though behind it were a strength it would prove in the long run useless to resist. It was Moyse who spoke first, muttering as it were to himself in an effort to make up his mind.

"I never did like murder," he said, almost whispering. "Gives you the shivers."

CHAPTER XXV

THE DICK MOYSE THEORY

BOBBY MADE A GRAVE gesture of assent, but he remained silent. He felt it might be better to let Moyse himself pursue his own thought to its own end, uninterrupted by outside comment. At last, with a final uncomfortable wriggle, Moyse seemed to make up his mind.

"O.K.," he said. "I've always heard you play straight—considering. Suppose you, knowing how to keep your eyes open, get to Cobblers, all innocent like, but knowing there's something a bit screwy somewhere, how long would it take you to spot Baldwin Jones was on the same lay? 'Soup's a bit thicker than sand,' you would soon be thinking; and if there was one of the maids was new, and if that maid went off every chance she got to a newcomer in a bungalow close by, and if you saw her making notes and not liking being seen, wouldn't you wonder more than ever what it was all about? There's a lot of valuable stuff lying round at Cobblers. Stamp collection worth a lot for one thing."

"Oh, yes," Bobby agreed. "You are interested in stamp collections, aren't you?"

Moyse looked very startled, and for a moment or two Bobby was afraid that this remark had been indiscreet and might possibly result in Moyse taking fright and refusing to say more. Men of his type have to be handled with the most extreme tact, the most delicate line must be drawn between letting them see a great deal is known, so they might as well talk, and making them feel so much is known they had better say no more. So Bobby produced his most friendly smile and said:

"Quite off the record, of course, and not even under investigation. Obviously, though, if a burglary or theft of some sort were being planned and you could do something about it, your position at Cobblers would be much stronger."

"Well, there was that," Moyse agreed, apparently somewhat relieved. "Anyway, I thought I might as well see if I could find out what was going on, and I kept an eye on Linda—the new maid, you know—and I followed her once or twice. To see if she met anyone or I could get any idea of what the game was."

"I can understand," Bobby said, "it was a big shock when doing that to stumble on the body of a dead man on the path where Linda had gone by."

"That's right," Moyse muttered. He had become very pale. He began to mop his face with his handkerchief and his hands were shaking. "Shock it was all right. Dark under those trees, and I switched on my torch and there was a foot sticking out from behind a bush. It was so still, if you see what I mean, I thought at first it must be someone took ill or asleep, only now I think I knew all the time, and when I looked he was lying there and me holding a dagger I must have picked up, though I didn't know it. All over blood it was, and me thinking: If I was seen now, I should be for it; be sure I had done it, they would, and next thing I knew I was running hard as I could. Proper scared I was and so I am still. You don't want to be mixed up in anything like that. You never know where it'll end."

"No, you don't, do you?" Bobby agreed.

"When I stopped running," Moyse continued, "because of not being able to any more, I was still holding the dagger. My first idea was to throw it away, only there was my fingerprints I remembered just in time, and then when I looked again I saw it came from Cobblers, from a show case in the Long Gallery. Made me think."

"It is catalogued as the Golden Dagger, attributed to Cellini," Bobby remarked.

"I didn't know what to do," Moyse said. "I cleaned up the handle best way I could and then I left it in a 'phone box I called you from. I wish I hadn't now. But for me doing that, nothing might ever have been known."

"Nothing," Bobby agreed gravely, and added: "Except by you, and you would never have forgotten."

"It wasn't that," Moyse said. "It was like as if that poor devil was there at my elbow all the time, wanting to know what I was going to do about it, not forgetting that if it was Lord Rone he might go on—if he knew it was me found the body and thought I knew more than I did."

"Mixed motives?" Bobby remarked. "Well, they generally are. Very mixed. 'All sorts' kind of minds we have, all of us. I don't think I quite follow why you think Lord Rone must be guilty?"

"Well, it was his dagger, wasn't it? Easier for him to get than anyone else."

"Other people could have got hold of it," Bobby pointed out. "Not very difficult. Linda herself, for example."

"I didn't think of her," Moyse said doubtfully. "No cause, had she? It was a man's hat that was found, wasn't it?"

"Oh, yes," Bobby agreed, but without saying that the story of the discovery of the hat rested solely on Linda's word.

"I never saw any hat," Moyse said. "But then I wasn't stopping to look. There might have been one. I thought it might give a lead if Lord Rone had been buying a new one. Very sporty they were at Bailey's, though, and wouldn't say."

"What made you go to Bailey's?" Bobby asked. "Did you know he dealt there?"

"Their name in all his other hats," Moyse said. "I looked."

"So far as the hat goes," Bobby remarked, "it may not have been left behind at the time of the killing. Mrs. Cato reports seeing lights the next evening, and that may have been when the body was moved from where you saw it, as it certainly was. The hat may have been forgotten then. Linda does not seem to have seen it the night the murder took place, though she may have passed before it happened. We haven't got the exact times fixed."

"Well, it was Lord Rone I thought of at once—his dagger, and he had a motive all right. You can take it from me Jones wasn't at Cobblers for his health, any more than me, though he had wangled it the easy way through the old girl he was making up to—Lady Watson, I mean. I mean to say, he knew all right there was something screwy, and what he wanted was to gate-crash so as to share—only on his own. Not doing a straightforward, honest job like me, but out for what pickings he could get."

"What were they?" Bobby asked, "and what was this straightforward, honest job of yours?"

Again Moyse hesitated, and again Bobby waited. This time Moyse made up his mind a little more quickly.

"The way you've jollied me along," he grumbled, "you might as well have it all. More fool me for talking. The only thing with a busy is to keep your trap shut." He was silent again, wrapped in gloomy meditation. Bobby once more waited in silence, thinking the while how strangely apt criminal slang often is. For in truth the too readily, too widely opened mouth often does prove itself a trap wherein men may easily find themselves taken. "Ever heard of Geoffrey Carton?" Moyse asked suddenly.

"Geoffrey Carton?" Bobby repeated, and then remembered the name had been mentioned by Maureen with the additional qualification of 'swine.' "Oh, yes, he said. "Next of kin and heir to the title and estates, but not on the best of terms with his relatives."

"That's right," agreed Moyse. "Fair poison to each other, if you ask me. And there aren't any estates either, only the title and Cobblers, which is like getting a millstone for your neck when you are swimming in deep water. No money. Doesn't come into the entail.

But there's the heirlooms all right and they are worth thousands—thousands, and they go with the title seemingly."

"Do you know what started this ill-feeling?" Bobby asked.

"Money," Moyse answered briefly. "Same as it always does, except when it's a girl—and girls mean money mostly." He paused, apparently slightly surprised himself by this profound aphorism he had just coined. "Seems Geoffrey tried to borrow money on the strength of being heir and he got some, but when Lord Rone shut down on it, there was a blazing row. Well, you see, Geoffrey is a writing bloke."

"Oh, not another," Bobby groaned, utterly dismayed.

"A lousy lot, aren't they?" Moyse observed sympathetically. "So he started writing about Cobblers and the family. Fair snorters. Lord Rone could have sued him for libel or scandal or something, only he didn't want. Make more stink. But he soon thought of another way of hitting back, or at least that's what Geoffrey says. Selling heirlooms on the Q.T."

"It's an idea," Bobby said as he had often said before. He was thinking of the Paul Potter painting, 'The Young Stallion.' If the original had been in fact disposed of and he had seen only a copy, that would explain a certain uneasiness Lord Rone had shown at Bobby's comparison of it with 'The Young Bull,' its companion picture. Perfectly safe, Bobby supposed, since it would be almost impossible to prove when the substitution of copy for original, if that were the case, had taken place. He said: "But if the heirlooms can't be sold, what good would they be to Mr. Geoffrey Carton?"

"He has two sons," Moyse explained. "The entail can be broken with the consent of next heirs. For good reason, such as poverty and keeping up the dignity of the title. That line of country."

"Well, I suppose if the heirs agree," Bobby said. "But is that all that makes you think Lord Rone may be guilty?"

"Well, there isn't anyone else, is there?" Moyse demanded.

"Oh, I don't know that I would go as far as that," Bobby answered. "There's always a possible someone else."

"You don't mean all that village talk, do you?" Moyse asked. "I mean about Mrs. Cato at the New Bungalow having done in her boss, or why hasn't he turned up, and Linda helping, and all that? Well, I mean to say . . . "

"I'm keeping an open mind for the present," Bobby told him.

"If you ask me," declared Moyse, "their game's plain enough. Old as the hills. Plant a girl somewhere. Easy doings now when people are so glad to get help they don't care a hoot about references. She gets to know where the good stuff is, best time to operate, lay of the house, all that, and there you are."

"Yes, I know," Bobby answered, "but it's a murder we have on our hands, and murder doesn't fit so well in that scheme of things."

"Oh, if you ask me," Moyse said, "you don't ever know. One thing and another," he said vaguely.

CHAPTER XXVI

TOY THEATRE

MOYSE WAS ALLOWED go then, a somewhat scared, disgruntled Moyse, wondering as he walked away how much he had told, why he had told it, whether he had been believed or not, and yet, in some odd way and much to his surprise, feeling considerably relieved.

"Jollies you along," he grumbled to himself, recognizing at last how he had been gently led from assumption to admission. He comforted himself with the reflection that now he wouldn't have to worry any more about what to do, since he had done it, and now no longer would he have to fancy a restless, disembodied Baldwin Jones, in whose continued existence he did not for a moment believe, might be whispering in his ear, a complaining ghost.

Bobby, too, was wondering if he could accept Moyse's tale as the plain, unvarnished truth. A guilty man does sometimes try to satisfy the old instinctive feeling that the spilt blood cries aloud for vengeance, by telling, though with most careful, misleading economy, some portion of the truth. No doubt also there is the mixed motive that a partial truth-telling is often the best way of concealing the greater part of it.

One thing, however, was clear. Moyse had been carefully, introduced into the Cobblers household to do what he described and apparently considered to be, the 'honest, straightforward' job of discovering whether valuable heirlooms were being illegally disposed of, though whether this was an offence under the criminal law or ground only for civil action, Bobby was not at the moment quite sure. But certainly, if anything of the sort had happened, Lord Rone would be extremely unwilling to let it become publicly known—indeed, 'unwilling' would be probably a considerable understatement.

Bobby surveyed this new complication with distaste, even though it was one he had already more than half anticipated. He put it out of his mind, as he had the most happy knack of being able to do with doubtful points until again they came up for consideration, and turned a carefully co-ordinated attention to the sandwiches he had sent for, since he saw no hope of any more substantial lunch, and to the latest reports on his desk. One to which he paid special attention was from the Hendon laboratory and concerned a two-inch-deep layer of soil removed from the scene of the crime. A small natural hollow in the ground had served to collect the blood of the murdered man as in a kind of basin, thus thoroughly soaking the earth there. Analysis of the layer of earth removed had given information of much interest, though sometimes information more of scientific than of practical interest. Bobby was, however, fascinated to see that it had even been possible to discover the exact blood group.

He had finished his sandwiches now, so he entered up his diary —the first duty of all good police officers—gave a few instructions to his secretary, and departed in his car to that small country hotel where Jack Longton was busy quarrelling with the author of the play he had been engaged to produce.

At the hotel, when he arrived there he was informed by a slightly nervous-looking receptionist that Mr. Longton had locked himself in his room and had left instructions that on no account was he to disturbed. Not even, he had said fiercely, if the hotel caught fire, and he had said this in such a threatening tone that the receptionist was still a little shaken. He had also informed her that his room telephone would be muffled and that anyone interrupting him would be at once thrown down the stairs.

"Very pleasant gentleman," the receptionist explained, "but very violent-tempered when upset. It's best not to," she added warningly.

"Too bad, too bad," Bobby said. "Is he still in his room or has he gone out?"

"Oh, I don't think so," the receptionist answered. "His hat's there still, at the end of the pegs," she added, looking at where two or three hats were hanging on a row of pegs. "It's that one at the end."

Bobby gave the hats an apparently uninterested glance, which told him, however, that none of them was a black Homburg—the last one on the pegs, as it happened rather apart from the others, was a grey felt. He asked the number of Mr. Longton's room. This the receptionist seemed unwilling to supply, and Bobby had to produce his card and explain he was on official business before he obtained it. He nodded approval when he saw it was on the first floor.

"It won't be so far if I do get thrown downstairs," he explained to an even more scared-looking receptionist, who knew only too well where managerial blame would fall if anything occurred to disturb the decorum of the hotel.

He ascended in the automatic lift, and when he knocked at the door of Longton's room there ensued an inarticulate roar from

within, indicating, Bobby supposed, extreme displeasure on the part
of the inmate. Proof, anyhow, that if the room's 'phone was muffled, the muffling did not extend to the room's occupant. So Bobby
knocked again—and louder.

This time that mighty roar became translatable into an injunction
to go away at once, before the worst happened.

Bobby hoped it wouldn't, and continued a rhythmic thumping
on the door to the accompaniment of a persistent rattling of the
handle that would, he thought, have an even more disturbing effect
on anyone trying to work.

Nor did it take long for these tactics to produce the desired result. There was a crash within as of a chair hurled to the floor, a
sound as of a hungry tiger leaping on its prey. The door was hurled
open and there stood Longton, shirt-sleeved, wild-eyed, hair almost
on end, his mouth open to emit a roar that died away, however,
when he saw who it was.

"Awfully sorry, Mr. Longton," Bobby said as he dexterously
inserted himself into the room. "Official, you know. Duty of every
good citizen, etcetera. If I've spoiled your afternoon's work, I'm
afraid that just had to be."

"Yes, it had to, hadn't it?" Longton said bitterly. "I thought it
was Bill."

"Who is Bill?"

"The bloke who wrote the stuff I'm trying to lick into shape for
the theatre," Longton explained, investing this last word as always
with almost religious significance. "What's it all about? Why had
you got to come along just when I'm beginning to get things
straight?"

"In every murder investigation every minute may count—does
count," Bobby told him.

"Oh, well, I don't see how I can help," Longton grumbled. "I
hardly knew the poor devil."

"It's partly that I wanted to ask you about," Bobby explained. "A
very little information may mean a good deal."

He went across the room to where by the window stood a small
table. By it was an overturned chair. On the table was a child's toy
theatre, on its stage and nearby various small toy soldiers. Unfortunately, when Longton, unable to bear any longer Bobby's
rhythmic thumping on the door and his handle rattling, had leaped
into action, he had not only overturned his chair, but had also upset
his careful arrangement of his toy soldiers, all placed in their appropriate places to illustrate the action of the play.

Longton had followed Bobby to the window. He picked up the chair and then swept his little soldiers together.

"Got to start again from scratch," he complained, "just when I was beginning to see how I could get rid of two characters altogether and at the same time improve the dramatic sequence." He smiled happily. "Bill will go pretty well off his head. All these authors always swear anything you have to cut is the best thing in the script. What do they care if cutting a character means cutting the salary list, too? Or if cutting a scene means letting the audience out in time for a drink and supper before going home? Expenses mean nothing to them, and Bill had the cold cheek to tell me audiences were the curse of the theatre. I should say—authors."

"Would anyone suggest producers?" Bobby asked.

Longton pondered. Then he shook his head.

"No," he decided. "I don't see how anyone could say that." He added, with some vague memory in his mind of a certain famous saying by a famous statesman: "Give us the stuff and we'll do the job."

Bobby was not only permitting, he was encouraging Longton to talk. He always liked to begin by a little casual chat, believing that thus was obtained a more natural, more easy approach. But he was as also wondering if Longton was talking to gain time and if this was due to an uneasy conscience, or if it was merely that to him the theatre alone was real and all that happened outside, even murder, was as it were in another world. Bobby, asking himself this, fiddling the while with the overturned toy soldiers, observed:

"Settling your exits and your entrances, and so on? With the toy soldiers for the characters in the play? How do you tell which is which?"

"Oh, you remember," Longton explained. "And then I always take the bigger ones for the chief characters and the small ones for the smaller parts. The bandsmen stand for the women. Because bandsmen as bandsmen are always playing and women as women are always talking."

"Have you explained that to Miss Maureen Carton?"

"As soon as I thought of it," Longton answered proudly. "Set her off all right. She's jolly good in a temper, too. I told her she would be fine as Katherine in *The Taming of the Shrew*. So now she's studying the part."

"You know," Bobby said, still fiddling with Longton's soldiers, "I'm rather taken with this idea of yours. It might be useful to try to reconstruct the crime in that way. A sort of game, so to say. The French do it—with the actual persons concerned, of course."

Longton was at once interested. The toy theatre stage was too small for what Bobby had in mind. He put it on one side. With Longton's help, he placed a pot of shaving cream to represent Cobblers. A hair-brush and a comb, one on each side of a piece of string, served to show the plantation through which ran the path where the body had been found. A packet of cigarettes at the other end of the bit of string stood for the New Bungalow. Longton joined in quite happily. Bobby picked up one of the toy bandsmen to represent, he said, Linda walking down the path that night. He had noticed, too, that one of the figures had had its head broken off.

"This will do for the murderer," he remarked. "No head and therefore unidentifiable, as is the case—at present. We must hope to find a head to fit. And a stud will do to mark the place where was found the hat the murderer apparently left behind. By the way, you bought a new hat from Bailey's recently, didn't you?"

"Bailey's? Good Lord, no," Longton answered. "They charge about twice what anyone else does. Why?"

"Not even," Bobby said, "if it was a bet you had won and someone else would have to do the paying?"

"You mean about Oxendale?" Longton asked. "How on earth did you get hold of that?"

"Our information," Bobby said, "is that you told Mr. Oxendale you were getting the new hat he owed you at Bailey's and that he told you to send him the bill?"

"That's right," Longton admitted. "I suppose it was Oxendale told you? He didn't tell you also, did he, that I never sent him the bill for the very good reason that I never bought the hat and so there was no bill to send? I never meant to. I only wanted to rub it in that I had been right. Oxendale isn't so flush as all that. Three or four guineas counts for most of us."

"You haven't bought any new hat recently, then, and never one from Bailey's?" Bobby asked.

"No, I haven't," Longton said. "Not for a year or two. My hat's downstairs in the hotel lobby on a peg. And it's a grey felt, not a black Homburg either."

He went back to the table and swept aside the brush and comb and shaving cream and so on Bobby had arranged with such care.

"I don't like this game of yours," he said.

CHAPTER XXVII

MRS. CATO AGAIN

BOBBY MADE NO COMMENT. But he found the gesture interesting. Longton glared defiance at him. A gong sounded from below.

"Tea," Longton said. "I think I'll go and get some."

With that he walked out of the room, leaving Bobby in possession. Bobby could not help wondering if this were another gesture, aimed at demonstrating that here there was nothing to conceal and that Bobby was at full liberty to search as much as he liked. More likely, though, that it was spontaneous, a result of his anger at Bobby's questions and apparent suspicions—or perhaps by fear? Or even due merely to Longton's theatre sense of an effective exit?

Bobby began to push, somewhat aimlessly, Longton's toy soldiers about the table. He was still thinking it might on occasion be useful to reconstruct, so to say, a crime in this manner. Too unorthodox, perhaps, and would the more stolid, self-contained Englishman be likely to react in the way in which it was said the Frenchman did at times? A rattle of tea cups sounded from below to remind Bobby that at any rate tea was always a good idea. So he returned to his car and soon was driving back to Lower High Hill village, where he hoped the tea ritual, essential to every proper Englishman's afternoon, could be suitably performed.

This accomplished, he spent some time reading and considering reports and listening to what his assistants working on the case in the locality had to say. Ford, for instance, had managed to unearth a worker on a neighbouring farm who stated he had seen Baldwin Jones, whom he knew by sight as a visitor at Cobblers, leaving the New Bungalow, and leaving it as though he had not been made very welcome. This visit had, however, been made the Saturday before the murder, but all the same Bobby thought it might be worth following up, especially as he felt he would like to know, and that for more reasons than one, how seriously his warning not to use the plantation path had been taken.

Not very seriously, he soon discovered, from what Mrs. Cato had to say when he found her at the bungalow. That might, of course, be due to the genuine inability to accept such warnings often shown by those who, having always lived a quiet, safe, well-regulated life, find difficulty in admitting that lawless violence can suddenly intrude upon it. Or, a grimmer thought, from a knowledge that no such danger could menace those who were themselves its source and origin.

However, it did seem that Linda, though she still visited the bungalow every day, did now sometimes come by the long way round, through the village. If she returned, as she generally did, by the much shorter plantation path, then Mrs. Cato herself went with Linda as far as Cobblers.

"I take the hatchet with me," Mrs. Cato added with a little nod at Bobby, as if to ask him what he thought of that. "What's more, I've had it sharpened up. I'll tell you something else. There's been someone watching, hiding in the trees and watching."

"Who was it?" Bobby asked. "Did you see?"

"What I wondered," Mrs. Cato said without answering either of these questions, "was whether it was the murderer come back to look for his hat he knows he left behind."

"Yes, there's that," Bobby said thoughtfully. "Might be something else, though."

"Makes you think," Mrs. Cato said; "makes you wonder. I mean, hiding there in the trees and, it may be, near desperate when for all he knows you've got hold of it and are only just waiting—waiting your time."

"Yes I know, Bobby said. "The snag is that as a matter of cold fact we haven't got it and if the murderer hasn't either, who has? Have you?"

Obviously taken aback by this direct challenge, Mrs. Cato first stared and then gave a short, hard laugh.

"No," she said. "Why should I? If I had, I wouldn't keep it. You could have it and welcome."

"If it is the case that the murderer is really trying to find it," Bobby remarked, "that may spell danger for anyone he suspects has got it. He may very well believe that his safety hangs—and that's a nasty word in this connection—hangs on getting hold of it again."

"Oh, well," Mrs. Cato said, though she was beginning to look a trifle uneasy, "I don't see why it couldn't have been picked up by a tramp or gipsy or someone like that. He may simply be wearing it without ever connecting it with what's happened."

"We've been making inquiries on those lines," Bobby told her. "We can generally trace gipsies, but tramps are a lot more difficult. They don't read papers much and if they do they may have their own reasons for not coming forward. I'm afraid the hat is a very illusive kind of clue," and again he did not add that even for the very existence of that clue there was no evidence beyond the unsupported word of Linda Blythe, whose repeated and continuing visits to Mrs. Cato had as yet received no satisfactory explanation. Nor had, for that matter, Mrs. Cato's interest in Linda. Bobby said instead:

"You have not told me yet who it was you saw?"

"I only said I thought I saw someone," Mrs. Cato answered. "I didn't mean to mention names. It might be libel and I don't want to be hauled into court. You have to be careful with the law as it is."

"So you have, and just as well," retorted Bobby. "People are lot too fond of talking. They've been saying things about you yourself in the village, you know. Scandal, of course, not libel, and I hope we've stopped it. But anything you say, or write for that matter, to police engaged on an investigation is privileged. I think I must ask you to give me the name."

"I didn't know it was privileged," Mrs. Cato said. "Besides, I expect lawyers could get round that all right. They can generally. You can libel people without ever having heard of them." She paused for a moment, frowning as if at some past, unpleasant, unforgettable memory. "Oh, well," she said, "if you must know, it was that tubby little man staying at Cobblers."

"Sir William Watson, you mean?" Bobby asked. "Are you sure?"

"It's what I thought at the time," she answered. "I was rather glad it was only him." She smiled grimly. "I was getting my axe ready," she admitted, "after what you said. But then I saw who it was and I thought it was all right. Only afterwards I did begin to wonder. But it was dark and it may have been someone else. Linda says she has seen Lady Watson there once or twice, and she thought perhaps it might have been her I saw. That's silly, though. It was certainly a man. I don't know why I'm telling you all this. It doesn't amount to anything."

"Oh, even the tiniest detail helps," Bobby assured her. "Noticing a button is missing may be the key to the whole thing."

"Well, don't look at me like that," she snapped. "I've no missing buttons, have I?"

What she had just said had in fact induced him to look at her with a renewed and closer attention. Not indeed because of any missing buttons, though Mrs. Cato was hardly remarkable for any very special care in her attire. But he did notice now that her finger and thumb were freshly stained with ink, that on the table near the window lay an uncapped fountain pen she had apparently just laid down and several sheets of paper covered with writing. A typewriter nearby was still covered, and close by was an unopened packet of typing paper and some carbon sheets.

It was almost mechanically, and because it was his habit and his trade to notice things, that he tucked these details away in his memory, but now he was wondering, too, if they tended in any way to confirm the vague, indeed fanciful idea that had been floating for some time at the back of his mind. Hard, though, to see their relevance to the fate of the unfortunate Baldwin Jones. Mrs. Cato was still watching him with a kind of indignant challenge, and he said:

"Oh, yes; sorry. No, no, no missing buttons. Nothing like that. Is there anything else you think you can tell me?" He thought she seemed to hesitate for a moment, but then she shook her head. So he went on: "Or that Linda could say? But it would be better if I spoke to her myself, wouldn't it?"

"No, certainly not. What for? She doesn't know anything," Mrs. Cato told him angrily, again with that half-unconscious air of protection she was apt to assume when the girl's name was mentioned. "She's worried enough already, frightened out of her wits of having to appear as a witness or something, and lawyers bullying her and all that."

"Lawyers don't try to bully nowadays," Bobby answered smilingly. "At least, not unless they want to make a present of their case to the other side." But he was remembering that the girl had given him the impression of being badly frightened on his first visit to Cobblers when he announced himself and his companion as police officers. He went on: "There is another point. I understand Mr. Baldwin Jones was an acquaintance of yours?"

"Then you understand wrong," she retorted. "He wasn't."

"We have information," Bobby said, "that he was seen calling here two or three days before his death."

"Oh, that," she said, and gave him a distinctly unfriendly look. "You've managed to rake that up. I sent him away with a flea in his ear, if that's what you call being acquainted."

"Well, it does seem to suggest you weren't total strangers," Bobby remarked. "He had some reason for calling?"

"I had never set eyes on him before in my life," she declared emphatically. "He said Mr. Tudor King had employed him recently. To get some facts for some of the stuff he writes—for *Glamour of the Footlights*. It's selling better than most of the rest of the tripe he turns out," and these last words were pronounced with an undisguised contempt, as if in her mind she were comparing it very unfavourably with her own novels of earlier days that the public had so lamentably failed to appreciate. Bobby found himself wondering if she used a similar tone when Mr. Tudor King was present, and thought also that contempt so deep, scorn so scathing, would be difficult to hide successfully. However, that was no business of his—or was it? Mrs. Cato was still speaking. She was saying. "But he really is extremely careful to get all his work exactly right in every detail. Goes to all kinds of trouble. It was information about stage life he wanted, and he thought Baldwin Jones could get it for him."

"Theatre again," Bobby observed with a kind of sad resignation in his voice.

"Well, why not?" Mrs. Cato demanded, this time as if defending, and even admiring, such care for detail. "Any slip, and you soon hear about it. To make people think you know what you are writing about is half the battle. Mr. King would tell you that if you can use professional slang in a familiar sort of way, then it's taken for granted you know all about the profession."

"I'm getting to know quite a lot of technical detail," Bobby observed, "but I don't know that it's getting me much further forward. But wasn't it generally known that Mr. Tudor King had not arrived here yet?"

"Oh, yes," Mrs. Cato agreed. "Jones was only trying to do a bit of snooping. That's why I packed him off again in a hurry. I thought what he was really after was trying to get hold of Linda. I wasn't going to have that," she added, again with the protective air she so often assumed when Linda's name was mentioned. "It was through him Linda got to Cobblers and then through Linda that Mr. King heard of this bungalow. Baldwin Jones knew Linda was looking for a new place to go to, as Mr. King was leaving England, and Linda knew Mr. King wanted somewhere to live till his Capri house was ready. I expect he felt he couldn't start flirting with her at Cobblers, but he thought he could here. He found out different."

CHAPTER XXVIII

THE ILLUSIVE CLUE

IT WAS A VERY perplexed and worried Bobby Owen who from the New Bungalow drove on to Cobblers. He had the impression that he had been told a good deal, including, he thought, more than Mrs. Cato had intended. One thing he felt certain of was that she had deliberately given him a hint of her own belief—or was it knowledge? Or again, had she merely attempted to divert suspicion from herself? But he was little inclined to accept her tale that Baldwin Jones's call at the bungalow had been an attempt to start or continue a flirtation with Linda Blythe. In Baldwin Jones's reputation as a picker up of unconsidered trifles in the way of bits of information of which he could afterwards make use for his own profit and advantage seemed to lie a much more probable explanation.

"Flirtation story not a very good invention," Bobby told himself disapprovingly. "Hasty improvisation," added as a kind of excuse. "Ten to one Jones thought he was on the track of something."

If that were so, then his being sent away with what Mrs. Cato had called 'a flea in the ear' was explained. But, an uncomfortable thought, blackmailers are at first very frequently sent away with this 'flea in the ear,' till presently their victims weaken and are tempted to take the fatal path of surrender—appeasement as it is called to-day, as a more respectable word. Was it possible there had been a second meeting in the plantation on that fatal Monday night? If so, had 'appeasement' been abandoned and 'flea in the ear' seemed inadequate?

A possibility that had to be considered.

Of one thing alone was Bobby sure. He had seldom met a personality more puzzling, more interesting even, than that of Mrs. Cato. Those deep eyes that could flash with such sudden fire, the firm, even fierce, lines of the mouth. There were moments when her whole being appeared to throb with a controlled yet passionate appetite for life. Put that against the background of a broken career that seemed to have started so promisingly to the applause of those who are supposed to be the arbiters of literary fame, only to be followed by a slowly growing indifference ending in complete oblivion. Then a necessity to gain a livelihood watching the success of a Tudor King whose work she made it so devastatingly plain she hated and despised from the bottom of her heart. What sort of psychological complex might not such a situation produce?

Had, for instance, that contempt and hatred slowly extended from Tudor King's work to Tudor King's person?

Once again a possibility that had to be considered.

Or was it that Tudor King had made his projected move to Capri an excuse for getting rid of a housekeeper of whose feelings he must have been aware, and was it that decision that had precipitated a crisis?

Bobby shook his head at himself, feeling he was becoming lost in a welter of incompatible, improbable theories. Yet in a murder case everything is improbable by the very nature of the deed, and still he could not get wholly out of his mind that first glimpse of her he remembered when she had come striding out from behind the bungalow—a Judith, a Jael, a Jeanne de la Hachette in modern dress.

There was that hat, too—that illusive, possibly non-existent hat. Mrs. Cato's prompt and firm denial, her hard, brief laughter, at the suggestion that it was in her possession, had not altogether satisfied him. He thought the denial a little too prompt, the laughter a little too hard. But it was not a point he dared press. A hat is too easily destroyed, and he had no right or power to search the bungalow, as he would have liked to do.

"An investigator in this country is tied hand and foot," he grumbled to himself, but knew all the same he would not have it otherwise, since proof of murder must be not only proof but proof above doubt.

But all these thoughts, buzzing interminably through his mind, had brought him no nearer a solution, and now he had reached Cobblers. He stopped his car and alighted, and when he knocked at the front door it was Maureen who opened it.

"I was expecting you," she said. She stood there, regarding him with a grave, measured, reproachful disapproval, much as a mother might regard a too forward child who had disappointed her. "The first time I saw you," she announced, "I thought you seemed fairly intelligent in a way."

She paused as if expecting to see Bobby wither slowly, or even swiftly, away. No sign of this being apparent, she turned and went back into the house. He followed her. She led the way into the inner lounge hall where she had apparently been sitting. A book was open on a chair, and Bobby saw it was a copy of Shakespeare. He said as sadly as he could:

"Does that mean you've felt you must change your opinion?"

"Well, I ask you," she said. "Suspect Jack—Longton—of—murder!" and between each word as she uttered it she left a pause as if to give it time to sink into the universal consciousness—and Bobby's in particular.

"Has Mr. Longton been over here to tell you?" he asked.

"I expect," Maureen went on, still grieved, still reproachful, "you'll be suspecting me next thing?"

"Why next thing?" Bobby asked.

"You don't mean you do?" she cried at this, forgetting at once entirely her air of grieved reproach. And when he nodded she breathed an "Oh, I say!" that might have meant either dismay or mere surprise, or even—gratification.

"At this stage of an investigation like this one," Bobby repeated once more, "we suspect every one automatically." She looked a little disappointed and then said:

"I'll have to tell Jack he's not the only one," and this time there was certainly in her voice a faint note of satisfaction. "Of course, he is the most awful bully and I simply hate the very guts of him. But he wouldn't ever murder anyone, and I don't think—" Here she paused, plainly giving the most careful consideration to what she was going to say: "I don't really think I ever would either—unless it was Jack himself."

"Is he such a bully as all that?" Bobby inquired.

"Worse," Maureen answered. "I'm studying 'Isabella'—*Measure for Measure*, you know."

"I thought it was Katherine in *The Taming of the Shrew*, Mr. Longton said."

"Oh, no," Maureen exclaimed with fervour. "That's such a silly part. I can't imagine what Shakespeare was thinking of."

"Well, you know," Bobby said, "in our job we do meet women like Katherine and even more of a shrew for that matter."

"I don't mean that," Maureen explained indignantly. "Why can't you stand up for yourself without being called a shrew? I mean the way Shakespeare makes her knuckle down. Didn't the man know that any woman who can't make life plain hell for her husband till he does the knuckling down just simply isn't worthy the name of woman at all?"

"How old are you?" Bobby demanded abruptly.

"You asked me that before," Maureen retorted, "and you were rather insulting about it, too."

"So I did," Bobby agreed. "I had forgotten. Let me see now." He did a little mental arithmetic. "Your exact age is five thousand, nine hundred and fifty odd."

"Oh, it isn't," cried Maureen, quite appalled. "What do you mean?"

"Well," Bobby explained, "you are evidently as old as Eve, and she dates from four thousand and four B.C.—see Archbishop Usher. Add the present date and there you are."

"I think that's rather silly," replied Maureen, dignified now. "Don't you?"

"Why is Mr. Longton bullying you over *Measure for Measure*?" Bobby asked, in his turn ignoring her question.

"Well," Maureen explained, picking up her book, "the Twenty-first Century Club is putting it on for a Sunday performance and I'm doing Isabella. She's the most awful, cold-blooded prig imaginable, you know, and of course that was how I was going to play her. Only when I told Jack he went simply mad—and was most abusive as well. I slung the book at his head." This with great satisfaction. "Only it missed." This with equal disappointment. "He dodged. Just like him, the mean thing." She went on, quite carried away by her sense of grievance: "He says she isn't a prig at all, only she's of her age, and being a virgin then was most awfully impressive and important, most likely because it was so jolly rare, and if you were, then you were sort of supernatural and liable to do miracles any moment almost. Giving it up to save your brother was like asking you to-day to save someone by torturing a small child. That's what Jack says I've got to get into what he had the cheek to call my empty head."

"Too bad," Bobby agreed. "Rather insulting, in fact."

"And then he said," she went on, "I had to study every other character in the whole play just as carefully, so as to understand how they felt towards her and she felt towards them. So I said there wasn't time and he simply went in off the deep end. He told me"—she paused impressively—"unless I wanted to be just a fashion plate on the stage, then I had to work like a donkey day and night till my hind legs fell off. I haven't got any hind legs," she concluded, almost in tears.

"Well, I must say I think that's simply too bad," Bobby declared, though without making it quite clear whether he referred to the absence of hind legs or the prospect of such unremitting toil. "Is Lord Rone in?"

"Yes. Why? Is it about hats? I expect you want to look at all we've got, don't you? Silly, I call it."

"You've heard about that?" Bobby asked.

"It's what everyone in the village is talking about," Maureen answered. "Didn't you know?" And her opinion of him evidently fell to even lower depths. "You can look in the cloak-room if you want to." She indicated a door in the outer hall. "In there," she said. "All Dad's things are there and everyone else's, too—Oh, here is Dad."

Lord Rone was in fact approaching from the inner recesses of the house. Maureen hailed him to explain that Bobby wanted to see all his hats, just in case one of them might be what she called 'the murder hat everyone's talking about.'

"And if he finds it, you'll be for it, Dad," she added.

"Be quiet, Maureen," said her father mechanically. "Hat?" he went on to Bobby. "Oh, yes, of course. Certainly. Quite right." He led the way to the cloak-room, followed by Bobby, and indicated a row of hats, coats, scarves, and so on, hanging on pegs. "They are all there, I think."

"Are they all yours?" Bobby asked.

"Oh, dear me, no," Lord Rone answered. "I'm not so well provided as all that. Moyse's will be there, and Watson's as well: There may be others, too." He went to the door and called: "Maureen. Maureen. Where's the new one I got from Bailey's the other day? I don't see it anywhere."

"I'm most awfully sorry, Dad," Maureen said, answering his summons. "You know that parcel I sent off to Oxford for displaced persons if you remember? I'm awfully afraid it went off with that by mistake."

"Really, Maureen," said Lord Rone, very crossly indeed. "You must be more careful. You did that once before—with my second-best dress trousers, and I'm almost certain there was a five-pound note in a pocket. This time I shall stop the cost of a new hat out of your allowance."

"I expect it would teach me to be more careful," Maureen admitted, putting a penitent thumb inter mouth and looking her saddest. "But you won't, Daddy dear, will you?"

"Certainly I shall," declared Lord Rone with great firmness, but knowing perfectly well he wouldn't.

"What was it like?" Bobby asked.

"A black Homburg, quite new," answered Lord Rone, and Bobby saw that Maureen was looking at him sideways.

CHAPTER XXIX

WORLD OF MAKE-BELIEVE

POSSIBLY IT WAS BECAUSE she saw Bobby had noticed—and noted—that sideways glance of hers that Maureen now said abruptly:

"I expect you want to see Uncle Bill, too, don't you? I'll tell him," and therewith ran off, while Bobby watched her go and was not pleased.

He felt he could never be quite certain which Maureen he was talking to, so swiftly did she seem to change from one mood to another. As for scruples, he was inclined to believe that she simply did not know they existed. Both Maureen and Jack Longton seemed to him as if they existed in a kind of borderland between the everyday world and the theatre world of make-believe; and which of these was to them the more real, he was not sure. He heard Lord Rone saying, half to himself, in a confidential, meditative voice:

"Besides, I don't really see what use dress trousers could be in a refugee camp in Germany."

"Well, if there was a five pound note in a pocket, that might help," Bobby suggested.

"True, true," Lord Rone agreed, evidently much impressed by this observation.

Maureen came hurrying back, and after her, though at a more mature pace, came Sir William, smiling and alert, and Lady Watson, wearing a formidable frown.

"I must say I entirely fail—" she began, but her husband cut her short.

"Oh, come, my dear," he said, "the police are simply bound to make inquiries when a thing like this happens—inquiries everywhere," and if she frowned the more at this, at any rate she said no more. Sir William continued to Bobby: "It's about this story of the hat you've found that's all over the village that you're here again, isn't it? Everyone with a different version. Anyhow, it can't be mine, unless by some miracle the one I lost on my way here has turned up again somehow."

"Nonsense," said Lady Watson very loudly, and then repeated the word more loudly still: "Nonsense."

"Now, now, my dear," said Sir William.

"You lost a hat on the way here?" Bobby repeated question-

ingly, and he noticed that Lord Rone looked surprised and that
Maureen had eyes and mouth both open to their widest.

"I was stupid enough," Sir William confessed, "to put my head
out of the window, trying to read the name of the station we were
passing. It was as small and inconspicuous as usual. I don't know
why the railways like to keep the names of their stations to themselves in the way they do. Cost me a hat. It blew off as I was trying
to see where we were."

"Too bad," Bobby said, and reflected rather grimly that hats
seemed to have a most unfortunate habit of disappearing just now,
and that if the papers got to know they would probably at once
produce headlines 'Missing Hat Murder.' "Did you make any inquiries?" he asked.

"Well, it hardly seemed worth while," Sir William answered. "I
couldn't have said within fifty miles or so where I had lost it. We
were coming up from a visit to Cornwall, and I don't know the line
at all."

"Did you say anything about it to anyone?" Bobby asked.

"Dear me, no," Sir William exclaimed. "One doesn't bore one's
friends with all the little misadventures that happen to one." He
paused to smile broadly at his wife. "Besides," he continued, "it
was rather a sore point at the moment. I had had a thorough good
scolding for my carelessness, and I didn't want to hear another
word about it."

"You deserved to hear a lot more," Lady Watson said severely.

"You got here bare-headed then?" Bobby asked, and now they
were all looking at him with a kind of puzzled and uneasy attention.

"Luckily, no," Sir William answered. "Or I should probably
have got a bad cold. My golf cap was in our hand baggage."

"Could you identify it again if it were found?" Bobby asked.

"Oh, dear me, yes—a black Homburg, nearly new, bought recently from Bailey's in Mock Street, near Piccadilly. And it has my
initials in it, hasn't it, my dear?" he asked Lady Watson.

"And your address, too," Lady Watson said. "It's not the first
time you've lost your hat. May I inquire the purpose of these questions?" she asked, turning suddenly on Bobby.

He did not reply to this question. They were still all watching
him with that kind of puzzled, uneasy attention they had begun to
show. It was Maureen who broke the silence, either because she did
not wish any answer or perhaps because she had remained silent as
long as, for her, was possible.

"Are you going to grill Mr. Oxendale, too? I'll ask Linda to try to find him, shall I?" she demanded. "And oughtn't you to have warned us that anything we say may be taken down and used in evidence against us?"

"No," said Bobby with more than a touch of temper in his voice.

"Well, don't get crass," Maureen said in her most injured tone.

"Be quiet, Maureen," said her father.

"Well, Dad," Maureen protested, "he has been a bit third-degreey, hasn't he?"

"You probably most of you know," Bobby said, "what with all this talk that seems to be going on, that the housemaid here, Linda Blythe, reported having seen a hat that may have been the murderer's. Could I have a word or two with her alone?"

"I'll tell her," Maureen said, and was starting off.

"One moment, please," Bobby called after her. "I should be glad if you would merely say I wanted to ask her a question or two without going into details."

His tone was severe, and Maureen looked offended.

"I don't know why you are always so horrid to me," she said over her shoulder as she vanished.

Lord Rone had an air of wishing to support his daughter's protest, but also of not quite knowing how.

"She's a little chatterbox," Lady Watson said. "But then, what girl her age isn't?"

"Or what woman of any age?" asked Sir William with a little private chuckle, all to himself. "Present company always excepted of course, my dear." He turned to Bobby and spoke more gravely: "Lady Watson," he said, "asked a moment ago what was the purpose of your questions. May I take it you are merely following a very proper and necessary routine or have you something more serious, more direct in your mind?"

"All questions in a murder investigation are serious," Bobby answered. "Any may lead direct to—the gallows."

Lady Watson gave a low cry and collapsed on a chair near. Indeed, she would probably have fallen had not her husband caught her in time to support her. A momentary confusion ensued. Maureen came running back and said Linda wouldn't be more than a moment or two.

"What's happened?" she asked, seeing them clustered round the half-fainting Lady Watson. She pointed an accusing finger at Bobby, a kind of 'thou art the man' finger. She asked severely: "What's he been saying now?"

"Be quiet, Maureen," said her father. "I must say, though, that I think a little more consideration might be shown."

"Not much was shown to Baldwin Jones," Bobby said.

"I'm all right," Lady Watson said, trying to get to her feet and pushing aside with apparently unnecessary vehemence the solicitous help her husband tried to offer. "I don't know what came over me. It made me think all at once what it all meant. I think I'll go and lie down for a time if I may."

"Come, Maureen," her father said, speaking with unusual authority. "We had better leave Mr. Owen alone to say what he wants to Linda."

Maureen, slightly more subdued than usual—it was seldom her father spoke to her in that tone—trailed away after him and the other two. Bobby went to stand with his back to the fireplace. Linda appeared, slightly nervous. She seemed to hesitate, seeing him alone, and Bobby said:

"I shan't keep you more than a minute or two. I only wanted to ask if you are sure there's nothing more you can tell me about the hat you picked up that night? Or about anything else for that matter." When Linda did not speak, but only shook her head, he went on: "The rain had stopped, I think, but the hat would still be very wet?"

"That's right," she answered then. "Everything was soaking. That's why I picked it up and hung it on the bush, out of the wet."

"You left it there," Bobby went on, "and when you returned on your way back to Cobblers, it wasn't there?" She nodded confirmation. "That does suggest, doesn't it, that the murderer had returned for it? And that does back up my warning to you not to use that path through the plantation? Mrs. Cato tells me that when you do, she comes with you?"

"That's right," Linda said. "She isn't afraid of anything. She brings the axe with her she uses for chopping firewood."

"I don't know that that would be much use against any sudden attack from an armed man," Bobby remarked.

"She's as strong and quick as any man," Linda said with a sort of affectionate pride. "I wouldn't want to be any man who tried."

"A man's strength against a woman's," Bobby said gravely, and then went on: "You think you saw Sir William Watson one night?"

"It was only an idea," she answered hastily. "Very likely it wasn't him at all. I couldn't be certain. There was someone. That's all can be sure of."

"It might be the murderer back again," Bobby said. "Nervous. Can't keep away. It's a big strain, knowing you are being looked for and may be found at any moment. Not everyone can stand up to it."

He was watching her attentively, but she was showing no sign of any marked interest or emotion. Nor did she try to speak, but waited quietly, less nervous now indeed than when she had first appeared in answer to Maureen's summons. He would have liked to question her further, especially about the missing hat. But he did not dare. It could so easily be destroyed, as might indeed have happened already. He almost abandoned all hope of ever finding what might so well have given him the proof he needed—or might do nothing of the kind.

"You are sure there's nothing else you can tell me?" he asked again.

"Oh, no, I don't think so," she replied, and in fact he had asked more as a matter of routine than with any hope of getting a satisfactory answer.

"Well, thank you very much," he said. "I'm sure you are doing your best to help. I think that's all I want just now. Shall you be visiting Mrs. Cato again this evening? If you are, do be a good sensible girl and go round by the village, even if it is a whole lot farther."

"Well, even if I do," she reminded him, "there are still those two fields to cross. And it's just as dark and lonely."

"Yes, that's true," Bobby agreed. "Why not stay at home for the time till all this has been cleared up?"

"It's a change, going out," she answered. "It's all strange here. They aren't very nice—the others, I mean. They talk about things I don't know anything about. And if I ask them anything, they say I'm nosey."

"Too bad," Bobby said thoughtfully. "Is that why you make notes so as to be sure of not forgetting what you want to know? Or to show to other people who wouldn't call you nosey? Mrs. Cato, for instance."

"I don't know what you mean," she exclaimed, angry and indignant. "It's all rubbish. I never do—make notes, I mean. Who's been telling you that?"

"My dear young lady," Bobby said, and he spoke the last word very clearly, "this is a case of murder, a thing which does not seem to be quite realized in this house. No detail is unimportant even though it may turn out in the long run to be without significant relevance."

"It's irrelevant anyhow," retorted Linda, "about taking notes —significant or not."

CHAPTER XXX

PLANNED COME-BACK

LINDA WAS DISMISSED then with instructions to see if Norman Oxendale could be found. He appeared almost at once, explaining that he had been in the garage, tinkering with his little runabout car, and had not known of Bobby's visit. And then he had had to wash his hands.

"What's up?" he asked. "They are all there with their heads close together, talking away like one o'clock, but they won't say a word—all except Miss Carton. She's sitting quiet as a mouse. Must be something pretty serious for her to be like that."

"Well, there does happen to have been a murder," Bobby reminded him, "if not actually of an inmate of this house, at any rate a guest who had only just left it. Enough to make anyone quiet—or for that matter to set people talking. One murder is sometimes followed by another, you know."

"You don't mean you think that's going to happen here?" Norman asked, looking very disturbed.

"I said 'sometimes,' " Bobby answered. "There's one point I should like you to clear up if you will. You remember saying you had lost a bet of a new hat you made with Mr. Longton? You told him to get one and send you the bill. Did he?"

"Well, he wouldn't give it a miss, would he?" Oxendale demanded. "Not likely. Went to a swell shop in Mock Street, where they charge double. Let me see now." He hesitated, frowned. "I can't quite remember." He sighed. "One gets so many bills, doesn't one?"

"Don't you remember paying it?"

"Oh, yes. Let me see now. I'm sure I paid something round there. Does it matter? If I didn't, Bailey's will let me know all right."

"Mr. Longton tells me he has neither bought a hat nor sent you any bill."

"Well, if he hasn't, he will," Oxendale said comfortably. "No need to worry about that. But I rather think I had his bill. I can't be sure."

"Anyhow, Mr. Longton doesn't seem to be wearing a new hat at present," Bobby remarked.

"Isn't he?" Oxendale said. "I hadn't noticed. Look, has all this anything to do with the talk in the village about a hat being found where Jones was murdered, and so now you know who did it?"

"You may take it," Bobby answered cautiously, "that hats have become of interest to us. That is why I should like it cleared up. At present it seems that Mr. Longton denies having bought a new hat recently and you seem to think he has?"

"Oh, I don't know," Oxendale protested. "You don't seriously suspect Longton, do you? Doesn't make sense. He's got the devil of a temper, I know. There's a story of his half killing some chap he quarrelled with over a girl. Mayn't be a word of truth in it for all I know. Besides, why should he? They never had much to do with each other. No one had much to do with Jones if they could help it. Sort of chap you always have to buy the drinks for. Of course, if you were a woman—women fell for him all right. I thought everyone believed it was that old battle-axe at the bungalow near here somewhere. She looks the part all right, but why should she?"

"There seems to have been some sort of idea that he led a kind of double life," Bobby said. "Sometimes Baldwin Jones living by his wits and sometimes someone quite different and very important. Do you know anything about that?"

"Well, I always thought that was just a yarn he put about himself so as to have a better chance of borrowing half a crown when he was hard up. I don't think anyone took him seriously. I didn't. I don't know, of course. I do remember once a man asked him if he was Shakespeare in disguise and he sort of smiled and said, 'Not Shakespeare,' and walked away."

"If we could get any light on that," Bobby remarked, "it might help us to find out why he was killed—and then we should have a better chance of knowing who it was. There seems a suggestion he wasn't above a little blackmail, but only on a petty scale. More a handle for borrowing half-crowns when hard up than for any other reason. You are sure there's nothing more you can tell us?"

"No, I don't think so. Sorry. And sorry, I can't be clear about that bill for Longton's new hat. If it was a bill, I may have chucked it away without bothering to look at it twice. Bills always bounce, don't they? I hope that doesn't bring me into Jones's murder. Not a man I liked, but I don't go about murdering people."

As there seemed no more to be got out of him, Oxendale was allowed to go, and Bobby drove back to the village, where be found Ford was waiting for him.

"I don't know that I've got much," Bobby confessed to his young assistant. "What I did get was all pretty vague. Might mean anything. Strong scent, but never clear whether it was of red herrings or not. I got fed-up with the rather casual attitude they have about it, at Cobblers, as if no one could possibly suppose Cobblers could be involved. So I reminded them that at the end of it all there here was the gallows waiting. Rather crude, I know. Lady Watson did a near faint and Miss Maureen has become remarkably quiet. I think it is only now beginning to dawn on her that a murder in the last act and a murder at night in a wood near her home aren't quite the same. Longton had been in touch with her. By 'phone very likely. I expected that. Oxendale either can't or won't remember whether he got a bill for the new hat he lost to Longton. Or if he did get the bill whether he paid it. Seems to throw bills away without looking at them twice."

"Does he get away with it?" Ford asked enviously. "I wish we could."

"Putting off the evil hour, that's all," Bobby said. "Or possibly swank because he thinks that's how the artistic temperament behaves and he's got one. Told me it didn't make sense to suspect Longton, but gave me the idea he rather hoped I would think different. He may only be calculating that if we take Longton seriously, then he will have a better chance of a free run with Miss Maureen. I had a talk with Linda Blythe. I used some rather long words—relevant significance or something like that. She didn't seem to notice. And I called her my dear young lady. Of course, to-day, charwomen are obsolete. There are only charladies, and it's a gentleman who calls to ask if you have any rags to sell. Still, she was in her housemaid's uniform and I should guess that at Cobblers, while a housemaid is in uniform, she is still, so to say, an *ex-officio* non-lady. She used rather long words herself once or twice. She didn't like it, though, when I mentioned about her taking notes. Does all that add up to anything?"

"Well, sir," Ford said, "at any rate, it's not inconsistent."

"No," agreed Bobby, and added: "Neither she nor Mrs. Cato seem to be taking much notice of my warning not to use the plantation path in case they met the murderer there."

"Is that," Ford asked, "because they know they won't, being the murderers themselves?"

"They both make rather a point about Mrs. Cato taking the hatchet with her she uses for chopping firewood," Bobby continued. "I can quite believe she would be a nasty customer to tackle."

"So can I," agreed Ford. "All of it. It wasn't an axe that was used, though."

"I think," Bobby said after a pause, "the bungalow had better be kept under observation. Things may happen."

"If they try to do a bunk," Ford said, "that always shows, doesn't it?"

"I didn't mean that," Bobby said. "There's the chance that the bungalow is where the missing hat is."

"Yes, sir," agreed Ford. "At least, if there ever was one," for of this he had never felt convinced.

"Yes, of course," Bobby agreed in his turn. "There's always that. No corroboration. We have to spend our time looking for a vital clue that may not even exist. But if Linda did tell the truth and she did find a hat on that path through the plantation, it seems more likely that she would take it on to the bungalow with her. If she did, it may be there still. And if the murderer begins to suspect that—well, there you are."

"Get hold of it or swing for it," Ford commented grimly.

"I think," Bobby went on, "I should like you to take on the job yourself. Can you do without a night's sleep, do you think?"

"I'm a father," Ford replied with equal simplicity and pride. "Our first is teething," and he clearly considered that no further proof of his ability to do without a night's sleep was necessary.

"I don't much expect anything to happen just yet," Bobby said. "One never knows, though. Arrange for a relief for an hour or two—say, from two to four. Quote that as an order. It's not only keeping awake, but keeping alert as well."

"Very good, sir," said Ford, knowing this sort of thing was all in the day's—or night's—work for a C.I.D. man.

Bobby made one or two other arrangements and then started back to Town, driving as fast as safety and other traffic on the road permitted. Arrived, he went first neither to the Yard nor yet home, but on to Fleet Street. There, at the big *Daily Announcer* building, he sent in his card and a gentleman widely known as 'Cock-eye'—except on Sunday, when a much respected Vicar's church-warden could hardly be so addressed—promptly appeared and led Bobby into a sort of cupboard he called his office.

"Got anything?" he asked eagerly on the way. "Something broken?"

"I come," Bobby told him, "not to give, but to receive—a far, far better thing."

"I might have known it," sighed 'Cockeye' resignedly. "Don't you wish you may get it?"

"I do," Bobby answered promptly. "I may as well tell you that if I don't I shall send an anonymous letter to your Vicar, telling him your Fleet Street name."

"Blackmail," declared 'Cockeye'. "Won't wash, though. He wouldn't believe you. Oh, well, have a cigarette? Shoot," he commanded.

"Do you know anything about a writer called Tudor King—personally, I mean?"

"No one does," came the prompt answer. "Publicity-dodging stunt. It goes over big if you wing it off. Not easy. One of our boys traced him to his lair and ever since swears an old battleaxe chased him halfway down the street with a broom or a rolling pin or something. He asked for a rise on the strength of it. Danger money. Nothing doing. Never is when you ask for a rise. The story at the time was that it was because Tudor King didn't want to go into court that he agreed to settle a libel action against him—and on pretty stiff terms."

"Libel action?" Bobby repeated. "When was that?"

"One of his earlier books," answered 'Cockeye.' "I believe it was pretty serious. Might have been brought in as criminal libel, but they preferred to go for damages. Got 'em all right, too. Must have run Tudor King into something like £10,000, what with costs and all the rest of it the lawyers push in for make-weight. He couldn't have done much worse if he had fought the action, but that was what was said at the time—that he didn't dare show in court. Afraid of cross-examination. It nearly broke him up altogether. He had to borrow. Took him years to get clear. Talk about living dangerously! Try being an author or a journalist:"

"Not me," said Bobby with fervour. "Ever hear of Cynthia Cairn?"

"I have," said 'Cockeye,' looking surprised. "Have you?" and when Bobby nodded, he looked more surprised than ever. "Well, think of that," he said. "I thought only really intelligent people knew anything about her. Twenty or thirty years ago, she was the white hope of the highbrows. Only the more they plugged her, the smaller grew her sales, till at last there weren't any. There was a description of the smell of boiled cabbage in a boarding house that became a classic. The *avant-garde* claimed that her books were unmatched in the whole range of English literature for their sordid, unrelenting realism. If you wanted to commit suicide, but didn't feel up to it, then you read one of her books and you were."

"Sounds awfully jolly," Bobby murmured.

"Well, you see, at that time," explained 'Cockeye,' "sordid, unrelenting realism was the hall-mark of authentic genius with all the really, top-ranking critics. Then there was the w.c. era, when w.c.s were your only wear in the best literary circles. Now it has to be allegory and symbolism if you want to be taken seriously. I'll tell you something else. In confidence. Top secret. Can I trust you?"

"As far as you can see me," Bobby assured him.

"A come-back is being staged," said 'Cockeye' in his most dramatic tones.

"What's that mean?"

"Well, ever since Anthony Trollope was dug up from his peaceful grave to be the brightest star in the literary firmament, every publisher has been trying to work the trick with any other old-has-been he can think of. Natural, of course, to try again what's come off once."

"What we call the M.O., the *modus operandi*," Bobby said. "In other words, the same old beaten trail we all like to follow."

"Exactly," agreed 'Cockeye.' "Well, she's next on the list. She's to be put over big. Some of the B.B.C. blokes are very sympathetic. Talks on the Third and serials on Home and Light. Neglected genius stunt."

"Thank you very much," said Bobby, getting to his feet. "I must be off now, back to Central. Got a lot to do."

"You haven't told me yet what it was you came about, what you wanted to know," 'Cockeye' said, surprised by this abrupt departure.

"Because you have already," Hobby explained. "Most useful. A flood of light on dark places. It'll clear up a lot that's been worrying me, so now I can concentrate on what I'm pretty sure is the right line. Good night and thanks again."

CHAPTER XXXI

NOCTURNAL VISIT

BOBBY WAS EARLY at Lower High Hill next day, and there, when he arrived at the little police station, he found Ford sound asleep on a rug on the floor. On Bobby's appearance, however, the sergeant on duty inserted the toe of a substantial boot into Ford's ribs, and instantly Ford was on his feet, as wide awake and alert as though he had spent the night in a comfortable bed. Bobby noticed, too, with approval that he had shaved before settling down on his rug.

"Sorry, sir," he said apologetically. "I didn't hear you come in."

"Had your breakfast?" Bobby asked.

"Four new laid eggs, straight from nest to saucepan," Ford replied, this time ecstatically.

"For once the path of duty justifies itself," remarked Bobby—enviously. "Anything to report?"

"All lights in the bungalow were out by eleven three," Ford answered. "At eleven fifty-seven heard footsteps. Too dark to see anything. At twelve seven could make out a person near bungalow. Am certain it was a woman. Woman went to bungalow door. She stood there. I was unable to see what she was doing. Before I could take action someone whistled. It sounded like the opening bars of a tune. I didn't recognize it. It went something like this." He tried, not very successfully, to hum a few bars that Bobby also failed to recognize. "As soon as she heard it the woman slipped away. I don't think it could possibly have been a warning that I was watching. I hadn't moved or made a sound of any sort. I jumped up and ran after her. It wasn't so dark but that I could see her, and I made sure I could catch up. But she was a fast runner and got to the trees first. I was close behind and then a man ran up and barged into me. It was Mr. Longton. He grabbed me and began shouting. Before I could get free, the woman got away."

"Maureen Carton, I suppose," Bobby said.

"Well, sir, that was what I thought, but I couldn't swear to it."

"Had Langton anything to say to explain what he was doing there at that time of night?"

"Oh, yes, a lot, all at the top of his voice," Ford answered. "Very indignant he let on to be. Claimed he thought I was a burglar, and how was he to know I wasn't? He said I wasn't in uniform and if I was a policeman, why not? Claimed he had been out to study night effects for a play he was producing, he said. I told him that tale didn't satisfy me. But I knew his identity, and if I had taken him in charge I should have had to leave the bungalow with no one watching and it did strike me that that might be what he wanted. So I told him to clear off. He wanted to go on arguing. I think he would be talking still if I had let him. He shut up finally. Nothing else happened. I hope I did right, sir?"

"Oh, I think so," Bobby said. "It might have been better, as things turned out, if you had waited a little longer before showing yourself. There might have been developments. No telling. It is better as a general rule to wait till the last moment before the clock strikes—only sometimes it strikes before then."

"Yes, sir. I see, sir," said a slightly crestfallen Ford.

"Oh, I'm not blaming you," Bobby said quickly. "I expect I might have done the same. If you had been able to catch the girl and make sure who she was, it would probably have been worth while. It's practically certain it was Miss Carton, of course, but practically certain isn't proof. I wonder what on earth she was up to."

"Do you think, sir," Ford asked, rather timidly, "that perhaps Longton and the young lady know the hat Linda Blythe says she found is in the bungalow somewhere and they wanted to get it? It must have been something they thought urgent that took them there at that time."

"It might be that," Bobby agreed. "I was thinking of trying to get a search warrant. I don't know if I could, though. Some magistrates are very sticky about search warrants. And then a hat—takes about two seconds to push it on the kitchen fire and there's the end of your evidence. May have been done already. I think the best plan will be to try to get a chat with Mrs. Cato."

"I meant to tell you, sir," Ford said. "First thing this morning Mrs. Cato got the old car they let out as a taxi at the 'Blue Lion,' and went off in it. Hired it for the day."

"Hope she didn't take the hat with her," Bobby said gloomily. "Nothing to do now but wait till she comes back. You've left someone on watch?"

"Oh, yes, sir," Ford assured him. "Charley Eaton."

"Well, you had better finish your sleep," Bobby said. "I'll try to decide what to do next. I think I shall dream of hats for the rest of my life."

"Yes, sir," said Ford sympathetically and, settling down again on his rug, was instantly fast asleep.

Bobby went to the door of the police station and stood there, perpending, somewhat at a loss. He had been expecting a talk with Mrs. Cato would help to make his path clearer. Her unexpected departure meant more delay and might possibly mean the final disappearance of the hat—the most illusive hat, Bobby thought ruefully, in history or legend. A hat, too, that might prove entirely useless when discovered—if ever. Then there was the appearance of Maureen and Longton in the neighbourhood of the bungalow and the puzzle of what they were doing there at that time of night. To secure possession of the hat? And did that mean it belonged to Jack Longton? In any case, such a midnight visit bore no semblance of innocence. But appearances can be deceptive.

He told himself that perhaps neither of them—neither Longton nor Maureen—could be judged by everyday standards. All who practise the arts—creative, interpretive, representational—all, by the necessities of their nature, tend to be excitable, emotional, inclined to rebel against the conventions of society. Their behaviour, which seems to them perfectly natural, may appear very differently to more sober folk, indeed at times to be quite irresponsible. In spite of the leading case of Cellini, the artist of the Golden Dagger, seldom, however, if ever, do they deviate into criminal courses, but none the less every criminal can also be described as something of a rebel against the conventions and as rather more than something of an actor. Nor was Bobby, a very ordinary Englishman, in spite of his touch of Celtic blood that gave him a more than ordinarily active imagination, entirely without the traditional British mistrust of all who meddle with the arts when they ought to be doing a 'job of real work like other people.'

A good deal worried, he strolled away down the village street and there met Sir William Watson, in plus fours and a golf cap, apparently also out for a stroll. He greeted Bobby with a friendly wave of the hand.

"I know I mustn't ask you questions," he said, "but I do hope this sort of thing isn't going on much longer. Dreadfully disturbing. You left an impression at Cobblers yesterday that you really suspected one of us. No, no. I'm not asking you to confirm or deny. No business of mine, I know. All the same, that's what we all felt. A very uncomfortable feeling, too. I noticed you didn't ask for young Moyse. All the same he seemed as disturbed as the rest of us, when he heard about your visit. And this morning, he's missing."

"Do you mean he has left Cobblers?"

"No one has seen him since dinner last night—a meal no one enjoyed, I can assure you. One of the maids—Linda, I think is her name—saw him going out last night. She didn't take any notice, of course, thought he was going for a stroll before bed, and she didn't notice if he was carrying anything. Most likely he would have been in time to catch the last 'bus for Town. I don't know if you think that at all important, but I thought I would let you know."

"Yes, thank you," Bobby said. "It may be important, of course. I hear Mrs. Cato went off early this morning in a car she had hired."

"Can there be a connection, do you think?" Watson asked eagerly.

"I think I had better go on to Cobblers and make some inquiries there," Bobby said, without answering this. "Can I give you a lift? I've my car here."

Sir William thanked him, but declined, and Bobby, as he drove off, was sure that Sir William's early morning stroll had been undertaken to inform him of Moyse's departure and to note any reaction that might be apparent.

"Growing uneasy—all of them," Bobby said to himself. "No wonder," and, looking after him, thought that Sir William's bearing was less confident, his manner less jaunty than usual. 'Getting them all down,' Bobby thought again, and again he said: "No wonder."

At Cobblers Linda answered the door, and showed him into the lounge hall. Nor did she display any inclination to stay or talk, but hurried away as fast as her legs could carry her with a murmured promise to let his presence be known.

It was Maureen who appeared first, with a message from her father that he would join Mr. Owen in a few minutes.

"Going to pinch one of us?" Maureen asked with a not very convincing air of bravado. "Or have you heard that Mr. Moyse has bunked off? Isn't that always taken for a confession of guilt?"

"Not always," Bobby said. "Sometimes it is mere, unreasoning panic. Did you sleep well last night?"

"Like a top," Maureen answered, gazing at him with pensive, innocent eyes. "I went to bed early and I never woke till morning. How sweet of you to ask."

"How nice of you to say so," Bobby retorted. "So few of those I have to put questions to think them sweet."

"One up to you," murmured Maureen, looking now, however, just a trifle less innocent. "I can hear Dad coming. Oh, by the way, did you know? I take an extra small size in handcuffs—junior miss."

Therewith she vanished, leaving Bobby with two convictions, (*a*) that he would greatly enjoy fitting the young lady with a suitable pair of handcuffs as described, (*b*) that in matters of truth-telling she could practise a quite remarkable economy.

CHAPTER XXXII

HEIRLOOMS

BOBBY WAS NOT LEFT long to indulge in solitude the luxury of such day-dreams. Almost at once Lord Rone appeared. In reply to Bobby's inquiry, he confirmed that Moyse had taken himself off the previous evening without informing anyone of his intention. His departure had not been known till that morning when he had failed to appear at breakfast and his room had been found unoccupied, his bed unslept in.

"One of the maids," Lord Rone said, "appears to have seen him leave the house last night, and she thinks he was carrying a suitcase, but doesn't seem at all sure. She didn't tell anyone. When I spoke to her, she said so many queer things had been happening, she didn't know what to think. She started to cry. I detest women who cry."

"They do seem to find it a sure refuge in all times of trouble and adversity," Bobby agreed, speaking with much sympathy, for how often had he not been baffled and delayed by a burst of tears from a woman he was questioning? "If I may make the suggestion," he went on, "have you noticed if any article of value is missing? Have you, for instance, checked up on your stamp collection? I'm told it's valuable."

"Why, no," Lord Rone exclaimed, considerably startled. "I didn't think of that. You don't mean . . . ? I thought it was on account of this other business he had gone off."

"Well, that's possible," Bobby agreed. "We've been making inquiries. That story about saving you from being knocked down by a car and the recovery of your dispatch case didn't satisfy me. There doesn't seem any direct evidence connecting him with the murder, but there is the possibility that he and Baldwin Jones were associates and that a quarrel, possibly over the Golden Dagger, ended fatally. He has confessed to making the 'phone call that gave the first information we had. And it is a fact that the first information of a crime does often come from the guilty person. There is a kind of instinctive feeling that being the first to call attention to it gives a kind of automatic assurance of innocence. Quite a mistaken idea, but it exists. Or it may be that the burden of such a secret becomes too heavy to be borne any longer alone."

"Well, in that case," Lord Rone exclaimed excitedly, "why hasn't he been arrested?" With some naïveté, he added: "It would be a tremendous relief."

"I said 'possibility,' " Bobby reminded him. "There has to be evidence, even clear evidence. At present I have no more against him than against some others. There is no proof again, but information received leads us to think that a young man, more or less answering to Moyse's description, was on the spot when two recent robberies of stamp collections occurred. Probably you know stamps are very valuable booty in these days. Portable, easy to dispose of, almost impossible to identify, and easy to smuggle abroad. But no proof. I think I should tell you, however, that Moyse offered a more or less plausible explanation of his presence here and of why he faked up that little scene to get an invitation to Cobblers. Nothing to do with the murder, he claims. With the Cobblers heirlooms instead. I am wondering if you would care to answer a few questions about them."

"I don't see where they come in," Lord Rone said, but he was beginning to look uneasy. "What do you want to know?"

"It is common knowledge, of course, that they are of very considerable value," Bobby said. "In his statement to me, Moyse confessed that that very elaborate and amateurish set-up I mentioned just now—you must please forgive me for saying it oughtn't to have deceived a child—was faked to plant him here on behalf of a gentleman I understand to be heir-presumptive to the Rone and Saine title and all settled property going with it. I'm told also that that property is worth comparatively little—except for the heirlooms."

"Well, yes, that's all correct," Lord Rone admitted when Bobby paused. "I dare say they would fetch high prices in a saleroom. They can't be sold, of course."

"Not legally, that is," Bobby said. "Not without consent of the heirs and, I suppose, permission of the courts. But the gentleman I referred to appears to believe—I don't know why—that some have been, or are being, sold privately. Moyse's job was to find out if that were so, and if so, which and when. The possibility I spoke of before still remains, of course—that he and Baldwin Jones were acting together—that in short he tried to double-cross both his employer and his accomplice. Hence the result—a quarrel and the use of the Golden Dagger."

"But you've let him slip through your fingers?"

"We can't take action without satisfactory evidence," Bobby repeated. "Are you willing to confirm or deny this heirloom story?

Speaking as a layman, I must say that the Paul Potter picture—'The Young Stallion' I saw here—didn't strike me as genuine."

"I remember," Lord Rone said. "I thought it good enough to deceive an expert. If a policeman can suspect it's a copy, seeing it for the first time, I shall have to keep it out of sight. Most disconcerting."

"Then it is a fake?" Bobby said.

"Not the original; a copy," retorted Lord Rone in a very offended tone. "I do not at all care for the use of the word 'fake.' And it is not an heirloom. I consulted my lawyer. He was in full agreement. The circumstances are unusual. Cobblers was very badly damaged by fire early in the last century. Nearly all family documents were destroyed. Other things—including some heirlooms—were also destroyed, or else simply stolen or lost in the confusion. A fresh list of heirlooms was drawn up. I do not accept it. My lawyer supports me. I admit nothing as entitled to be regarded as an heirloom unless there is satisfactory confirmation. Nor is there, for that matter, anything to show that this particular list was ever accepted by my great-grandfather. I see no reason why the person you refer to—he has shown no regard for my wishes, in fact he has gone out of his way to be extremely offensive—should inherit what he has no right to. I prefer everything, when there is no other proper claim, to go to my daughter." He paused and then continued, speaking with more care: "Not that I was I anxious to have these family matters made public. I had no wish to be involved in tedious and expensive legal proceedings. There would have been a good deal of gossip. Unpleasant. Other matters could have been dragged in—matters of some delicacy. I considered it all very carefully indeed and I feel I am fully justified—more than justified—in what I did. An entirely private matter."

What Bobby thought was that his lordship of Rone and Saine was a good deal less sure of his position than he wished to appear. What Bobby said was:

"Naturally, all that doesn't concern me. Not a police matter. I must thank you for being so frank. A great help. I think I must be equally frank. There is evidence that Baldwin Jones occasionally practised a kind of petty blackmail. Another possibility therefore comes into the picture. No direct evidence, of course. That's my trouble all the time. This theory and that, but nothing much in the way of proof or disproof. But it will be pointed out by others, if not by me, that Baldwin Jones may have known what you have just told me about the Cobblers heirlooms, that he may have thought he saw prospects of blackmail on a much bigger scale, that a meeting on the path through the plantation was arranged, that the Golden Dagger was produced—as a guarantee of good faith perhaps or for other reasons—and that at any rate in the end it was used for an altogether different purpose."

"I understand what you mean," Lord Rone said. "You have made it quite plain. I am, of course, always at your service, and I thank you for being as you said—frank. I shall see my solicitor as soon as possible and in the meanwhile, if you have nothing more to say, I will make sure that my stamps are safe. I should be sorry if any of them are missing."

He made a little stately bow and without another word walked away. Bobby, watching him go, saw that his form was less erect, his step less steady than usual. Almost immediately Maureen came in, a fierce little Maureen with flushed cheek and flashing eyes, with an angry, stuttering speech.

"What have you been saying to my father?" she demanded.

"You must ask him," Bobby answered. "Not me."

"Will you please go?" Maureen said. "I hope to God I shall never see you again."

"I fear that you will," Bobby said heavily. "I fear that that must be."

CHAPTER XXXIII

APPROACHING CRISIS

BACK AT Lower High Hill, Bobby remarked to Ford in a rather dispirited manner that his visit to Cobblers did not seem to have got him much further forward.

"One thing, though," he added. "They've all got the wind up pretty badly, and no wonder. It's a strain on me and a very much bigger one on them. Innocent or guilty, they all feel they are poised on a tight-rope above an abyss, and when it's like that the final crack may come at any moment. And to-day I think I saw the real Maureen for almost the first time."

"You still think—" Ford began, and paused, not quite sure he ought to ask.

"There is always the discrepancy in evidence I told you to look out for," Bobby said. "It may mean nothing. Impossible to tell, but in a case like this even the tiniest clue may put you on the right road. Have you found it yet?"

"Well, no, sir," Ford answered, looking rather crestfallen. "I haven't had much time to go over things."

"No, I know," Bobby agreed. "Well, take an hour or two off this afternoon and see if you can. Nothing much we can do for the moment. Though . . . though . . . " and his voice trailed off into an uneasy silence.

"Sir?" Ford said, when Bobby still did not speak.

"Though," Bobby said, rousing himself from his troubled thoughts, "though I've a queer sort of feeling that there's a crisis coining. A 'hunch' they call it—a kind of inner warning that the tension has been stretched to a point where something's bound to break."

"At Cobblers, sir?" Ford asked.

"Not only there. Everywhere. I expect that's why Moyse has taken himself off. Who was it whistled to Maureen last night? Long odds it was Jack Longton. The emotional, sensitive, artistic type is always liable to crack—crack with violence sometimes. Mrs. Cato, has she gone off like Moyse? If she doesn't come back to-night, I shall want to take action. I'll drive back to Central now. One or two things to see to there. I'll be back before dark." He laughed uneasily. "Zero hour, and what will that bring?"

It was in fact fairly early when Bobby returned and then, a little before dusk, a message arrived to say that Mrs. Cato was back at the bungalow. Bobby started off at once in his car, taking Ford with him.

"You wait here with the car," he said when they reached Higgles Lane, whence was the easiest access to that isolated bungalow. "But keep a look-out. If I want you, I'll flash my torch three times."

"Very good, sir," said Ford.

Bobby walked on across the fields, following the faint footpath which led to the bungalow. A thin, chill mist was rising as the night drew on. Easy to lose one's way even in these two fields if the mist grew worse. He could see now the lamplight showing against the curtained windows of the bungalow. When he pushed open the garden gate with its little tinkling bell, the bungalow door opened almost immediately and Mrs. Cato appeared, framed in soft lamplight. She called out:

"Is that you at last, Linda? Where ever have you been?" She stopped abruptly as Bobby's tall figure emerged from the enveloping mist. "Oh, you," she said.

"Were you expecting her?" Bobby asked. "She may not have been able to get away."

"I told her to be here before this," Mrs. Cato complained, clearly of the opinion that what she wanted was much more important than any wishes of Linda's employers. "You had better come in? What is it now?"

Bobby followed her into the bungalow. Mrs. Cato began to be busy, lighting an oil cooking stove and putting a kettle on to boil. Bobby, watching her, thought she had a flushed, excited look. She said:

"I've had no tea; no time for it. I expected Linda to have it ready. I can't think what's keeping her. I told her particularly."

Bobby waited patiently while she completed her preparations. Again he thought there was something different, new, about her. Brisk, eager, excited she seemed, with a look in her eyes he had not seen before. He remembered seeing a girl just after she had accepted an offer of marriage, and, absurd though the comparison was, he thought that this worn, elderly woman had something of the same air. As of a new life opening to both. She asked him if he would like a cup of tea and he thanked her and said that he had had his tea before he left Town.

"I was really hoping for a chat with you this morning," he went on. "One of our men has been busy at Somerset House. I got his report first thing to-day."

"Somerset House?" Mrs. Cato repeated, giving him a doubtful but challenging glance. "What for? What's that mean?"

"He hadn't much luck," Bobby said. "He couldn't find any trace of the birth of either Miss Linda Blythe or of Mr. Tudor King. Or, for that matter, of the issue of identity cards to either of them."

"Why should you expect to?" Mrs. Cato asked. "Oh, the kettle's boiling." She began to make the tea. "Have you never heard of people changing their names? Or of writers using a *nom-de-plume*?"

"Have you heard from Mr. Tudor King lately?" Bobby asked, replying to neither of these questions.

"Not for some time," she answered. She put the teapot on the table. She said: "Three or four minutes to draw." She was looking at him quizzically, still with that curious air of shining anticipation as of the weary traveller who sees at last his destination, rest, food, comfort, all at hand. Then she said: "Do you know I'm beginning to be afraid I never shall? Can something have happened on this Continental trip, I wonder? An accident perhaps? Something for you to chew on, Mr.—Owen, isn't it? Or influenza? Influenza is so very prevalent."

"I wonder," Bobby said, "'if in that case he will share a common grave with Mrs. Harris?" At that she nearly dropped the teapot she had been putting out her hand to pick up. She stared at him with an expression of almost ludicrous dismay, but did not speak. He went on: "Or—less tragic—has he merely suffered a sea-change into Cynthia Cairn, by way of Mrs. Cato?"

"Is all that any business of yours?" she asked presently, and now she had forgotten all about her tea.

"It would be none," Bobby agreed, "if it hadn't got so tangled up with a murder investigation—and a murder investigation is a very serious matter with which nothing can be allowed to interfere. Also I have reason to suspect that you have in your possession important evidence."

"You mean that hat Linda picked up and that the little fool must needs bring along here with her? I had quite forgotten. She says I saw it. I don't know. I never thought about it. You can have it and welcome. But you'll have to wait till Linda gets here. I've no idea where she put it." She was beginning to rally now and was drinking the tea she had poured out for herself. "I don't admit anything," she said. Then abruptly and inconsistently, she asked: "How do you know? I don't see what it has to do with anyone else. You've no right to go prying into my private affairs."

"I've no wish to," Bobby assured her. "It is part of the duty of police to respect privacy—any failure to do so would be a most serious breach of discipline. But—do please understand this—I must get straight your connection, and that of Miss Linda, with what's been going on. Am I right in thinking that Miss Linda Blythe is your daughter?"

"You've guessed that, too, have you?" she said angrily. "Good at guessing, aren't you?"

"That isn't fair," Bobby protested. "We don't guess. We observe all sorts of small, insignificant facts till we can be sure they all point one way. And then we follow. It's not adding two and two to make four. It's adding tiny fractions together to make one unit and then, when we have one unit, getting more fractions to make another unit till at last we have four units. The four we want. Nothing dramatic or exciting about it. Just plain plodding till you get there. Of course, at first, I took more or less at its face value the idea that Linda was lonely at Cobblers and felt more at home with you, as you had apparently been in Tudor King's employment together. But I remembered Linda seemed oddly alarmed when I called at Cobblers the first time. As soon as I mentioned I was a policeman and had come on police business. I wondered why? Then I heard that she made frequent visits here and apparently didn't talk about them much. I had to ask myself if it was only because at one time you had both been in Tudor King's employ. It all seemed—well, unusual. I began to notice other little things. As an instance, the way she flared up when Miss Maureen Carton referred to Tudor King's work as 'slush,' I think she said. It almost seemed personal. And then again there was a certain protective attitude you showed—a tendency to come rather quickly to Linda's defence at any sort of a hint of disapproval of anything she had done. I even thought I noticed a bit of a likeness between Linda and the Tudor King photograph I showed you and I noticed you appeared a little disturbed at seeing it."

"It was Linda. Linda sat for it," Mrs. Cato admitted. "'I hoped no one would recognize it—moustache and all. We told the photographer it was for a fancy dress ball. Some story like that. I forget."

"The whole set-up seemed to need explanation," Bobby went on. "In fact, at one time it seemed so peculiar that we had to consider very unpleasant possibilities. That there had been another murder—of Tudor King. That possibly Baldwin Jones was Tudor King, or, if not, that he had been an accomplice in getting rid of Tudor King and then had been got rid of himself. The motive, of course, would have been to secure money earned by Tudor King or possibly again for Mrs. Cato to come forward and claim that she herself was Tudor King. We got near the truth then; and if the rest seems rather wild, none the less, it had to be taken into account. You must admit it seemed peculiar that a writer of popular romantic fiction should have in his employ as housekeeper an extremely realistic novelist of former days whose books had had less success. And though you claimed to be Cynthia Cairn, I had only your word for it. My first idea indeed was that Tudor King was the real personality and Cynthia Cairn the name he used at first. We got near the truth there, didn't we? Only the wrong way round. Two things that helped me—not to guess—to deduce the truth were first the extreme, almost fierce dislike you showed for the Tudor King stories. It seemed rather different, more personal, than the merely half-amused contempt of a house-keeper for the work her employer does to earn the money to pay her with. Again, you spoke with a good deal of feeling about libel actions. Well, ordinary folk don't think much about libel actions, but I'm told libel actions are the author's nightmare, and only an author realizes you can libel people you have never heard of. And apparently Tudor King had been sued for libel and had to pay very heavy damages. It all seemed to add up, and I remembered I had been told that Linda liked to make notes about her work and also that something had been said about the lengths to which some writers will go in order to get material—copy they call it. Dress up as a vagabond, for instance, to get to know a tramp's point of view. Did the fact that there had been rather damaging attacks on Tudor King's description of life among titled folk come in there? My first idea was that Linda herself might be Tudor King pursuing researches into the aristocratic life—the tramp idea in reverse so to speak. But I soon gave that up. Which meant it had to be you."

"It was Linda's own idea," Mrs. Cato said gloomily. "I didn't want her to. She was more upset about those reviews than I was. Some of her friends were giggling about it all, trying to poke silly fun at the Tudor King books, and it worried her. Her idea was that if she got work as a housemaid for a time somewhere she would get to know little details that I could put in and I could make it plain Cobblers was what I was writing about. That would stop the reviewers trying to be clever. Besides, it would put people off the scent. Everyone would be sure it must be some friend of the family and they would never be able to find out which. I gave in in the end. I didn't like it, but Linda was very keen—and it might have helped. That's what frightened her when you called. She thought it might be about her. Well, what are you going to do?"

"Nothing, I hope," Bobby assured her. "That is partly why I am alone. I have left my car and assistant in Higgles Lane so that you may be sure no one else knows. But I must be entirely sure of the facts, if only to be also sure that no more of them need be made public than have to be. Of course, too, it will have to be explained in my report and lawyers may have to know. They are used to keeping secrets. But there is one point in which I think you may have been guilty of an offence. Are you quite sure you had no suspicion that the hat your daughter found might not be important and even decisive evidence?"

"No. How could I?" she demanded with more defiance than was needed, so that her words did not carry to Bobby much conviction.

"There has been a lot of gossip about it in the village," he reminded her gently.

"Some don't listen to village gossip," she retorted, sullen now. "Some of it was about my having murdered the man. Silly, even if you seem to have thought so, too."

"Was that all," Bobby asked. "Are you sure there was no stronger motive? A question of reputation—literary fame and standing?"

"You know it all, don't you?" she sneered.

"No, but I do know a good deal from experience about human nature—and this case has taught me as well a good deal about the human nature of writers and artists generally. One thing I know is that a come-back is being planned of Cynthia Cairn's books. B.B.C. broadcasts—always always very effective—reviews, interviews, so on. Were you afraid that if a story like this became public it would rather spoil things for you?"

"It would set every fool in England giggling," she said darkly. "It would have stopped the B.B.C.—they are scared of their own shadows there. The critics would have been on me like the flock of vultures they are. It would have prevented me from taking my rightful place as the greatest realist novelist of the century." She was speaking quite simply now, without a trace of egotism, as of one merely stating a plain, simple fact with which the speaker had no personal connection. "The symbolism, the allegorical inner meaning of my books is beginning to be recognized as having the fundamental importance it must possess for all who desire to understand the relation of man to life. When I depict the gradual slow decay of the soul of man into utter rottenness, I am giving a warning of how inevitably that happens also in human society. You understand? You realize the significance of this warning that an earlier generation refused to hear, but that to-day may be listened to and even understood? Was I to allow it to be smothered by the idiotic laughter of the rabble because I had allowed my daughter to gather material for Tudor King's slush novels by masquerading as a maid in a house like Cobblers? Was I to submit to the sneers of those who would hunt through the Tudor King novels to compare them with Cynthia Cairns's so infinitely different work? I tell you it was not to be borne."

"Well, of course, I can see your point of view," Bobby said, slightly overwhelmed by this torrent of eloquence. "I must tell you quite candidly that I am not altogether sure that it will be fully appreciated elsewhere. That evidence must never be suppressed is of—er—fundamental importance in all police work. In fact, you might say we are rather touchy about it. And, of course, in some cases it could be regarded as what is called 'accessory after the fact.'

It was at this moment that they both heard a loud and sudden cry as of one in the last extremity of fear and dread.

CHAPTER XXXIV

IN THE MIST

THE ECHO OF THAT strange, distant cry was still hanging in the air as Bobby sprang to his feet, as he was running to the front door. Mrs. Cato was close behind. Bobby tore the door open—and stood dismayed. There had been in the air, as he came across the fields by the footpath leading from Higgles Lane where he had left Ford and his car, floating, baffling wisps of mist. Now, while he had been in the bungalow they had grown, come together, formed a great, pale, billowy mass. The lamplight streaming out through the open door fell back helplessly against that soft, impenetrable barrier.

Bobby stood hesitating. He listened. Then he shouted. There was no answer. Nor was there repeated that great cry he and Mrs. Cato had both heard. What he looked upon was an ocean of silence and invisibility. Already the mist was creeping into the bungalow, as though there too it would smother all sight, all sound, beneath its white, all-pervading shroud. Mrs. Cato pushed past him. She seemed about to plunge into the mist, but she drew back before the great billowy mass, so easily brushed aside and yet so formidable in the deadly menace it concealed. She cried out very loudly:

"Linda! Where are you? Linda! Linda!"

And if Bobby had not known it before, he would have recognized in that great piercing cry all a mother's love, all a mother's fear.

"Do you think it was her?" Bobby asked quickly. "It might have been someone else. Wait here. Get a bell if you have one—a tea tray, anything you can bang and make a noise with. Keep it up, the louder the better. I'll try to find her. Understand?"

Without waiting for an answer, he plunged into the mist that closed around him at once with a soft, dreadful tenacity. It took him into itself without so much as the splash that is caused when a pebble is dropped into the depths of the sea.

Almost at once he lost the path he had expected to be able to follow till he reached the gate. He blundered on, blundering then against the garden hedge with no idea whether the gate was on his right hand or his left. He swore aloud in his frustration, anxiety, exasperation, and next he stumbled against some obstacle and nearly fell. He heard Mrs. Cato call:

"What's the matter? Where are you? What are you doing?"

"I can't find the gate," he shouted back.

"It's just there. I'll show you. Wait a minute," she cried her reply.

But he, rather than lose more time, for who knew how urgent might not be the need of her who had cried through the darkness and the mist her appeal for help, broke or burst or forced an angry way through the hedge into the field beyond.

He began to run. He flashed his torch, but it was of little use against the soft persistence of the clinging mist that seemed to grow thicker with every yard he advanced. Very soon he knew that he had lost all sense of direction, for indeed he was running like a blind man set down at random in a place where he had never been before.

He slackened his pace to a walk. No object in running, no use in hurrying when he had no way of knowing in which direction it would be best to go. No sound broke the utter stillness and silence around, no sound of human footstep or of human voice, no sound at all, no sound of bell or hammered tray or metal pan such as he had asked for. He did not know whether this meant that Mrs. Cato had not obeyed his request or whether the sound of it was being muffled by these dense waves of mist.

"Only hope," he muttered, half aloud, "she hasn't tried to follow and got lost herself."

He walked on, more slowly still, pausing frequently, hoping against hope that the mist might presently lift, in part at least. Once he ran into another fence, once into what seemed a post stuck in the ground. He cursed it and pressed on. Because he had read, or thought he had read, that lost travellers tended always to stray to the right till presently they walked in circles, he tried at every fifth or sixth step to take one sideways to the left.

How far this was effective he had no idea. He began to think he must wander helpless here all the long night through till dawn came and daylight to chase away the faint, fatal enmity that held him captive.

Every few moments he stood still and shouted. Never came there any reply, listen he never so closely. But now, when he shouted his loudest once more, he thought, but was not sure, he heard a sound close by that might have been a human footstep. He listened, but there was nothing. He called again and now, suddenly, silently, there became visible a faint shadowy form, so faint indeed he could not tell whether it was man or woman, or even be sure that it was human. It was indeed no more than a faint wavering darker outline against the pale nothingness of the mist.

He ran towards it, if indeed it had been at all. But no sign or shape of it remained, nor any trace or sound to show it was more than some passing trick of the changing wreaths of mist. He could almost have believed he had seen nothing and yet was sure he had, and somehow he felt too that that passing form had concealed a dark and dreadful threat. He flashed the torch he was carrying, the useless torch whose light was instantly lost as utterly in the mist as he was lost himself. Nevertheless, still shouting, he pressed forward, and suddenly there was Maureen, clinging to his arm, breathing in great gasps, sobbing, clinging to his arm as a drowning man to a lifebelt.

"Thank God! Thank God!" she was panting. "Thank God it's you!"

"What on earth—" Bobby began, completely taken by surprise. "What's been happening?" he asked.

"It's Linda," Maureen stammered. "Linda . . . her face was all over blood . . . there was a man . . . masked. I ran . . . I couldn't help it . . . I saw you and I thought it was him after me and I think it was but then it was you . . . thank God!" She was speaking more quietly now. "I said I hoped to God I would never see you again and now I'm thanking God it's you."

"Pull yourself together," Bobby said sharply. "What's this about Linda? Where is she?"

"It's the fog," Maureen said. "After I ran away I couldn't find her again. Or the hat. She threw it away. It's what he wanted. He must have known. He must have been waiting for us. He came a out of the fog all of a sudden and I screamed and Linda threw it away—the hat I mean . . . and then she was on the ground all over blood and I ran away . . . her face I mean . . . he followed me, but I don't know . . . and then I was lost till I saw you."

"I'm lost, too," Bobby said. "Keep with me. If you move a yard away, we may never find each other again. You and Linda were bringing a hat, the one she found on path through the plantation, was it? You were taking it to the bungalow and a man attacked you. He was masked. Who was he?"

"I don't know," she answered. She spoke quietly now, simply and quietly. She repeated: "I don't know. How could I? He had a mask and he came all of a sudden out of the fog and it was all over before I knew. And I ran and I know it was being a coward, but I couldn't help, and when I tried to go back I couldn't because of the fog. If we don't find Linda she'll die."

"You must keep with me," Bobby said again. "Catch hold of my coat and don't leave go whatever you do. If we could even find the bungalow it would help. Or the stile into the next field. If we do find Linda I shall have to ask you to stay with her while I try to find the bungalow or anything to show where we are. Shall you be afraid to stay alone with her?"

"Oh, yes," Maureen answered fervently. "I never knew I was such a coward. But I'll stop with her if you say so. Only I think if that man finds us he will kill us both because he'll be afraid we knew him. Only, of course it's the hat he wants, but how can he find it when it's like this?"

"I think both you and Linda knew well who he was," Bobby said. "Will you not tell me?"

He waited for a reply. It did not come at once. Then she said the one word:

"No." Correcting herself quickly, she said: "How could we know? It was all so sudden and he was masked and then the fog."

"Loyalty may become a crime," Bobby said. "Please think that over. Now I'm going to walk in as straight a line as I can. I am hoping in that way we may reach the hedge. Then if we follow it round we may be able to get to the bungalow or the stile into the next field. I left one of my men in the lane. I told him to stop there, but he may have sense enough to try to find out what's happening. He may have heard you calling. I'm going to shout as loudly I can. When I stop, you shout. As loudly as possible. Your voice may carry further than mine in this mist. I don't know. But whatever you do, don't leave hold of my coat."

"I won't," Maureen assured him with great firmness. "Me hanging on to a man's coat-tails," she added ruefully, "and awfully afraid of letting go."

They walked on accordingly, Maureen clinging very tightly indeed to his coat-tail. As he walked Bobby shouted as seldom he had shouted before, then listened for a reply. Maureen, too, at intervals, with all the vigour that her fear gave her, fear both for herself and Linda. Nor was it long before these tactics succeeded, for presently there came a reply. Bobby shouted again. This time the response was nearer. Maureen added a scream by way of helping and Bobby told her not to, for fear of confusing the direction.

"It may be the man in the mask," Maureen whispered with sudden, renewed fear.

"I hope so, but it won't be," Bobby said. "If it were, I would not have to ask you or Linda to tell me who he was."

"Perhaps Linda's dead," Maureen said in a little low whisper he could hardly hear, and he had not time to remind her that Baldwin Jones at least was dead before he heard Ford calling.

"That you, sir?" Ford was saying. He loomed huge and indistinct from out of the all-embracing wreaths of mist. "When I saw how bad the mist was getting I thought I had better come along, but it wasn't anything like it is now or I would have bumped the car through the hedge somehow—lamps and all. I thought I heard someone scream," he added, aware now of Maureen half hidden behind Bobby and still clinging firmly to his coat-tail.

"It was me," Maureen said, peeping out from her shelter. "It's Linda been hurt. You must find her."

"They were attacked on their way to Mrs. Cato's," Bobby explained. "By a man in a mask. Keep on the look-out for him. He may be dangerous. He used the Golden Dagger once. Perhaps he will again. They had the hat we've been looking for. Linda is probably unconscious somewhere about here. I hope he hasn't found the bungalow. Mrs. Cato is there, alone. Thank God!" he exclaimed as at this moment, and apparently from no great distance, they heard a banging, as of metal upon metal. "That'll be her. Hurry, Ford. You go with him," he added to Maureen. "Don't get separated. Ford, tell Mrs. Cato to lock the bungalow door and not open it to anyone except us. There's risk our masked friend may be there first. When Mrs. Cato and the girl are safe indoors, get all the string or rope you can and lay a trail from the bungalow so we can find it easily again. Look sharp. There's danger till we have got this masked man or know he's gone—and most likely he's still here looking for the hat he knows he has to find."

"I think the mist is lifting," Ford said.

"I think 'I saw someone over there," Maureen said. "I think perhaps he was near enough to hear. I think perhaps that he was listening."

"Well, that doesn't matter much now you've told us who he is," Bobby said loudly. He clapped his hand, none too gently, over Maureen's mouth, for he saw she had been about to protest. "Shut up," he said in an angry whisper as she tried to push his hand away, "If he thinks you've told us, he won't bother about you any more." Aloud he said: "Hurry now. I'll stay and see if I can find Linda."

A thin, high voice from behind, a voice he did not recognize, a voice he thought might be disguised, said:

"She's there, on your right, about ten yards away. If you don't get her into shelter at once, she'll probably die of cold—your re-sponsibility."

CHAPTER XXXV

A SCRATCHED FACE

"OR YOURS?" Bobby called back into that pale invisibility. "Hadn't you better stop this sort of thing? I've always known who you were and now there's your hat for proof."

There was no answer, no sound. Except indeed one so faint, so muffled, so low, Bobby was not sure he had really heard it. Yet he thought that it had sounded like the low moan of a stricken animal, stricken to death. Now the impenetrable curtain of the mist that had withdrawn itself momentarily came rolling back, and again it was to Bobby as if he stood alone in a world where he alone had palpable existence. The voice from the mist had said that Linda was lying a few yards away, to the right, and that she was in danger of dying from exposure and cold. That, at least, was probably true. But was the rest true? Or was it merely an attempt to lead him astray or even to give to one evidently desperate a chance to take him unawares? Or again, and more probably, was it true but was the motive to get Bobby to a safe distance and so leave the unknown a better chance of finding the hat that Linda had thrown away, the hat which, if it gave proof of ownership as it well might, would give also proof of guilt?

And if what had been said could be trusted, if the direction had been given accurately, could he, he wondered, keep that direction for even so short a distance as ten yards?

Very cautiously, slowly, on his guard, for he still thought an attack might be launched at any moment from out of the shelter of a mist now as thick as before, Bobby began to move in the direction indicated. He felt himself tread on something that was neither the turf of the field, nor the beaten track of the footpath, nor yet one of the many stones scattered here and there. He stooped to pick it up and found he was holding a black Homburg hat, the one beyond doubt that the two girls had had with them and that Linda had thrown from her into the sure keeping of the mist. Though sought for with passion, since on the finding of it hung issues of life and death, it might well have lain there unseen till finally the mist cleared and day had come. Unsought, it offered itself to his foot. Holding it, feeling that the long pursuit had ended at last, Bobby moved on as cautiously as before—and soon was obliged to rec-ognize that he had gone much farther than the ten yards or so the voice from the mist had mentioned. No trace of Linda had he seen, though the discovery of the hat seemed to give proof that she could not be far distant.

He made an attempt to retrace his steps and immediately was as hopelessly lost as before. Perhaps the direction given him had been mistaken, too, since it was altogether likely that its giver had been as entirely confused and astray as Bobby himself had now become once again. He stood still, listening intently, hearing nothing. A faint slow breeze came creeping across the fields stirring the mist, stirring in Bobby a hope that if only it would strengthen, the mist would clear. It did strengthen, and then suddenly, as suddenly as in a theatre the curtain rises to show the prepared scene behind, so now the mist rolled back, dissolved, was not.

Above shone out a clear, cloudless sky, throwing down light from the stars and a young moon. At a little distance a human form became visible, that of a man, standing there silent and still, doubtless as much surprised as Bobby was himself by this swift change. Between them, equally distant, more or less, from the one as from the other, lay the huddled form of a prostrate woman.

Instantly Bobby sprang forward. As instantly the man thus so revealed turned and ran, ran with such urgency of flight that he went headlong into the prickly hedge that here divided this field from the next. He was on his feet again on the instant, dabbing at his face with his handkerchief, whether because it was scratched and bleeding or as a means of concealment, since his mask had been torn off in his fall.

"Look after her," he screamed, his voice high, shrill, distorted, unrecognizable. "Or she'll die—die."

The last word itself died away into the mist. Bobby's swift dash forward had brought him to Linda's side. He could see that in her condition she could not be left. He knelt down by her. She was moaning softly, but did not seem to be conscious.

The bleeding from an injury she had received to the head had stopped. But when he tried to feel her pulse it was scarce perceptible. Her hand was as ice, and he heard with anger the sound of running footsteps die away as the fugitive made sure his escape.

Bobby would have given much to follow in pursuit even now, but Linda's need for prompt assistance was obvious and paramount. She must not be allowed to remain any longer lying there in cold and damp, if indeed these had not already done their work. For well might it be that already it was too late. With some difficulty, he got the girl's prostrate form on his shoulder in what is sometimes known as the 'fireman's lift.' Carrying her thus, he began to run towards the bungalow. He saw Ford running to meet him. He called:

"I can manage. Fetch a doctor. Get to the car. Hurry. She's alive still; that's about all. Tell the doctor it's chiefly cold and shock and exposure. Quick."

Ford was already hurrying full speed to obey. Bobby pushed on towards the bungalow. Mrs. Cato was hovering near the gate. She had ignored the warning to keep inside behind locked doors. He noticed she was carrying in one hand the hatchet she used for chopping wood. Seeing him coming, she threw the thing down and ran to meet him. He called to her to go back and prepare hot drinks, hot-water bottles.

"All we can do till the doctor comes," he panted as he still ran with the girl upon his shoulder. "I've sent the car."

Mrs. Cato fled back at her best speed to the bungalow. Maureen had come now to the open door, reassured by Bobby's presence. Bobby put Linda down on a bed and left her to her mother and Maureen to undress and get between the blankets. He went back into the outer room and busied himself preparing coffee and boiling more water—the coffee both for himself, for he was chilled to the bone, and for Linda when she recovered consciousness. Mrs. Cato came out and began to fill and trim a portable oil stove. As she worked, she said:

"I was nearly lost, too. I tried to follow you and then I didn't know where I was. That's why I couldn't do anything at first till I got back and found a tea tray to bang. Thank you for bringing Linda back.

"How is she?" Bobby asked.

"We can't get her warm," Mrs. Cato said. "Not in herself."

"Her assailant got away," Bobby said. "But I know who he is. I have his hat," and he indicated with a gesture the black Homburg hat he had put down on a table in the corner and towards which he directed from time to time a glance of grim satisfaction.

Mrs. Cato hardly seemed to hear what he said or to notice it. She went back into the bedroom. Bobby sat down to wait. There was nothing more he could do. He found himself nodding off to sleep, so he got up and went outside. There was no sign yet of any doctor or of Ford. He waited impatiently, chafing at the inactivity forced upon him. But he dared not leave the women alone, for he did not know to what pitch of desperation Linda's assailant might not by now have wrought himself. He might be somewhere near at hand, watching, ready to attack again. He might appear even in innocent guise, claiming merely to have been lost in the fog and too confident in his disguise to believe he had been recognized. It might be he would make one last desperate effort to recover possession of his hat, which he could well feel was the only solid evidence against him. Nor, for that matter, did Bobby wish to let out of his sight for a moment that same piece of evidence for which he had searched so long.

"And even yet," Bobby admitted to himself, "I couldn't swear to identity. I know all right, but that's no good by itself. Even if either of the girls could and would, any clever K.C. could soon make a jury doubtful—and the girls themselves as well for that matter."

He drank some more coffee, and then went outside again. This time he heard approaching footsteps. Then out of the dim night there loomed up three figures. They were those of Ford, of another, plainly a doctor, and of Jack Longton, looking tired, dishevelled, muddy from a fall apparently, his face slightly scratched and showing traces of slight bleeding. Ford said:

"We met Mr. Longton in Higgles Lane going towards the village so I asked him to come with us," and in Ford's voice as he spoke there sounded a suspicion he made no attempt to hide.

"You are out late, Mr. Longton," Bobby said as the doctor disappeared into the room of which Mrs. Cato had just opened the door. "It's a long way here from where you are staying." There was suspicion, too, in his voice, as he began to wonder whether the trail he had been so persistently following had not been mistaken from the start. "You've been out all night?" he said.

"I got caught in that beastly fog," Longton answered. "Got lost completely. Walked bang into a ditch." He touched his face where the scratches showed. "Why? What about it? What's up? Your man won't say. Is it Maureen?"

"Why should you think so?" Bobby asked.

"Why shouldn't I? There's something. What is it?"

"Miss Carton and Miss Blythe were attacked earlier to-night," Bobby said. "Miss Blythe has been rather badly hurt. Their assailant escaped. I had a glimpse of him, but he got away in the fog. Shortly afterwards you were found not far away. I think an explanation is required."

"What do you mean?" demanded Longton angrily. "Are you trying to make out it was me? Don't be a fool."

"Can you tell me what you were doing here?"

"I don't have to," Longton retorted. "Why should I?"

The doctor came out of the bedroom. Mrs. Cato was with him. He was saying to her:

"You've done everything possible. Rest, quiet, warmth. Unless pneumonia sets in, I don't think there's much cause for alarm." To Bobby he said: "The injuries to the head are not serious. Concussion. No sign of any fracture. If she had been left out much longer, though, it would probably have killed her. Any idea who did it?" and in his voice, too, there was obvious suspicion as he looked at the bedraggled, dishevelled Longton.

"It's too early yet to say," Bobby answered.

"She's asleep," the doctor went on, though still with one eye warily on Longton, as though he thought it best to be on guard against any fresh outbreak. "Best possible thing. Don't disturb her on any account. I've told her mother what to do if she wakes, but I hope she won't. I'll look in again first thing in the morning. Can your man drive me back? He wouldn't give me time to get my car out."

"Of course," Bobby said. "Ford, drive the doctor home and then back here as soon as possible."

Ford and the doctor went off together to the car waiting for them in the lane beyond the fields. Bobby turned to Longton. He said:

"Mr. Longton, I'm not satisfied. There are some questions I must ask you."

Before he could say more, Maureen appeared from the room where Linda was sleeping. She stared blankly at Longton.

"What on earth . . . ?" she began and stood staring, open eyes and mouth, and in her eyes and in her voice, too, there was something that seemed as if it, too, might be suspicion.

CHAPTER XXXVI

THE SIZE OF A HAT

BEFORE LONGTON COULD answer or Maureen speak again, Bobby interposed. He said, speaking to Longton:

"Miss Carton and Miss Blythe seem to have been attacked in order to get possession of a hat they had with them. There is some reason to believe it belonged to the murderer of Baldwin Jones. You were in the vicinity, though you are staying at a considerable distance. You seem inclined to refuse any explanation of why you were here or what you were doing."

"I don't see why I should," Longton retorted. He turned to Maureen. "He wants to make out it was me," he said.

"I'm only asking at present for an explanation," Bobby said. "The man was masked and there was a thick mist as well. Miss Carton had no chance to identify him. No more had I, though I got a glimpse for a moment. Just possibly Miss Blythe may be able to tell us more presently."

"It wasn't Jack," Maureen said. "It couldn't be."

"I have the hat they were bringing here," Bobby went on, ignoring this. "You remember, Mr. Longton, I told you we had information you had won a new hat in a bet. You agreed about the bet, but not about having had the hat."

"It's not Jack's hat," Maureen said. "How could it be?"

"You take rather a large size, don't you?" Bobby went on. "Seven or over?"

"I take seven and a quarter, if you want to know," Longton growled. "What about it? I suppose it's a policeman's job to ask a lot of footling questions."

"To ask questions, certainly," Bobby agreed. "I've been rather interested in guessing what size hats people here take. Lord Rone has rather a small head."

"Six and seven eighths," Maureen said. "I do know that."

"Mr. Oxendale, too, I should guess," Bobby said. "You and Sir William Watson both have rather large heads. I should guess he takes seven and a quarter, too, or even larger."

"Are you trying to make out," Longton demanded, "that one of us two is the murderer? Well, it wasn't me, I know that, and Sir William of all people—that's nearly as silly."

Bobby turned to pick up the hat from where he had put it down. He looked inside. The size was plainly marked—not seven and a quarter, but six and seven eighths. He stood, holding it in his hand, frowning, contemplative, struggling to see his way clearly through these complexities and contradictions, while the other two watched him doubtfully, uneasily.

As they all three stood thus, silent, unmoving, there came a knock at the outer door of the bungalow. It passed unheeded—not so much unheard as unheeded, so lost was Bobby on the one hand in the maze of thoughts crowding in upon his mind, so absorbed were Jack Longton and Maureen on their side in their own fear and unease as they waited for what Bobby would say next.

The knock was repeated. The door opened. Lord Rone was there. He too had a dishevelled, disarrayed appearance. He was bareheaded. From where he stood, he could see Bobby and Longton, but not Maureen. She had not moved since she came out of the bedroom and was still standing with her back to the bedroom door. Lord Rone said:

"I've been wandering about in the fog—quite lost. No idea where I was. Then I saw a light here. Miss Carton went out rather late and hasn't come back. It may be the fog. Her mother was growing exceedingly anxious."

"It's all right," Maureen said, coming forward. "I'm quite all right. I got lost in the fog." Her voice suddenly rose, became shrill. "Everyone did. It's been rather beastly."

Lord Rone was looking at the hat Bobby was holding and that now he was holding forward as if to invite attention.

"Is that my hat?" Lord Rone asked. "The one I couldn't find?"

"No, it isn't," Maureen cried. "Of course it isn't."

"Whose hat is it, then?" Bobby asked. He addressed the question more directly to Maureen. She did not answer. He said: "Is it the hat Linda Blythe found on the spot where the murder took place?"

"I don't know," she answered then. "I don't know anything about it. It isn't Father's, that's all."

"Why had you it with you, you and Linda Blythe, when you were attacked?"

"I think I thought it was Norman Oxendale's," Maureen said.

"That's not what I asked you," Bobby said sharply. "Why had you it with you? Why were you bringing it here?"

Maureen remained silent. Lord Rone said:

"Well, Maureen, well?" This also failed to draw any reply. He went on: "Linda Blythe? The new maid we've just engaged? What's she to do with it?"

"She has been injured," Bobby said, "in an attack made on her and on Miss Carton."

"I ran away," Maureen said. "There was a man in a mask. Out of the mist. All of a sudden. I ran away and Linda screamed and I tried to get back, but I couldn't, because of the fog, and I didn't know where I was, and then there was Mr. Owen. I expect he saved my life, and I don't care if he did and I wish he hadn't."

All this came out in a sudden rush of words. Bobby thought that she was on the verge of breaking down. He said to her loudly and sharply:

"None of that. Pull yourself together. You've done mischief enough already without going into hysterics."

"I'm not. I never do," Maureen said indignantly. "You're horrid, trying to bully."

"Where is the hat Linda found?" Bobby demanded.

"I don't know. How should I know?" Maureen retorted. Bobby waited—waited in that grim, silent, commanding manner which at times he could assume, almost unconsciously. The expression of a fierce inner energy of will that all could feel and that few could resist. Not Maureen. She mumbled: "I shouldn't wonder if it hadn't got burnt or something. I don't know."

"I think," Bobby told her, "both you and your father had better consider your position. So far you have managed to bring both Lord Rone and Mr. Longton under suspicion. Either could be charged. If Linda Blythe dies, there may be another charge. You may be charged yourself with destroying evidence that might have provided proof of guilt."

"All right, go ahead and charge me if you want to," Maureen said at her most obstinate. "I don't care a scrap, not if you did save my life."

"I didn't do anything of the kind, so don't keep saying so," Bobby snapped, and added, rudely and indefensibly, but then he was tired, worried, and very cross: "I don't know that I should even think it worth saving."

By a kind of instinctive movement, both Jack Longton and Lord Rone had moved so as to stand between her and Bobby, almost as if they wished to form a kind of protective screen. She looked at them both, and somehow it seemed to make her change her expression, even in a sense it might have been said, her personality. With a gesture that was not without a certain dignity, she stepped between them, and stood facing Bobby. She did not speak, but just stood there. Now it was she who was waiting, and she managed to put into that waiting something of the same force and controlled energy Bobby had shown before. But he was still too angry to take much notice. He said:

"You've been acting like an irresponsible schoolgirl."

"Have I? Perhaps I have," Maureen said. She was speaking quietly now, quietly and steadily, without a trace of the hysteria that had at one time threatened. "I'm not going to say another word," she went on. "Not even if I have to go to prison."

"What is all this?" asked Lord Rone. Till now he had appeared so bewildered as to be unable to get out even a word of protest. "What are you talking about, Maureen?" he demanded. "What have you been doing? Something was said about charging me or Mr. Longton with something or another. Is that seriously meant? Does that mean—?"

He did not finish the sentence. It was as though he feared to put into spoken words the thought in his mind. Longton had no such hesitation. He said brusquely:

"It's seriously meant all right. We're both under suspicion of having murdered Baldwin Jones—jointly or severally, I suppose the lawyers would put it. Have you an alibi? I haven't. I could get in or out of my room at the hotel any time I wanted. Easy as winking. I did once when my car broke down coming from Town and everyone was in bed and asleep. I didn't want to wake them all, so I climbed in. They'll remember if you ask them—surprised to find me there in the morning. What about you?"

"Alibi?" repeated Lord Rone. "I don't know, I'm sure," and he had rather the air of not quite knowing what the word meant.

"A hat was found on the scene," Bobby said. "You all know that. By Linda Blythe. She says she left it there, meaning to take it back with her to Cobblers on her way home. But then it had gone. Or so she says. Unfortunately, she can't be questioned at the moment. I've been trying to find it for some days. It should provide the proof needed. I've suspected—indeed, felt sure of—the identity of the murderer for some time, but I hadn't enough evidence to act on. Now that evidence may have been destroyed."

"Whom do you mean?" Lord Rone demanded. "I think we have a right to know."

"Don't ask that, Daddy, please," Maureen said. "Please don't."

They heard steps approaching. The door of the bungalow opened. Ford was there. He was saying to someone just behind him:

"Please come in, Sir William. Mr. Owen is here and others as well."

CHAPTER XXXVII

"A LONG, LONG SLEEP"

SIR WILLIAM CAME forward slowly into the lamplit room. Ford followed. None of the others moved or spoke, but they all watched intently. He, too, was dishevelled, bareheaded, all his clothing in disarray, his expression one of utter fatigue. His face was slightly scratched and bleeding a little. He stumbled as he walked and when he sat down on the nearest chair, it was more as if he collapsed upon it, and might indeed have collapsed instead upon the floor but for Ford's guiding hand from behind. He said:

"You will excuse me. I am so tired. I have been wandering out there in the mist—in the mist like a lost soul for I don't know how long. Then I met our friend here." He indicated Ford with a gesture of one hand. "He insisted on my joining you."

"It was in Higgles Lane across the fields where I saw the gentleman," Ford said. "Almost the same place where Mr. Longton was."

"We are quite an assembly," Sir William said, blinking at them from half-shut eyes that seemed to shrink even from that soft lamplight. "What is it that has brought us all here together? Strange. No, thank you"—this was to Bobby, who had filled a cup with coffee from the pot keeping hot on the oil stove and had brought it to him, only to have it waved aside. "All I want is a sleep," Sir William said. "A long, long sleep. And sound. I've been wandering out there—I almost thought for years. Lost in the fog. Lost—for ever lost. I wonder—"

"Why?" Bobby asked. He was still holding the cup of coffee he had poured out—black and strong it was. He asked again: "Why were you out in the fog so late?"

"Ask our dear little Maureen," Sir William said as he waved a hand towards her. "Do you know, I think I'll have that coffee after all if I may? It may keep me awake and I don't want to sleep just yet—not yet. I won't either—not yet. Thank you." He took the cup Bobby gave him and began to drink. "Black and strong," he said. "Black and strong," he repeated and went on: "You know, Mr. Owen, I've been watching you. I've been afraid of you. I've dreamed of you. I expect the hunted man does tend to dream of the hunter close upon his tracks. Quite a long time before I understood my danger came rather from dear little Maureen, little fool Maureen, Maureen who hardly knows the difference between the stage and life, between acting and reality."

"I was trying to help you," Maureen said. "I promised I would. She made me take a Bible and I held it and I promised."

"What do you mean, Maureen?" Lord Rone demanded. "Promised who—what?" Without waiting for an answer, he turned sharply towards Bobby. "He doesn't know what he is saying. He must be out of his mind."

"I don't think so," Bobby said and he spoke to Maureen. "Then you knew what I only suspected?" he asked. "Did you?"

"Aunt Bella knew," Maureen said. "She told me. I heard her crying all one night through. Have you ever heard someone you rather liked and had always known crying all a night long? That wasn't acting; that was real enough. If I never knew the difference before, I did then. I mean real crying, not just when you feel you want to, but crying because there's nothing left to you but to lie and cry. I think I almost knew before, because I knew what Uncle Bill said about the hat wasn't true, because he was wearing it when he came, and then you couldn't help seeing there was something between Aunt Bella and Baldwin Jones. I should have liked to kill him myself."

"He had letters from her," Sir William said, rousing himself from the slumber into which he had seemed to be falling, He held himself upright, fighting off by an effort of will the sleep that oppressed him. "After it was over," he said, "I took the letters from him."

"Not all she had written," Maureen said. "He kept half of them back. He was that kind of beast. Aunt Bella knew where he lived because she had been there, so she told me, and I went and I got them and I burned them. And then Mr. Owen came, and, of course, he would; he always does. So I said they were mine. I've told an awful lot of lies," she added meditatively. "Not that I care."

"Really, Maureen," said Lord Rone, even more hopelessly than ever before.

"I say, Maureen," said Jack Longton. "You have been going it. Oh, I say," and then he could say no more.

"Ought to be in the dock," muttered Ford from behind.

"I wasn't going to have anything horrid happening to Uncle Bill if I could help it," Maureen said defiantly. "I promised Aunt Bella I wouldn't, and I didn't want myself, and I don't suppose Uncle Bill ever meant to, not really. Aunt Bella kept saying it was a kind of accident and I expect it was."

"He wouldn't give me her letters back," Sir William said in his faint, slow, wandering voice. "I wonder—is there any more of that coffee left? Black and strong, blacker, stronger." His head dropped forward as if sleep were overcoming him as he spoke and then with an almost visible effort of the will, he jerked himself upright. He took the coffee Bobby brought him and drank it off. It seemed to revive him for the moment. He said: "Never kill anyone, not even the man who is trying to take your wife from you, trying to make her run away with him, not even if there's a figure on a knife that's come alive and whispers, whispers, whispers: 'Kill, for that's what I was made for, what you were born for. Kill, kill,' she whispered and never stopped. You see, I got it out of Bella that she was going to meet him that night. But I went instead of her and he grinned and laughed and said she would come to it sooner or later. And I thought perhaps that was true, so I killed him."

There was a silence then. It lasted only a moment, but it was a long, strange moment, a moment that seemed as though in it there passed long hours, long days. Ford was the first to break it. He murmured, but in a murmur, that in that strange silence sounded like the blast of a distant trumpet:

"He's said it now."

"He is in no state to say anything," Lord Rone protested. "In his present condition he can't be held responsible."

Sir William, unheeding, went on:

"Excusable, no doubt, in the circumstances, but still an error, a mistake. I recognize that now. But he really shouldn't have laughed. I really don't know why I am rambling on like this. An intolerable old bore, you must all be saying."

"Sir William," Bobby said, "do you realize it will now be necessary to charge you with the murder of Baldwin Jones?"

"Oh, I don't think so," Sir William said, smiling at him in the friendliest way. "No. Definitely no. No," he repeated. "I don't think that will ever be."

"I repeat," Lord Rone insisted, "that he is not fully aware of what he is saying. That is perfectly clear. He is clearly suffering from hallucinations caused by strain and fatigue. No significance can be attached to what he says at present. I am sure Mr. Longton agrees. You, too, Maureen."

"Definitely," Longton said. "Anyone can see he is near dead for sleep and hasn't an earthly what he is saying."

"Anyhow, the hat's burnt," Maureen said, staring defiantly at Bobby. "Linda and I burnt it. I was jolly sure she had really picked it up that night and taken it on to the bungalow. No one would just have left it there. So I asked her, and I told her it was no good telling me lies because I wasn't a man"—this last word was given an accent of a gentle, tolerant contempt—"I was a woman, too, and I knew. So then she owned up, and she was awfully upset, and cried a lot—I mean she cried the way you do when you want to, not the way Aunt Bella cried all that long night. Only then she got saying nobody must ever know about something, and I didn't know what she meant, and it didn't matter, anyhow, and she was only being a housemaid for the experience, and that made me ask her if she was writing a play, and she said she was, and I said I always thought her a bit of a fool and now I knew, and she said no one must ever know, because everybody would laugh and laugh, and there was something about her mother coming into it, I don't know how, but I didn't bother, because she had given me the hat and I was burning it, so nothing mattered any more. And that's all, and Mr. Owen can do what he likes, but I've done what I promised Aunt Bella, and he can't touch Uncle Bill. Uncle Bill, wake up. Did you hear?"

"Yes, I heard," Sir William said slowly, and indeed for the moment he seemed more alert, more wide awake, than he had been previously, more fully aware of his surroundings. "Burnt, you say? How very odd. But then what hat is that?" and he pointed to the one Bobby had replaced upon the table near him. ,

"It's the one Linda and I were bringing for Mr. Owen to find," Maureen said simply.

"Maureen," Lord Rone exclaimed, "will you ever learn to hold your tongue?" Maureen retired with an air of being about to consider this proposition, though somewhat doubtfully. Her father continued: "Nothing Sir William has said to-night here can be held as carrying the least significance. He is clearly under the influence of extreme fatigue. As for the burning of some hat or another—a schoolgirl's trick, a stupid schoolgirl's trick—that, too, cannot be considered of importance. Why, he has dropped off to sleep again while I was talking. Can't keep his eyes open."

Bobby stepped forward and jerked Sir William roughly to his feet. Sir William opened his eyes now, but only with difficulty. He said:

"Oh, you are still there. What have I been saying? Oh, yes, yes, of course. That hat of mine. Maureen says she burnt it, doesn't she? And I've been thinking of her as dear little Maureen." His features became twisted in a queer sort of smile—if smile it were. "Ever read Thomas Hardy?"

"That shows," Longton cried. "Just as I told you—hasn't an earthly what he's saying. Thomas Hardy!"

"Ford, someone," Bobby exclaimed, a new sense of urgency in his voice. "Quick—mustard, salt. Quick. It's morphia. Quick."

"The Spirit of the Ironies, Mr. Longton," Sir William said, and his voice was loud and clear. "I heard Mr. Owen calling that he had the hat I thought was my hat. Because I knew it was the only proof against me I tried to get it back—I didn't much mind how. But if he had it then I knew it was all over and only one thing left." Ford came running back with a glass of water to which he had added a handful of salt. Sir William began to laugh when he saw it. "An emetic," he said. "My good man, I used a hypodermic needle."

~   ~   ~

It was not till the day of the two inquests that Bobby saw Maureen again. A merciful verdict of 'Temporary Insanity' had been returned in Sir William's case. In the general view; it was a verdict more than justified by those last murmured words about the Golden Dagger figurine having come alive and urged him on to do what had been done.

The other verdict, that on Baldwin Jones, had been one of murder against 'person or persons unknown,' and this, too, had become inevitable, since the police, though admitting that the arrest of Sir William had been contemplated, admitted also that they had no really conclusive evidence in their possession. Nor were the names of Mrs. Cato, of Linda, or of Maureen, ever mentioned, though all three had been warned to be in attendance.

To Bobby when they were leaving the court together, Maureen said:

"I think you always knew, didn't you?"

"We almost always know," Bobby told her. "But knowing's not proving. I knew there had been heavy rain only on Monday afternoon and Monday night. Sir William told me himself, without at the time realizing what the remark meant, that he had got wet through and caught a bad cold as a result. But you, before you knew anything about a possible murder, mentioned that Sir William was in the Long Gallery all that Monday afternoon. So it wasn't the Monday afternoon when he got wet and caught cold. Then Lady Watson went out of her way to complain he had kept her awake all Monday night by his continuous snoring. So apparently, according to you and her, he hadn't been out in the rain at all. But he himself said the opposite. And why had Lady Watson said all that unless she was trying to establish an alibi—though, of course, an alibi that covered her, too. I had to keep that in mind. There were other pointers as well. Small, but pointers all the same. For instance, your saying that he kept an eye on what you called Lady Watson's lap-dogs and took care they didn't go too far. Suppose one had, though? And then I could see for myself he could assert himself pretty strongly when he wanted to. All the same, I never managed to get the substantial evidence you have to have to satisfy a jury. Especially after you burnt the hat I was looking for. For which," he added, "if there were any justice in the world, you would now be in gaol."

"Are you sorry I'm not?" she asked in her character of the sweet, innocent young thing.

"Very sorry indeed," he told her severely.

"Now it's you that's telling lies," she retorted. "I'm so glad it's not only me. Because you aren't really, now, are you?"

"At any rate," growled Bobby, "I'm jolly sure I'm more than sorry I never got a chance to fit you with those junior miss handcuffs you talked about once."

"Oh, well," she sighed, "you needn't worry. It's come to much the same thing. I'm getting married next week, and, of course, getting married does so utterly mess up your career when you're a woman. Handcuffs nothing to it. Of course, if I hadn't been just simply blackmailed into it, I shouldn't have ever."

"How do you mean—blackmailed into it?" Bobby asked, a little startled, such convincing emotion, such protest, such melancholy indignation had she managed to convey in the tones of that expressive voice of hers.

"Well, you see," she explained, "Jack Longton's signed up for three years with some big theatrical people in Australia as their producer, and they want him at once. It's to be the biggest splash ever out there, apart from just visiting tours. And as soon as it was all fixed up, he had the cheek and impudence to go off and get a special licence. It costs an awful lot, you know, and I couldn't very well start our married life letting him waste all that money, could I?"

THE END

RAMBLE HOUSE's

HARRY STEPHEN KEELER WEBWORK MYSTERIES

(RH) indicates the title is available ONLY in the RAMBLE HOUSE edition

The Ace of Spades Murder
The Affair of the Bottled Deuce (RH)
The Amazing Web
The Barking Clock
Behind That Mask
The Book with the Orange Leaves
The Bottle with the Green Wax Seal
The Box from Japan
The Case of the Canny Killer
The Case of the Crazy Corpse (RH)
The Case of the Flying Hands (RH)
The Case of the Ivory Arrow
The Case of the Jeweled Ragpicker
The Case of the Lavender Gripsack
The Case of the Mysterious Moll
The Case of the 16 Beans
The Case of the Transparent Nude (RH)
The Case of the Transposed Legs
The Case of the Two-Headed Idiot (RH)
The Case of the Two Strange Ladies
The Circus Stealers (RH)
Cleopatra's Tears
A Copy of Beowulf (RH)
The Crimson Cube (RH)
The Face of the Man From Saturn
Find the Clock
The Five Silver Buddhas
The 4th King
The Gallows Waits, My Lord! (RH)
The Green Jade Hand
Finger! Finger!
Hangman's Nights (RH)
I, Chameleon (RH)
I Killed Lincoln at 10:13! (RH)
The Iron Ring
The Man Who Changed His Skin (RH)
The Man with the Crimson Box
The Man with the Magic Eardrums
The Man with the Wooden Spectacles
The Marceau Case
The Matilda Hunter Murder
The Monocled Monster

The Murder of London Lew
The Murdered Mathematician
The Mysterious Card (RH)
The Mysterious Ivory Ball of Wong Shing Li (RH)
The Mystery of the Fiddling Cracksman
The Peacock Fan
The Photo of Lady X (RH)
The Portrait of Jirjohn Cobb
Report on Vanessa Hewstone (RH)
Riddle of the Travelling Skull
Riddle of the Wooden Parrakeet (RH)
The Scarlet Mummy (RH)
The Search for X-Y-Z
The Sharkskin Book
Sing Sing Nights
The Six From Nowhere (RH)
The Skull of the Waltzing Clown
The Spectacles of Mr. Cagliostro
Stand By—London Calling!
The Steeltown Strangler
The Stolen Gravestone (RH)
Strange Journey (RH)
The Strange Will
The Straw Hat Murders (RH)
The Street of 1000 Eyes (RH)
Thieves' Nights
Three Novellos (RH)
The Tiger Snake
The Trap (RH)
Vagabond Nights (Defrauded Yeggman)
Vagabond Nights 2 (10 Hours)
The Vanishing Gold Truck
The Voice of the Seven Sparrows
The Washington Square Enigma
When Thief Meets Thief
The White Circle (RH)
The Wonderful Scheme of Mr. Christopher Thorne
X. Jones—of Scotland Yard
Y. Cheung, Business Detective

Keeler Related Works

A To Izzard: A Harry Stephen Keeler Companion by Fender Tucker — Articles and stories about Harry, by Harry, and in his style. Included is a compleat bibliography.
Wild About Harry: Reviews of Keeler Novels — Edited by Richard Polt & Fender Tucker — 22 reviews of works by Harry Stephen Keeler from *Keeler News*. A perfect introduction to the author.
The Keeler Keyhole Collection: Annotated newsletter rants from Harry Stephen Keeler, edited by Francis M. Nevins. Over 400 pages of incredibly personal Keeleriana.
Fakealoo — Pastiches of the style of Harry Stephen Keeler by selected demented members of the HSK Society. Updated every year with the new winner.

RAMBLE HOUSE's OTHER LOONS

The Triune Man — Mindscrambling science fiction from Richard A. Lupoff
Detective Duff Unravels It — Episodic mysteries by Harvey O'Higgins
Mysterious Martin, the Master of Murder — Two versions of a strange 1912 novel by Tod Robbins about a man who writes books that can kill.
The Master of Mysteries — 1912 novel of supernatural sleuthing by Gelett Burgess
Dago Red — 22 tales of dark suspense by Bill Pronzini
The Night Remembers — A 1991 Jack Walsh mystery from Ed Gorman
Rough Cut & New, Improved Murder — Ed Gorman's first two novels
Hollywood Dreams — A novel of the Depression by Richard O'Brien
Four Gelett Burgess Novels — *The Master of Mysteries, The White Cat, Two O'Clock Courage, Ladies in Boxes*, with more to come from Surinam Turtle Press
The Organ Reader — A huge compilation of just about everything published in the 1971-1972 radical bay-area newspaper, *THE ORGAN*.
A Clear Path to Cross — Sharon Knowles short mystery stories by Ed Lynskey
Old Times' Sake — Short stories by James Reasoner from Mike Shayne Magazine
Freaks and Fantasies — Eerie tales by Tod Robbins, collaborator of Tod Browning on the film FREAKS.
Five Jim Harmon Sleaze Double Novels — *Vixen Hollow/Celluloid Scandal, The Man Who Made Maniacs/Silent Siren, Ape Rape/Wanton Witch, Sex Burns Like Fire/Twist Session*, and *Sudden Lust/Passion Strip*. More doubles to come!
Marblehead: A Novel of H.P. Lovecraft — A long-lost masterpiece from Richard A. Lupoff. Published for the first time!
The Compleat Ova Hamlet — Parodies of SF authors by Richard A. Lupoff – New edition!
The Secret Adventures of Sherlock Holmes — Three Sherlockian pastiches by the Brooklyn author/publisher, Gary Lovisi.
The Universal Holmes — Richard A. Lupoff's 2007 collection of five Holmesian pastiches and a recipe for giant rat stew.
Four Joel Townsley Rogers Novels — By the author of *The Red Right Hand: Once In a Red Moon, Lady With the Dice, The Stopped Clock, Never Leave My Bed*
Two Joel Townsley Rogers Story Collections — Night of Horror and Killing Time
Twenty Norman Berrow Novels — *The Bishop's Sword, Ghost House, Don't Go Out After Dark, Claws of the Cougar, The Smokers of Hashish, The Secret Dancer, Don't Jump Mr. Boland!, The Footprints of Satan, Fingers for Ransom, The Three Tiers of Fantasy, The Spaniard's Thumb, The Eleventh Plague, Words Have Wings, One Thrilling Night, The Lady's in Danger, It Howls at Night, The Terror in the Fog, Oil Under the Window, Murder in the Melody, The Singing Room*
The N. R. De Mexico Novels — Robert Bragg presents *Marijuana Girl, Madman on a Drum, Private Chauffeur* in one volume.
Four Chelsea Quinn Yarbro Novels featuring Charlie Moon — *Ogilvie, Tallant and Moon, Music When the Sweet Voice Dies, Poisonous Fruit* and *Dead Mice*
The Green Toad — Impossible mysteries by Walter S. Masterman – More to come!
Two Hake Talbot Novels — *Rim of the Pit, The Hangman's Handyman*. Classic locked room mysteries.
Two Alexander Laing Novels — *The Motives of Nicholas Holtz* and *Dr. Scarlett*, stories of medical mayhem and intrigue from the 30s.
Four David Hume Novels — *Corpses Never Argue, Cemetery First Stop, Make Way for the Mourners, Eternity Here I Come*, and more to come.
Three Wade Wright Novels — *Echo of Fear, Death At Nostalgia Street* and *It Leads to Murder*, with more to come!
Four Rupert Penny Novels — *Policeman's Holiday, Policeman's Evidence, Lucky Policeman* and *Sealed Room Murder*, classic impossible mysteries.
Five Jack Mann Novels — Strange murder in the English countryside. *Gees' First Case, Nightmare Farm, Grey Shapes, The Ninth Life, The Glass Too Many*.
Seven Max Afford Novels — *Owl of Darkness, Death's Mannikins, Blood on His Hands, The Dead Are Blind, The Sheep and the Wolves, Sinners in Paradise* and *Two Locked Room Mysteries and a Ripping Yarn* by one of Australia's finest novelists.
Five Joseph Shallit Novels — *The Case of the Billion Dollar Body, Lady Don't Die on My Doorstep, Kiss the Killer, Yell Bloody Murder, Take Your Last Look*. One of America's best 50's authors.
Two Crimson Clown Novels — By Johnston McCulley, author of the Zorro novels, *The Crimson Clown* and *The Crimson Clown Again*.

The Best of 10-Story Book — edited by Chris Mikul, over 35 stories from the literary magazine Harry Stephen Keeler edited.

A Young Man's Heart — A forgotten early classic by Cornell Woolrich

The Anthony Boucher Chronicles — edited by Francis M. Nevins
Book reviews by Anthony Boucher written for the *San Francisco Chronicle*, 1942 – 1947. Essential and fascinating reading.

Muddled Mind: Complete Works of Ed Wood, Jr. — David Hayes and Hayden Davis deconstruct the life and works of a mad genius.

Gadsby — A lipogram (a novel without the letter E). Ernest Vincent Wright's last work, published in 1939 right before his death.

My First Time: The One Experience You Never Forget — Michael Birchwood — 64 true first-person narratives of how they lost it.

The Black Box — Stylish 1908 classic by M. P. Shiel. Very hard to find.

The Incredible Adventures of Rowland Hern — Rousing 1928 impossible crimes by Nicholas Olde.

Slammer Days — Two full-length prison memoirs: *Men into Beasts* (1952) by George Sylvester Viereck and *Home Away From Home* (1962) by Jack Woodford

Beat Books #1 — Two beatnik classics, *A Sea of Thighs* by Ray Kainen and *Village Hipster* by J.X. Williams

Ruled By Radio — 1925 futuristic novel by Robert L. Hadfield & Frank E. Farncombe

Murder in Silk — A 1937 Yellow Peril novel of the silk trade by Ralph Trevor

The Case of the Withered Hand — 1936 potboiler by John G. Brandon

Finger-prints Never Lie — A 1939 classic detective novel by John G. Brandon

Inclination to Murder — 1966 thriller by New Zealand's Harriet Hunter

Invaders from the Dark — Classic werewolf tale from Greye La Spina

Fatal Accident — Murder by automobile, a 1936 mystery by Cecil M. Wills

The Devil Drives — A prison and lost treasure novel by Virgil Markham

Dr. Odin — Douglas Newton's 1933 potboiler comes back to life.

The Chinese Jar Mystery — Murder in the manor by John Stephen Strange, 1934

The Julius Caesar Murder Case — A classic 1935 re-telling of the assassination by Wallace Irwin that's much more fun than the Shakespeare version

West Texas War and Other Western Stories — by Gary Lovisi

The Contested Earth and Other SF Stories — A never-before published space opera and seven short stories by Jim Harmon.

Tales of the Macabre and Ordinary — Modern twisted horror by Chris Mikul, author of the *Bizarrism* series.

The Gold Star Line — Seaboard adventure from L.T. Reade and Robert Eustace.

The Werewolf vs the Vampire Woman — Hard to believe ultraviolence by either Arthur M. Scarm or Arthur M. Scram.

Black Hogan Strikes Again — Australia's Peter Renwick pens a tale of the outback.

Don Diablo: Book of a Lost Film — Two-volume treatment of a western by Paul Landres, with diagrams. Intro by Francis M. Nevins.

The Charlie Chaplin Murder Mystery — Movie hijinks by Wes D. Gehring

The Koky Comics — A collection of all of the 1978-1981 Sunday and daily comic strips by Richard O'Brien and Mort Gerberg, in two volumes.

Suzy — Another collection of comic strips from Richard O'Brien and Bob Vojtko

Dime Novels: Ramble House's 10-Cent Books — *Knife in the Dark* by Robert Leslie Bellem, *Hot Lead* and *Song of Death* by Ed Earl Repp, *A Hashish House in New York* by H.H. Kane, and five more.

Blood in a Snap — The *Finnegan's Wake* of the 21st century, by Jim Weiler and Al Gorithm

Stakeout on Millennium Drive — Award-winning Indianapolis Noir — Ian Woollen.

Dope Tales #1 — Two dope-riddled classics; *Dope Runners* by Gerald Grantham and *Death Takes the Joystick* by Phillip Condé.

Dope Tales #2 — Two more narco-classics; *The Invisible Hand* by Rex Dark and *The Smokers of Hashish* by Norman Berrow.

Dope Tales #3 — Two enchanting novels of opium by the master, Sax Rohmer. *Dope* and *The Yellow Claw.*

Tenebrae — Ernest G. Henham's 1898 horror tale brought back.

The Singular Problem of the Stygian House-Boat — Two classic tales by John Kendrick Bangs about the denizens of Hades.

Tiresias — Psychotic modern horror novel by Jonathan M. Sweet.

The One After Snelling — Kickass modern noir from Richard O'Brien.

The Sign of the Scorpion — 1935 Edmund Snell tale of oriental evil.

The House of the Vampire — 1907 poetic thriller by George S. Viereck.

An Angel in the Street — Modern hardboiled noir by Peter Genovese.

The Devil's Mistress — Scottish gothic tale by J. W. Brodie-Innes.

The Lord of Terror — 1925 mystery with master-criminal, Fantômas.

The Lady of the Terraces — 1925 adventure by E. Charles Vivian.

My Deadly Angel — 1955 Cold War drama by John Chelton.

Prose Bowl — Futuristic satire — Bill Pronzini & Barry N. Malzberg .

Satan's Den Exposed — True crime in Truth or Consequences New Mexico — Award-winning journalism by the *Desert Journal*.

The Amorous Intrigues & Adventures of Aaron Burr — by Anonymous — Hot historical action.

I Stole $16,000,000 — A true story by cracksman Herbert E. Wilson.

The Black Dark Murders — Vintage 50s college murder yarn by Milt Ozaki, writing as Robert O. Saber.

Sex Slave — Potboiler of lust in the days of Cleopatra — Dion Leclerq.

You'll Die Laughing — Bruce Elliott's 1945 novel of murder at a practical joker's English countryside manor.

The Private Journal & Diary of John H. Surratt — The memoirs of the man who conspired to assassinate President Lincoln.

Dead Man Talks Too Much — Hollywood boozer by Weed Dickenson

Red Light — History of legal prostitution in Shreveport Louisiana by Eric Brock. Includes wonderful photos of the houses and the ladies.

A Snark Selection — Lewis Carroll's *The Hunting of the Snark* with two Snarkian chapters by Harry Stephen Keeler — Illustrated by Gavin L. O'Keefe.

Ripped from the Headlines! — The Jack the Ripper story as told in the newspaper articles in the *New York* and *London Times.*

Geronimo — S. M. Barrett's 1905 autobiography of a noble American.

The White Peril in the Far East — Sidney Lewis Gulick's 1905 indictment of the West and assurance that Japan would never attack the U.S.

The Compleat Calhoon — All of Fender Tucker's works: Includes *The Totah Trilogy, Weed, Women and Song* and *Tales from the Tower,* plus a CD of all of his songs.

RAMBLE HOUSE

Fender Tucker, Prop.

www.ramblehouse.com   fender@ramblehouse.com

318-455-6847   10325 Sheepshead Drive, Vancleave MS 39565

www.ingramcontent.com/pod-product-compliance
Lightning Source LLC
Chambersburg PA
CBHW030333030726
47499CB00003B/752